Praise for the novels of John Shannon

"Tough and engaging . . . *Concrete River* is my kind of L.A. novel—hard as nails with a soft spot in the middle."
—Michael Connelly, author of
the Harry Bosch mysteries

"Shannon is a fine writer. Make no mistake, this is the real L.A., real people, some of them you cross the street to avoid, looking everywhere but at them. Take a walk with Jack Liffey, a brave and decent man."
—Kent Anderson, author of *Night Dogs*

"If Raymond Chandler had written *The Day of the Locust*, this is the book he would have written."
—Mike Davis, author of *City of Quartz*

"Like Graham Greene—and there are other admirable resemblances—he is an explorer of that shadowy area in which, as spurs to positive action, abstract idealism and personal psychology merge. The author has achieved one of the most stimulating of the form's uncountable possibilities."
—*Sunday Times* (London)

"A serious adventure . . . [that] draws much of its strength from a clear presentation of social and political tensions."
—*Times Literary Supplement*

"Fast and exciting action."
—*Daily Telegraph* (London)

"Racy, ambitious."
—Clancy Sigal, author of *The Secret Defector*

MORE MYSTERIES FROM THE
BERKLEY PUBLISHING GROUP...

DEWEY JAMES MYSTERIES: America's favorite small-town sleuth! "Highly entertaining." *—Booklist*

by Kate Morgan

A SLAY AT THE RACES	MYSTERY LOVES COMPANY
A MURDER MOST FOWL	DAYS OF CRIME AND ROSES
HOME SWEET HOMICIDE	THE OLD SCHOOL DIES

FORREST EVERS MYSTERIES: A former race-car driver solves the high-speed crimes of world-class racing... "A Dick Francis on wheels!" *—Jackie Stewart*

by Bob Judd

BURN	SPIN
CURVE	

THE REVEREND LUCAS HOLT MYSTERIES: They call him "The Rev," a name he earned as pastor of a Texas prison. Now he solves crimes with a group of reformed ex-cons...

by Charles Meyer

THE SAINTS OF GOD MURDERS	BLESSED ARE THE MERCILESS

FRED VICKERY MYSTERIES: Senior sleuth Fred Vickery has been around long enough to know where the bodies are buried in the small town of Cutler, Colorado...

by Sherry Lewis

NO PLACE FOR SECRETS	NO PLACE LIKE HOME
NO PLACE FOR DEATH	NO PLACE FOR TEARS
NO PLACE FOR SIN	NO PLACE FOR MEMORIES

INSPECTOR BANKS MYSTERIES: Award-winning British detective fiction at its finest... "Robinson's novels are habit-forming!" *—West Coast Review of Books*

by Peter Robinson

THE HANGING VALLEY	PAST REASON HATED
WEDNESDAY'S CHILD	FINAL ACCOUNT
GALLOWS VIEW	INNOCENT GRAVES

JACK McMORROW MYSTERIES: The highly acclaimed series set in a Maine mill town and starring a newspaperman with a knack for crime solving... "Gerry Boyle is the genuine article." *—Robert B. Parker*

by Gerry Boyle

DEADLINE	BLOODLINE
LIFELINE	POTSHOT

JOE WILDER MYSTERIES: Featuring struggling-novelist-turned detective Joe Wilder... "Crime fiction at its riveting best." *—Faye Kellerman*

by T.J. Phillips

DANCE OF THE MONGOOSE	WOMAN IN THE DARK

THE CRACKED EARTH

JOHN SHANNON

BERKLEY PRIME CRIME, NEW YORK

THE CRACKED EARTH

A Berkley Prime Crime Book / published by arrangement with
the author

PRINTING HISTORY
Berkley Prime Crime edition / February 1999

The Penguin Putnam Inc. World Wide Web site address is
http://www.penguinputnam.com

ISBN: 0-425-16732-1

Berkley Prime Crime Books are published
by The Berkley Publishing Group,
a member of Penguin Putnam Inc.,
375 Hudson Street, New York, New York 10014.
The name BERKLEY PRIME CRIME and the BERKLEY PRIME CRIME
design are trademarks belonging to Berkley Publishing Corporation.

PRINTED IN THE UNITED STATES OF AMERICA

10 9 8 7 6 5 4 3 2 1

For Pam

Catastrophes adapt themselves to their relevant cultural order. Los Angeles represents a horizontal break, a breaking open of spaces in an intellectual sense. There never was a foundation or a profundity, but only a cracked surface.

—JEAN BAUDRILLARD

THE CRACKED EARTH

1

COMPLETELY INSULATED FROM UNHAPPINESS

"YOU WAIT," THE TOUGH-LOOKING LATINA MAID SAID, AND then waddled away like a tugboat. There was nowhere to sit in the large tiled entry and his eye quickly ran out of things to look at, though a number of them had entertainment value while they lasted. A real elephant-foot umbrella stand out of Graham Greene, an oak coat tree from some monastery, and a Chinese vase as tall as his chest overflowing with unopened junk mail.

A single English phrase broke through a flood of Spanish: "Don't use the word 'kidnap.' . . ." That got his attention, all right. The woman's voice had a strange familiar timbre to it.

On his way up into the Hollywood Hills, he'd wondered idly who still lived up here in the big houses around the cul-de-sacs like Avenida Bluebird. The movie folk had mostly gone west to Bel Air and Malibu, leaving the hills to the coke dealers and the ruthless new music execs. He'd been sent to see a woman named L. Bright, and he'd guessed that she'd turn out to be the widowed third wife of a very rich dentist.

He heard that honeyed voice again, and then it was lost in the burring of a leaf blower that started up out front. The maid came back finally and beckoned him in. When the heavy door closed, it snuffed the sound of the leaf blower right out. The large room was craftsman, Norman, and

Moorish in equal proportions, with sunlight streaming in through motionless gauze curtains. But he didn't look at the furnishings for long. He couldn't help staring at the woman.

"Yes, I'm Lori Bright."

He wondered if the young lawyer who'd referred him had been playing a joke. But the young guys didn't know the older stars anymore.

"I'm shorter than you thought." She smiled with a rueful confidence and brushed back one side of the glossy blond hair that looked like it had been labored over by a half-dozen hairdressers. "And older."

"Hell, *I'm* older than I thought," he said. "Jack Liffey." He took her hand, small and firm, and tried to keep his eye from drifting across her body. Somewhere in the back of his brain, a calculator was working out her age. When he was fourteen, he'd probably masturbated to the famous *Life* picture of her in a half-off slip, but she'd only have been nineteen or so herself. She wore a kind of peasant getup that he associated with Ava Gardner.

"Can I get you something to drink?"

"What are you having?"

"Herb tea." She pronounced the *H* with that marvelous gravelly voice. He tried to remember if she was married to somebody British, but he had never followed who movie stars married.

"That'll be fine."

"I could have Anita get you something stronger."

He shook his head. He didn't drink—or smoke or do a lot of other things—but it was complicated to explain why and he wasn't there to talk about himself. She stooped to pick up a telephone, with a lot of bobbling going on under the peasant blouse, and punched in one digit.

"Two teas," she said, and set the phone down. "Please sit. You're making me nervous."

"Really?" He forced himself to tear his eyes off her for a moment and sat in a leather Mission chair that looked like it had once belonged to Will Rogers. Being ambushed by celebrity must have unsettled something in him. "Maybe it's because my curiosity would kill a whole bunch of cats."

She smiled and sat on a Mission sofa. "You'd best get over the awe before we talk. Then I'll have your undivided attention."

He didn't know quite what to say. He wondered if Marilyn Monroe had ever sat in the chair he was in, the spirit of her rump communing now with his, or maybe Jane Fonda, or Billy Wilder. *A Week in Palm Springs,* he thought. Lori Bright had lounged in the bubble bath while Cary Grant, caught in the wrong room in one of his last movies, tried to keep his eyeballs from ripping sideways out of their sockets.

"Don't feel bad. I see that reaction a lot. For the life of me, I can't figure out why we're envied. You've been to college, right?"

He nodded. He had a master's degree in English literature, but that was something else he wasn't there to talk about.

"Actors hang out with other actors. Maybe two in a hundred have been to college. They can say witty words, but they don't think them up. Mostly they can't cook or build things or carry a tune. They've been around the world but only in hotels and only staring in mirrors. Famously, their eyes go blank when the conversation wanders away from their own doings. What's to envy?"

"I think the money helps."

"But it's not the point, is it? You don't envy the CEO of IBM. I have no idea what glamour is supposed to be. As far as I can figure, it's just circular. You're enviable for being envied."

He never liked these instant overconfidings that were so common in L.A., and he was also annoyed at himself for reacting to her like an out-of-towner gaping in a restaurant. "When was your last movie?" he said.

Her eyes went hard as steel and everything about her

face stiffened. It was probably a trick, but it was really chilling. "You've got a mean streak."

"Look, you can't do this poor-little-rich-kid routine on me. You've got everything people want. The house, the friends, the travel, the money. And you were the most attractive star of the sixties for my money, because you always played smart."

She opened her mouth, but he forged on. "I've seen photos of you all my life, and you've never seen a photo of me. Okay? Offhand, since you bring it up, I'd say glamour is about the illusion of a life that's completely insulated from unhappiness. But I don't think you asked me up here to talk philosophy."

Once again a strange kind of confidence stole over her features. She cocked her head as if she'd just noticed one of his features, maybe an extra nose. "You really get your back up. That's a plus." She got up and pulled the curtain aside to look out in a strange theatrical gesture. "I wonder if you can be bought."

That really tore it. What movie was this? he wondered. He kept his mouth shut.

"It isn't an empty question, Mr. Liffey. My daughter has disappeared. I think when you look for her, you're going to have to ask questions of some pretty rich and powerful men."

"Gosh, maybe you'd prefer a rich and powerful detective."

"Don't be angry with me, please." Now she was vulnerable and defenseless, dark clouds scudding in over her sunny plain. Being around her a lot would be a real emotional whirlwind.

But then he decided he could use the money.

"Tell me about your daughter."

"Lee is fifteen going on twenty-five. Her retro style of choice at the moment seems to be beatnik. She's a sophomore at Taunton School, but she disappeared from there a week ago Thursday."

She seemed to lose interest in whatever was outside the window.

"I take it she boards."

Lori Bright nodded with her lips pursed. "I suppose you don't approve of private schools. A part of me doesn't either, but it seemed to settle her down. At some ages girls do a lot better when they're out of sight of the boys. She came home most weekends."

He got out a tiny pad, just to look professional. "What was her major?"

"They don't believe in that at Taunton. Everyone's a generalist until the last year. She thinks she wants to study film, heaven forbid."

"You don't want her following in your footsteps?"

"Or her father's. He's Lionel Cohn."

"I see. Is he still in the picture?"

She turned and stared thoughtfully at him. "Interesting diction. No, Lionel is not in the picture. Twelve years ago he started grazing in greener pastures, and I do mean greener. He sees Lee now and then between jobs. He's on location right now up in the Owens Valley shooting a killer-robot film. Poor dear. He despises them more than I do."

"She has a boyfriend?"

"Last year at Hollywood High there was a black football player, but I believe she's settled in chastely at Taunton. She's always been a very shrewd and unconfiding girl, at least with me. You'll have to ask her girlfriends at school."

The maid knocked twice and then glided in with the tea.

"Has she ever run off before?"

With the tiniest of gestures, Lori Bright requested he wait until after the tea was served. He wasn't even sure how she did it. He wondered if they gave acting classes in signals like that. The maid set the tray down in front of her.

"Thank you, Anita. If Bruce or Tennyson call, I'm taking *una pequeñita siesta*."

"*Sí*, madam."

She left quickly, loose flat shoes slapping against her soles, and shut the door softly.

"You don't want her to know?"

"She knows. It's just not polite to air intimacies in front of the help as if they didn't have their own curiosity. It's rude, don't you think?"

"It's not something I think about a lot. Has your daughter ever run away from home before?"

"Never. Oh, there was once. When she was very little I punished her unfairly—for something a playmate had done—and she pretended to run off and hid next door until after dark. She has a fierce sense of justice."

"Drugs?"

"No, thank you," she said quickly, and then laughed. It was so infectious he had to laugh, too. She was still smiling as she poured the tea. "I'm sorry, I couldn't resist. I had my own bout with cocaine when Lee was about eight and she disapproves mightily."

"What about religion?"

"No thanks again." She didn't laugh this time. He got up to take the steaming cup of perfumy tea. "Her father is Jewish, but secular. I'm just plain secular, and so is Lee, as far as I know. In my experience the only grown-ups who believe in anything are Catholics. Especially among actors. It's the hold of all that ritual."

"I was thinking cults." He took a long sip of the tea that smelled like some shrub you'd find on the hillside.

"I doubt it. She's not a joiner."

"How did you and she get along?"

"You and *she* in the nominative." Lori Bright smiled and raised her carefully plucked eyebrows at him, and he wondered why she was trying to charm him now. Maybe it was just a routine with her, a habitual approach to the postman, the store clerk, the passerby, a way of buying her way back from glamour to reality. "You *have* been to college. We spatted now and then. I'm fairly strict about her hours when she's staying here, in by midnight on Friday and Saturday. She just turned *fifteen*."

"Do you have a man friend she might object to?"

"I'm in between," she said, staring straight back at him, and he swore it was meant to be taken as flirtation. He was suddenly nervous again. He remembered her distress in *Enough Is Never Enough* and he couldn't imagine anyone not wanting to comfort her the way Mitchum had.

"Do you have any guess where she's gone? A friend, her father?"

"No. I'm sorry if I don't seem to be taking it too seriously. I'm sure she'll turn up, but Lionel would kill me if something happened and I didn't try to track her down."

"I need a contact at the school and a recent photograph if you have one. But first, I'd like to see her room." He swilled down another mouthful of the abstemious tea, and that was plenty. His spartan urges had their limits.

"Privacy has always been a luxury in my profession." She stood up. "But it's a bit of a trial having a stranger actually prowl the house. I suppose you're not *such* a stranger now." She took his upper arm in one strong hand and led him through an archway beside a baronial fireplace.

She let go, but his arm still burned where her hand had been. I'll bet you do that to all the boys, he thought.

"At the top of the stairs, just on the left. I think I'll let you look by yourself."

"I'll try not to soil things. By the way, is her name Cohn or Bright?"

"Borowsky. It's Lionel's legal name. I'm tired of the story about it. You can ask him if you see him."

She was already walking away and for a moment he watched her buttocks reciprocate against her gauzy skirt, speculating on dance training, and then he tried to get his head working clearly. He took hold of that terribly inviting, vulnerable-tough image of her and pushed it down hard into the interior white suspended space where he kept everything else he had lost, or fucked up, or never had. He knew he could keep her there and get on with things because he had a hard selfish streak.

The first thing that struck him in the girl's room was the

large black lapel button taped to the wall that said EAT SHIT
AND DIE, but any kid might think that was funny. There
were Victorian colored prints of stringy pastel flowers and
a rather silly poster of a birthday cake being run over by a
big snow tire. He drifted to the single shelf of books—S. E.
Hinton, the beat poets, Khalil Gibran, *The Fountainhead,*
Alan Watts, Aleister Crowley's book on black magic, and
Henry Miller. It was a sampler of all the cul-de-sacs of
Western culture. There was an expensive-looking boom
box and a pile of tapes with names like Thrashing Apes,
violent names without wit or imagination. He saw an over-
size deck of cards and guessed they were probably tarot,
but when he turned a few up he saw the star, square, tri-
angle of Rhine cards, popular with the ESP crowd.

He went through the drawers one at a time, prodding
gently and feeling the undersides for taped-up secret messages or keys. He found only expensive black underwear,
padded black bras, a hundred used batteries, black tank
tops, and an old stuffed elephant, worn from being clutched
in bed. The clothes in the closet were mostly black, too,
blouses, tight skirts, black jeans on hangers, and a long
shiny leather coat like something from the panzer korps.
The closet shelf held a year-old high-school yearbook from
Hollywood High. He found her by name in a group photo,
skinny and innocent looking in a pink dress, obviously from
before she'd joined the Waffen SS. He wondered what had
happened there, only a year earlier, to drive her to private
school.

He stopped at the door and looked around. The bedroom
had a weird volatile quality that kept defying his focus, like
a layering of several lives. In the bathroom he found a lot
of creams for vaginitis and dark makeup and a giant plastic
bag of puffballs.

He waited in the hall a moment and then he went back
to the bedroom closet and felt all the pockets. In the leather
coat he found a movie stub, a Kleenex with dark purple
lipstick on it, and a crude Xeroxed leaflet demanding death
to the "mud people who are stealling are birthrite."

Up until then he had dismissed the ESP cards, the punk music and black leather, imagining a celebrity daughter who was just working overtime trying to make herself interesting to herself, but now he realized that kids like that were on a breakneck merry-go-round that spun them through adolescence. With a little luck the wheel might stop at a graduate school back east or a coffeehouse in the Valley, but who knows what hitch in the mechanism might toss her off into a Buick driven across the plains of Idaho by a handsome serial killer out of the local militia.

The maid met him in the hallway and gave him a note with the contact numbers at the school, plus a check for one thousand dollars. The señora was asleep. A retainer, he thought, staring in awe at the check. He'd been hunting missing kids for two years and finally he had a real retainer. He was in the big leagues.

"How well did you know Lee?" he asked the maid.

She seemed not to know English, which was unlikely, but he let it go.

He stepped out into a balmy crystalline day, smogless and warm, one of those late-winter–early-spring California mornings that should have promised endless satisfaction. Flowers glowed, the air smelled of eucalyptus, a seagull swooped across the sky, but he wasn't moved by it. He seemed to have lost the knack of that kind of satisfaction.

He watched a Latino gardener clipping the hedge in a fussy way. There was no truck in the cul-de-sac, and Jack Liffey wondered if the man was staff, maybe even the maid's husband. That would be tidy.

"*Compañero, buenos días*. Did you know Lee? The little one?"

Jack Liffey would never know what the answer might have been, for just as the man glanced up, there was a faint deep rumble and the lawn gave them both a thrusting jolt.

"Eeeee," the gardener said softly, and his eyes filled with perfect panic. A car alarm went off somewhere, and they both held their breath, but there was no more.

The gardener got hold of himself quickly and sighed. *"Terremoto,"* he said.

"Yeah, three-point-five." Of course, if it wasn't an aftershock of the Pacoima quake a year earlier, his guess was meaningless. Everyone in L.A. got to be a fine judge of the Richter scale, but it only worked when you knew where the epicenter was.

The gardener left the clippers on the hedge and scurried around the house.

One thing for sure, the car alarm wasn't his. He climbed into the white 1979 AMC Concord wishing someone would steal it. He and his wife had had a nice, tight trouble-free Accord, but that had left with her and his daughter, and then there was the secure aerospace job that had gone south earlier still.

His satisfactions now lay in disdain and self-control, in his resistance to all the easy compensations that had once sustained him—cigarettes or drugs or drink or even the tough, edgy novels he had once read endlessly and that now seemed to be weirdly leaking back into his world.

"HEY, Dick Tracy."

A bunch of black kids were hanging by the steps of the complex. Usually he'd greet them as he passed and they'd nod sullenly or offer a grudging sampling of the current salutations.

" 'S up," he said.

"Hey, check it out, man."

They looked like they wanted to tell him something. He sat on the retaining wall to put himself on their level. He was pretty good with kids through the simple expedient of having burned out all his own ambition. Most people didn't realize how threatening an adult's ambition was to the teenagers who inevitably felt the last crop of adults had grabbed all the available decent space in the world and would go on rusting over their heads for the rest of their lives. Jack Liffey never felt he had to top their jokes.

"You really private detective?" He had a rough idea of

which kid was which and this had come from one of the leaders, a fifteen-year-old who hunched his shoulder regularly like a tic. Jack Liffey knew he was called Ducks.

"Nah, not really. I look for kids who are missing and I get them out of trouble sometimes. If the parents have a bit of money, they even pay me for it."

They looked confused, but he couldn't help that.

Ducks hunched his shoulders. "Check this out, you was gettin' ran up on. We caught a couple cowboys tryin'a bust in your window."

"Two months ago?"

"That's it."

He knew about the cowboys, all right. It was over, but the emotion and terror of the ordeal was still fresh. A woman he'd loved had left him because of the terror, and worse, he'd had to kill someone for the first time in his fifty-two years, even counting thirteen months in Vietnam.

"The cowboys are out of the picture now. How come they didn't get in my window?"

"Me an' Li'l Hammer drew on 'em."

"No shit. Why'd you do that?"

"You got to represent, man. This our 'hood, down or die." It was nothing to joke about: the head cowboy had been a psychopath sack of shit, and Jack Liffey was impressed the kids had taken him on. Kids grew up even faster than he thought these days.

"I guess I owe you guys one."

HE PICKED UP A *TIMES* AT THE COIN RACK. THE MAYOR WAS in a feud with the police chief about a citizen's arrest performed by one of the mayor's aides who'd caught the chief smoking in an airliner over Fiji, the President was chopping wood in front of a circle of admiring Asian diplomats, and the celebrity killer whom they'd taken to calling Manson 2 had left another music cassette full of rhymed taunts at a radio station. Random notes from a universe that was getting a lot stranger than the one he'd grown up in.

It should have been Marlena Cruz's nephew running Mailboxes-R-Us over the noon hour. He'd taken to avoiding her, mainly to save her embarrassment. They'd had a bit of a thing until he'd accidentally caught her in bed with a cop, and a cop he *really* didn't like. But it wasn't Rogelio looking up to see him open the mailbox, it was Marlena herself and she gave a strangled little cry.

"Jack."

"Hi." He decided not to tiptoe. "How are you and Quinn doing?"

"I don't see him no more, not since he hit me and called me a wetback." She'd put on a couple of pounds since he'd had a good look at her. She still didn't look bad in it, but she'd be lighter on her feet with a lot less. The tight dress emphasized a mannish paunch and he felt a real tenderness for her.

"I bet that's not all he said."

"There was another bad word, too, means my private parts. He's got a mean streak."

"Taken as a whole, he's got a tiny little nice streak. Thanks for tidying up my place after it was wrecked."

"I do it for you anytime, Jack." Her eyes were begging something, but he wasn't ready for that.

"Thanks. I'll see you later."

The mail was all solicitations for services he couldn't afford and bills he couldn't afford either, but only one was the red one you really had to pay or go without something. The check from Lori Bright was already earmarked for last month's condo mortgage and penalty, and a couple of other red bills.

"Just coffee and toast," he said to Dan Margolin as he stepped into the Coffee Bean that was two doors down the strip mall from Mailboxes-R-Us and directly beneath his own office.

"How 'bout those Lakers?" Dan Margolin said.

"I'm not up on the doings in Minneapolis." Margolin knew he hated everything to do with sports.

Liffey thumbed through the paper. Somebody had found a new way to deny the poor health benefits, a plane had crashed into Lake Michigan, some study had just revealed that the steel trussing they'd been doing for earthquake reinforcement for twenty years wasn't all it was cracked up to be. Dan Margolin brought his coffee with toast and the little pot of homemade jam. He had a ponytail, a dry sense of humor, and a real knack for cooking simple things, and Jack Liffey liked him.

"These two *yentas* are just off the bus in Miami Beach and they unfold their sand chairs and settle in.

" 'Say, Ruthie,' one of them says, 'you been through the menopause yet?' "

" 'Menopause-shmenopause, I haven't even been through the Fontainebleau yet.' "

Jack Liffey didn't glance up. "What's a yenta? Speak English."

"You live in the town MGM made, for chrissake. You've got to learn a little Yiddish."

"I don't have to do anything."

Ever since Jack Liffey had moved into the old travel agency upstairs, Dan Margolin had been telling him Yiddish jokes and he'd been playing Mike Hammer back. It was just a way of passing the time.

He took the coffee up to his office and looked up the Taunton School in his collection of phone books. He'd picked up most of the directories for the L.A. basin, which was the most overtelephoned area on the planet. He even had the thin neighborhood books with the cheerful majorettes on the cover.

The machine was flashing at him, two calls.

"Jack, Kathy. It's getting kinda dumb me going on denying you visitation month after month. Where's the surprise, right? Maeve really wants to see you and the lawyer says maybe let you see her for a couple months and then it'll break your heart and you'll come through with some child support. I know, I know. We agreed we'd be adults, but I can't just let you go on being irresponsible. Anyway, you're on this weekend. Pick her up Saturday at nine. Don't be late."

What that meant was Kathy had red-hot plans for Saturday with the new guy she was seeing.

"Mr. Liffey, this is the Bright residence. It's eleven-forty. I think you'd better come back here as soon as you can." The Bright *residence*. It was her voice, all right, but she didn't say Lori, or Lori Bright, or Mrs. Bright. Weird. There had been a tremor in the voice and then she seemed to be working up to tell him something, or wanting him to think so. It was hard not to be cynical with actors. "Just come back, please."

According to the map, Taunton School was near the Wilshire Country Club smack in the heart of Hancock Park. That was the last bastion of old money in L.A., though *old money* in L.A. only really meant electric railways or graft or oil at the turn of the century. Behind every great fortune is a great crime, somebody had said. He'd loop down to the school after Avenida Bluebird.

He got stuck in a jam on Bronson when he forgot they were diverting traffic around the giant crater where two square blocks of Hollywood had caved in on the Red Line tunnel, carrying down twelve souls—nightwatchmen, two winos, and a CPA burning the midnight oil. The hole was so big no one had figured out how to fix it yet, and the contractors were too busy pointing fingers at one another and gearing up for court.

He filed slowly past where one end of the hole had become an unofficial public dump. Every day the police tried to stop it with barriers and every night the barriers seemed to be pulled down. He could see an alluvial fan of mattresses, old stoves, TV cabinets, tree trimmings, and black plastic bags. He could also see thirty or forty children and old women, mostly Latinos, clambering over the slope to pick through the trash, like something on the outskirts of Bombay. Another small step in the transformation of North America into a scavenger economy.

He diverted west to Gower and drove up through the Plains of the Locust, the infamous Gower Gulch where in the 1920s dimestore cowboys from New Jersey had hung out to be seen by the shabbier little film studios. The traffic broke up and the car spurted up out of the gulch into the hills where the more successful cowboys had settled. He had once got a kick out of knowing things like that.

Lori Bright waited for him on a stone bench beside a fountain in a Spanish cloister garden. Nice to have money, he thought, and enough taste not to use it to build a kidney-shaped swimming pool. The maid waddled away and Lori Bright squinted up in annoyance at a helicopter that circled the neighborhood, "orbited" as the cops called it.

"The blonde pop singer down the slope sunbathes in the nude and the sheriff gives her extra-special protection."

"I could see the tendency," he said.

She sighed. "I suppose it means my house is safer, too. How the neighborhood has fallen. That house used to belong to Malcolm Lowry before all the British exiles moved to Santa Monica Canyon. He played the ukulele in his backyard.''

"It didn't have very far to fall then."

She smiled thinly without looking at him. "I can't always work out your attitude."

"We all have our problems."

He sat on a second stone bench, waiting for whatever it was. What was she fishing around for? Maybe she was just lonely.

"I once walked along a jetty with a lover, sun setting in the distance, and I asked him whether he would choose courage or happiness. This was in a film, of course."

"Children of Light," he said.

She nodded, unsurprised that he recognized it.

"With happiness you don't need courage, but it never lasts. With courage you can outlast unhappiness, but it's no fun." She shrugged. "Of course this is the town that thinks courage was personified by that draft-dodging drunk John Wayne because John Ford taught him how to huff and puff."

"You couldn't take your eyes off him," Jack Liffey said.

"It's true," she conceded. "Clint Eastwood, James Coburn—they're like snakes coiling up in front of you, but John Gielgud shows up, you can't bear to look at him. Voice like a god, acts like a god, but you can't look at him." She laughed once, softly. "They always say I had a dusky sensuality, whatever that is."

He wondered what she was after. Why would she need compliments from him?

She unfolded a sheet of paper and set it on the bench in front of him. It was a fax, apparently reproducing an original on which words and letters cut out of a newspaper had been glued down to eke out:

WE HAVE GOT LEE GET $50 GRAND   NO COPS

Most were whole words in various fonts, though they'd had to go to individual letters for LEE.

"When did this show up?"

"It came to my husband, on location. The publicist at Monogram called and then faxed it to me an hour ago."

"You seem to be taking it rather oddly."

"Do *you* believe a ransom note that shows up after ten days?"

"You mean you think she's hoaxing?"

Lori Bright jiggled her head, maybe not even a denial, just as if shaking off a persona to leave behind a clearer-headed, more focused person.

"It's not beyond her. I don't know."

"You have to call the cops."

"Lionel already did. Or he had the studio call them. I thought you should know."

"Before the cops notice me sniffing around and pick me up. Does anything in the note ring any bells?"

She reflected. " 'Have got' is British idiom. An American would just say 'have' or maybe 'got' in some social circles."

"Anything else?"

"Fifty thousand dollars isn't very ambitious."

"It'll do in my social circles."

"My husband could get his hands on quite a bit more, without much trouble."

He took a last look at the note. "Where's the original?"

"I didn't ask. Presumably the studio gave it to the cops or couriered it up to Lionel in the Owens Valley with the day's call sheets."

"I'll go check the school. Would you phone ahead and say I'm okay? I think it's necessary now."

"Don't get too worked up about kidnapping, Mr. Liffey. Something is fishy."

"Mr. Liffey's my dad. I'm Jack."

"My friends call me Mary Ann," she said. Her smile cut through him like sun dispersing a cloud. "It's my real name."

He nodded.

As he was leaving she looked into her lap and then up at him. "So which is it, Jack?"

"Pardon?"

"Courage or happiness?"

"Beats me."

FIRST, his car wouldn't start. The old Concord had more miles on it than a fleet of taxis, and he guessed one of the cells in the battery was going dry. It was one of those batteries that said you never had to add water, but they invented them back east, where they had humidity. In Southern California you still had to add water, and now you had to pry the top off with a four-foot crowbar to do it.

There was enough hill on her cul-de-sac to roll-start in second, and just as he got it going he noticed the white Lumina start up behind and follow. They should buy beat-up Hondas or yellow BMWs, he thought. They were so conspicuous it was funny. The plainwrap almost hit him when he crammed on his brakes abruptly where the cul-de-sac fed onto the steep part of the hill just as some kid facedown on a big skateboard went by very fast. The kid was wearing a bicycle crash helmet, which wouldn't have helped all that much at the speed he was going and he was giving the world, or maybe God, the finger with both hands. Might as well offend all the fates at once, Jack Liffey thought. He looked back up the street before starting, and sure enough two more boards clattered toward him, one piloted by a girl with bright red hair leaking out of a football helmet. He followed them down, staying far enough back to avoid running over anybody who fell off, and saw a little clot of bystanders around a fat kid with a stopwatch and walkie-talkie.

In the rearview mirror, Jack Liffey could see the cop in the passenger seat surreptitiously on a microphone. They followed him down into the dreary industrial end of Hollywood and then he made four right turns, just in case it was a fantastic coincidence. The Lumina stayed behind and he found a block with some homes on it so there'd be witnesses to whatever it was, and he stopped. They stopped fifty yards back, neither trying to hide nor close the gap.

He got out and strolled toward them, watching the two dim faces watch him. He concentrated on the driver, heavy-set and impenetrably calm. The window came down silently as he approached. The passenger side, younger and Latino, with a tidy mustache and mobile face, was holding a microphone softly, and both of them watched him the way you'd watch something you might soon decide to eat.

The radio fizzed softly, then startled all of them: "Forty-four Alice, Forty-four Alice. Come back *immediately,* over. Do you still see the intruder?"

Jack Liffey thought he sensed a minute upward roll of the driver's eyes.

"This is four-four Alice," the passenger said. "Everything is just swell, sir. Over."

"You should still be seeing the intruder. Do you see him?"

It was then Jack Liffey realized *he* was the intruder.

The driver took the microphone away from his partner and looked at it for an instant disgustedly before keying it on. "We got the *intruder* in the crosshairs, sir, but there's a thousand VCs in those pointy hats. I think they got heavy weapons, and I don't know if we can hold out. Can you give us an air strike? Over."

"Who is this?"

The cop studied the microphone.

"I said, who is this? This operation is not a figure of fun."

Still the driver didn't reply.

"Forty-four Alice, I order you to identify yourself immediately!"

The driver clicked the microphone ostentatiously a couple of times. "You got to say 'over' at your end . . . sir. Over."

"Who is this? *Over.*"

"This is forty-four Alice. It's against procedures to use our names, sir. I got the intruder standing at the window right here and I think maybe you ought to shut the fuck up now. Over and out."

Jack Liffey heard a small sucking sound of air drawn through the man's teeth as he hung up the microphone and turned an impassive face to the window.

"Intruder?" Jack Liffey said.

The man shrugged lightly. "They sent an FNG down from the top because this is a very big show. He's got an oar in the water some of the time."

"Fucking New Guy," Jack Liffey said.

"You been in the Big 'Nam, too."

"My name is Jack Liffey. I was hired by Mrs. Bright to find her daughter."

"We know that. I'm Lieutenant Malamud, and this is Sergeant Flor. This here *operation* is something of a high-profile portion of a long-running story, and we're here to see nobody hurts theirself."

"First missing kid I've seen get this treatment."

"Uh-huh."

"Is there something I should know?"

"You tell us."

"Mrs. Bright doesn't seem very worried. Like it may all be a mistake."

"Really?"

"C'mon, that's all I know. I'm on my way to the girl's boarding school, Taunton in Hancock Park. Can't you tell me anything?"

Lieutenant Malamud moved his lower jaw back and forth thoughtfully, like a guy who never really got excited about anything. "I spent a lot of years in Hollywood Division, and while I was driving around, you know, I took pictures of the real places that Raymond Chandler was always writing about, like his office, which a lot of people think is the Security Pacific Building on Cahuenga but I like the Guaranty building on Ivar better. Anyway, that was all fiction and it doesn't mean I like a real private eye much."

"I worked at Rockwell down in El Segundo, pretty nice office with a window," Jack Liffey said. "I was a technical writer back when they were still making planes with guns in them. Then I was the peace dividend. I got child support to pay, so I do what I can. I look for missing kids."

The lieutenant turned to his partner. "What do you think, Flor?"

The younger man shrugged.

"Cut me some slack," Jack Liffey said. "I'll let you know anything I find out."

"Uh-huh. Look, there's a war going on here, on a scale of, like, maybe not on the order of the ones they used to give numbers, but right up there for meanness, and you don't want to get your dick caught in it, believe me."

"You couldn't tell me who's fighting whom?"

"I can tell you Jamaica is a pretty island, but it's got the highest murder rate in the western hemisphere."

"That's supposed to help?"

"There it is."

"Thanks a lot, guys. I hear Puerto Rico's pretty, too."

He felt a tremor in the asphalt as he walked away and wondered if it was another aftershock. About 3.0. It might just as easily have been somebody working on the subway tunnel, trying to dig it out again. Nothing worked quite right in L.A. except the stuff made for the rich.

A few blocks north of Taunton School he had to come to a stop for a party spilling onto the street from a broad lawn in front of a faux-southern mansion, all black tuxes and ball gowns like models trying to simulate a slick magazine ad. But the guy in front had a tux cut to ribbons and hanging off him like party streamers and he fled ahead of the others, who were laughing and chasing him with pointy pairs of scissors. Jack Liffey knew there was no way on earth he would ever figure out what was going on there.

Taunton itself took up most of an old-money block, high walls hiding a couple of modern wings that were plugged into a huge Tudor estate at the corner. One discreet sign at ground level announced the name and nothing else. He wedged his old Concord between a Lexus and a lime-green Facel Vega and found the entrance up a broad staircase between sleeping lions.

A smell of some flower rose as he mounted the steps and a kind of brief annoyance at privilege rose as well. It subsided quickly when he saw a little girl standing in the hall, looking lost and sad, and he thought of Maeve with a pang. He wondered how she would look in the blazer and tweedy skirt, but there was little chance of that.

Inside the first door he found the headmistress. She was named Miss Rebecca Plumkill and she had round wire glasses and was dressed so severely she looked like she ought to be in a Nazi hat on the cover of a man's magazine tying up another woman.

"Mrs. Bright called. You don't look like a detective."

"What did you expect? Dragon tattoos?"

She burst out laughing and sent him to see the girl's housemother, Myrna Kleis. The headmistress hadn't seemed any more worried than the girl's mother. He wondered if their girls went AWOL all the time.

Myrna Kleis met him in a tiny cluttered office just inside the door of one of the modern wings. She had a froth of pure white hair that looked suspiciously acrylic, and a strong European accent, and she looked sickly and fluttery in the fluorescent light. A pinned-back curtain seemed to lead into a residence room and the whole thing reminded him of a motel sign-in.

His occupation had preceded him there, too.

"Mr. Liffey, I will assist you however I can." She offered a limp, dry hand. "Our girls are so precious."

"Do they go missing a lot?"

"No, they do not. Could I make you some tea, please?"

"Sure." He was getting a lot more tea offers than he wanted, but he guessed the fussing would put her at ease.

"Come into the sitting room, please."

Two stiff sofas faced each other over a low spindly table, probably for tête-à-têtes with the girls, and on a cart there was a fancy British teamaker with a lot of glass tubes and knobs, like something bolted together by a mad scientist.

As she fiddled with the tea machine his eye was drawn to a small oil painting in a heavy frame. It had pride of place in the room and it looked like a maelstrom of a dozen shades of blue, with streaks of sleet across it.

"It belonged to my father, in Vienna," she said when she noticed. "It is my most prized possession."

"Kandinsky?" he guessed.

She smiled. "His colleague and friend and admirer Theo Harten. They were in a group called *der Blaue Reiter,* though Harten never became well known and he died in the ovens at Birkenau. Does the painting speak to you?"

"Not really."

"It speaks . . . volumes to me." She clanged the lid of her teapot shut. "I look at it for some time every day, the way some people will listen to the *Brandenburg Concertos* or read a favorite poem. It's my music."

"I see."

"No, I don't think you do, Mr. Liffey. That's an Irish name. Do you like Yeats?"

"Most Irishmen are familiar with Yeats, or Seamus Heaney these days. I like Auden more."

The machine began to steam and hiss softly, and then brown liquid dribbled into a pot. "The sounds of Yeats are reds and browns, with flecks of gold.

> *The falcon can no longer hear the falconer,*
> *Things fall apart . . .*

she quoted. "The color is so *intense.*"

Myrna Kleis shook her head and then drifted across the room and stared intently at the painting from maybe two feet away.

"It sings, but I have no way of knowing it sings the same song for me it did for Harten or Kandinsky. They were both synesthetes, you know? Though I have a feeling that it is possible Harten only pretended to be, to please his master. Do you know what synesthesia is?''

He figured he was about to learn, so he kept his mouth shut.

''It is a peculiarity of the psyche of some people who have the ability to shut down the yackety-yak of their analytic mind and have their senses cooperate, actually to fuse. Kandinsky could hear colors and see sounds. He was tested by skeptics and he would always make the same associations. His one-act opera was called *The Yellow Sound*.''

She tore her eyes away from the painting and looked at him.

''I believe current research suggests that synesthesia has something to do with a deficit of serotonin in the brain, but it would be a shame to explain away Kandinsky like that, wouldn't it?''

''I take it you have this capacity.''

She nodded. ''I don't often speak of it. People think you are crazy.''

Nutty as a fruit bat, he thought. He took a guess. ''Did Lee have this ability?''

She nodded. ''That's why I brought it up. One afternoon a few weeks ago she came to me very upset. She told me she had been listening to Bach and she'd started to lose the color. At first things went pastel and then she was only hearing the music as music and it scared her so much she shut the CD off. She was terrified she might be growing out of any natural talents she had for color.''

Great, he thought. He could start looking for her at Standard Brands paint store.

Myrna Kleis poured tea into two delicate Chinese cups. ''Milk? Lemon?''

''Nothing. Do a lot of painters experience this thing?'' he asked.

She shook her head and brought him a cup. She remained standing with her cup. ''More musicians, actually. Rachmaninoff, Liszt, Olivier Messiaen. He went to Bryce

Canyon in Utah on a commission and he said later that *Des Canyons des Étoiles* wrote itself out of the scenery. It's a weird piece, but everybody likes it. He's dead now. David Hockney is the only living synesthete painter that I am aware of.''

''Do you think this has anything to do with her running off?''

''If I didn't, I wouldn't be opening myself to the possibility of ridicule. She was very upset at starting to lose her colors.'' Her eyes begged him not to scoff.

''So where has she gone?''

She shook her head sadly. ''Ask Bronwen King. I was Lee's adviser and friend, but she was her confidante. I'll get her for you.''

The housemother sipped at her teacup, then left him alone in the room. He looked at the painting again. He was beginning to like the edgy swirl of it, but he didn't hear anything. Then, he didn't really expect to. He felt no urgency to have remarkable powers. Though being able to pick horses would have been nice.

A bell rang in the hallway outside and it gave him a chill of sensory recall. *That* was the way senses got to him—the involuntary memory of the oppressive orderings of high school. Six minutes to get to a book locker that wouldn't open half the time and swap books. Neither college nor the army nor fifteen years in aerospace could erase the dream of standing there naked and suddenly realizing he had only six minutes before French finals and he had forgotten to go to French class all year.

He was actually sweating a little when Myrna Kleis led in the girl, tall with short shiny black hair.

''Mr. Liffey, this is Lee's friend Bronwen.''

''Hello, Bronwen.''

The girl stared at him neutrally, hugging a Peechee to the chest of her blue blazer.

''Could I speak to her alone?'' Jack Liffey said.

''Of course.'' The housemother was offended, but she nodded curtly and went out.

"I'll disturb your day as little as possible," he offered. "I'm sorry to pull you out of class, though when I was in high school I think I would have welcomed any interruption."

"Cut to the chase," she said.

He chuckled. "Okay. I think you know Lee is missing. I need to speak to her, just to make sure she's okay, and Ms. Kleis thought you might have an idea where she is."

She started humming something softly, and he waited a few moments.

"I get it," he said. "If I recognized the tune, the lyric would probably be an insult."

" 'You know something is happening here, but you don't know what it is, do you, Mr. Jones?' "

"If your humming was better I'd know 'Ballad of a Thin Man.' 'And he says, How does it feel to be such a freak, and you say, Impossible, as he hands you a bone.' "

Despite herself, she gave a small smile.

"Go on, sit down. If Lee doesn't want to go see her mom, I won't make her. I've been finding missing kids for a long time and I never make them do anything they don't want to do."

She didn't sit. She mastered her urge to be polite and looked away from him as she spoke slowly, judiciously, "If bullshit falls in the forest and nobody's there, does it make a sound?"

"Look at me," he said sharply.

She did, suddenly an obedient fifteen-year-old.

"You're endangering your friend's life. I don't have time to waste convincing some spoiled rich kid that I know the score. There's a ransom note and Lee might be in trouble. If you know anything at all, tell me *now*."

"I'm not spoiled," she said defiantly.

He thought about it, then nodded once, giving her that one.

"She's been working all her free time with a filmmaker named Dae Kim. She's been his PA."

He immediately thought of "public address," but that couldn't be right.

The question must have showed. "Production assistant. Kim is a well-known underground filmmaker, but she said he was going mainstream in an interesting way. Some company hired him to do an interactive movie for CD-ROM."

"Where would I find him?"

"The company is called PropellorHeads. It's on Little Santa Monica near Sepulveda."

"Thanks."

There might have been tears in her eyes. "Do you think Lee's okay?"

"Yes, I'm sure she is." He pointed at the painting. "Can you hear it?"

She shook her head. "I can't do that either. Lee has all the luck. She even had lunch with Brad Pitt once."

3

DIFFERENT PARADIGMS

THE RECEPTIONIST SQUINTED AT HER COMPUTER SCREEN, AP-
parently unable to get the words on it to do what she
wanted. "Way bad," she murmured.

The logo on the dark gray wall behind her was a stylized
beanie with a propeller on top, and beside it were six TV
screens let into the wall, all but one showing duplicates of
a video game where a little round-faced boy with a sword
flailed away at what looked like a crushed Buick with legs.
As fast as the multiple swords dispatched the Buicks with
bright puffs, new ones waddled out of the scenery. The
sixth screen, on the right edge of the array, was dead.

"I'd like to see Dae Kim."

"So would I," she said. She might have been about nineteen and the heavy eye makeup gave her a permanently
startled look. Office professionalism seemed to have gone
south with the California economy. She leaned in over a
dozen toppled vitamin bottles and a pile of Skittles to peer
at the screen.

"Do you know Lee Borowsky?"

"Sure. Do you know WordPerfect?"

"A bit."

"How do you get it to turn that list of numbers into
columns?"

"No one in the known universe has been able to get

WordPerfect to do columns. Could you, perhaps, tell Dae Kim I'm here?''

"He doesn't really work here. He's, like, whatayacallit, *contract*. Dae's doing Matrix for us, mostly he's out shooting or something. I could put something on his E-mail for you.''

"Could I talk to someone else?'' He opened a leather ID wallet briefly, the kind police and feds carried, but his had a card with a gold stamp and a fine-print statement that he'd passed a course on investigation and dispute mediation at World Wisdom College of East Orange, New Jersey. Even that wasn't true.

"Oh, like, sure. Sorry. Maybe you better see Bruce.''

She hit a function key and what looked like an architect's blueprint of the floor came up on her screen. Superimposed on the rooms were small grinning faces, sometimes two to a room. She tapped a face that had a tiny dark goatee and the loudspeaker on her computer came on with a hiss and a faraway voice.

"Uh, Bruce, uh,'' canting her head, as if she needed to get the icon's attention. "There's a guy here, a cop, wants to see Dae. Could you, like, talk to him?''

"I'll be right out.''

She punched the screen back to word processor and grinned. "Cool, isn't it? I can track 'em all over, even to the bathroom. 'Course, they're always dumping their trackers in somebody else's lunch bucket when they get in their question-authority mood.''

"I think I can understand.''

Two young Asians with fade haircuts walked past kicking a hackey sack to one another.

"... So I go, 'It's just a cubicle,' and he goes, 'Man, don't tell me doors aren't important. Doors are mega-important. They're the defense of your identity.' ''

"I think you are your favorite application.''

"Unless you're just empty-file.''

They went in the inner double door and then the man with the goatee peered out into the reception area. He was thirtysomething with a dark ponytail below his shoulders.

"G'day, Officer," he said. "I'm Bruce Parfit. Why don't we shoot on through."

The man barely opened his mouth when he spoke, and he had one of the strongest Australian accents Jack Liffey'd ever heard.

"Jack Liffey."

He followed into a long corridor with a lot of doors. It had oyster-colored walls and plum carpeting. "I'm not actually a cop. I'm an investigator."

"Stone the crows," Parfit said with a thin smile.

They passed an open door where two young men played Whiffle basketball. One was in a wheelchair. Above the Far Side cartoons taped up beside their door was a sign: THE IMMINENT DEATH OF THE NET IS PREDICTED. Inside the next door, a woman was being fitted out in a pink antebellum ball gown. Over her head was a big inflated shark. A bay off the corridor held a dozen young people working at screens that all seemed to show the same 3-D view of glowing pipelines receding in perspective.

"That's Dae's show," Parfit said. "Backgrounds. That's the matrix. We're going flat out on it."

Parfit took him into a big sunny office that looked out over the city. They were on the fourth floor and Little Santa Monica bustled below, split off from Big Santa Monica by a dirt strip that had once been the red-car line. A billboard to the east had flickering neon digits that professed to report the exact number of smokers who had died since the beginning of the year.

"Take a pew."

Jack Liffey sat in a black leather Mies van der Rohe chair. The wall displayed a lot of stills from video games behind a long band of Plexiglas. On a sideboard was an open jar of chunky Jiff with a spoon in it and a pyramid of Tab cans.

"Thanks."

"You're interested in Dae Kim?"

"I'm more interested in Lee Borowsky. I think she was his part-time production assistant."

The man seemed to go very still. "I knew that one was trouble."

"Why is that?"

"She's the daughter of a director who does a lot of work for Monogram Pictures. PH and Monogram have been in a feud for a year. A real argy-bargy."

"PH?"

"That's us. Monogram would love to sink us without a trace and this girl showing up was just too big a coincidence, so I told Dae to keep her out of the building. She's also like fourteen or something, and there are labor laws. Now, can I ask what you're on about?"

Suddenly there was a crash and they both jumped. A naked pink Barbie doll had caromed into the room off the open door. A sheepish-looking twentysomething peered in clutching a nine iron. "Sorry, Brucie."

When the golfer had left, Bruce Parfit got up and shut the door.

"Bruce, the damn sprite keeps disappearing when you change the level of armaments." It was a tinny voice out of the dark computer.

"Not now, Bobby." He hit a key, but there was no discernible change in the machine. Peace seemed to return to the room gradually, like liquid filling a pool.

"Lee is missing, and her mom wants me to find her. Probably off with a boyfriend. I just want to talk to Dae Kim."

He rattled his fingers on the desktop. "Too right. Maybe I best have him call you."

"You mean in case the girl is holed up in his bedroom, being underage and all?"

"Something like that. Frankly, Matrix is half shot in a very distinctive Kim style and I don't need to lose my director and rubbish the project. We needed a director of his horsepower and his particular sensibility and he's damn good."

Jack Liffey noticed all of a sudden that one of the man's eyes was blue and the other was green. It made him look like a Siamese cat. "I'm not going to the cops."

Parfit beckoned and the two of them stood shoulder to shoulder at the floor-length glass wall. The height made him nervous, the glass going right down to his toes. The man pointed and he saw the Lumina, parked conspicuously on a red zone with an elbow out the window.

"I saw them roll up just before Bambi buzzed you in. They following you?"

"You spend that much time watching the window?"

"A bit."

"If this were a video game, I suppose you could zap them with your ray gun."

"If this were a video game, I don't think I've got the juice yet. My worlds are very rational, in a plodding sort of way. You've got to earn your power to kill."

"What's your problem with Monogram Pictures?"

He seemed to think about it.

"I don't know if you'd understand."

"I'll probably get the little words."

The Australian smiled. "It's differences of metaphysics, or maybe just meta-*phors*." He seemed pleased with himself. He unscrewed a little metal vial, shook it between thumb and forefinger, then rubbed his nostrils. It was just a taste, but Jack Liffey was astonished the man would be so blatant. He'd stepped into another world.

"How do you know I'm not a narc?"

"They're all little guys with long hair."

"That's vice."

"Whatever. Monogram is an old-style Hollywood studio, run by fat guys with cigars, even if a lot of them aren't fat anymore and don't smoke cigars. What's crucial is the way they think of the world—they want to build a big dam, store up a lot of water, then bust the dam and everybody grabs as much water as they can when it's rushing out. The dam is a Schwarzenegger movie, and everybody snatches what they can off the profit train as it steams past. Him most of all, but also the studio and the director and the publicists and all the crafts. Then they go out and build another dam. What's important is being there to grab the water.''

Down on the street a black-and-white police car pulled up next to the Lumina. Words were exchanged and the hand dangling out of the Lumina seemed to give the finger. The patrol car revved up and pulled away. Bruce Parfit chuckled.

''We're Silicon Valley. We want to build the widest swiftest river that we can and keep it flowing past all the time. We know people are going to siphon off as much as they can, so we just keep making it faster and wider so they'll want to use our river. What I'm saying is, we rely on our expertise and being light on our feet to stay ahead of the game rather than a narrow sense of property rights. It's a different way of thinking, so you can see you could have two companies, both operating within their lights, both feeling justified and honorable, and there could be serious misunderstandings.''

Suddenly a riderless horse appeared on the dusty median between the two Santa Monicas, galloping westward. It had an English saddle and looked panicky. Sergeant Flor got out of the Lumina and tried to wave it down, but the horse reared and ran past. Then it was out of sight, the kind of thing that left you wondering if you'd seen it at all. The only proof was a bit of dust on the air and Flor standing there with his hands on his hips.

''Is that a way of saying you stole some of their product?''

Bruce Parfit smiled and his ponytail swished a little from side to side as he made a theatrical shrug. ''Information wants to be free.''

For some reason, Parfit gave him the address of Dae Kim's studio, and on his way out Jack Liffey noticed that the receptionist had given up on the computer and was hunched forward nearsightedly, nose too close to a New

Age paperback with a misty picture of an East Indian with a lot of hair on the cover.

"Wow, killer," she said. "The baboo says only the present really exists."

He leaned close to her and whispered, "But it'll be over any minute now."

THE address was on the north edge of Koreatown, where the mansions of Hancock Park petered out into big frame houses and stucco apartments with those doodad lamps plastered on the front like giant bugs on the windshield. It was a no-man's-land between Korea and Central America. In some areas the old homes had been cut into eightplexes and the lawns were shaggy, and ailing Oldsmobiles with signs that said YO AMO QUERETARO leaked oil onto the crowded streets. Whole pockets of the area, however, had been done up and tidied and had grilles on the windows. Aging Korean grandmothers squatted beside empty bus benches, caught between two or three worlds, and the old churches had been resignboarded for Missionary Korean Baptist denominations.

He slowed past a big Italianate house that a crew of workers was painting up in horizontal bands of bright green and purple, right across doors and window sashes and the too skinny Corinthian columns. He stopped to stare, wondering if it was possible that somewhere someone liked a paint scheme like that, or if it was an elaborate practical joke. It was like living in a damaged reality.

Actually he hadn't been slowing to see the house, but to twit the cops who pulled to the curb a half block behind. Jack Liffey picked up a black water bottle someone had given him that was shaped like a car phone and pretended to talk to someone for a long time. He hoped they had some kind of scanner and were frantically trying to trace his call.

Then he drove to Serrano Avenue. Two blocks north of Wilshire, but it looked like something from the Midwest, big two-story single-family homes behind trees. Dae Kim's house had a telescope dome on the roof and an old panel van in the driveway. Parfit had called it Kim's studio, but it looked like an ordinary house. The front door had a little sign that said, DO GO AROUND BACK. DO-BE-DO.

In back, a screened vestibule had its door open and Jack Liffey stepped inside gingerly to a kitchen piled with Styrofoam cups and hardening Danish on paper plates, like the kitchenette of a real estate office. "Dae Kim?"

"Is that the gumshoe?" The voice came out of the front room, so nasal and suburban he pictured some blond surfer.

"Jack Liffey." Bruce Parfit must have called ahead to make sure no half-dressed fifteen-year-olds were lolling on his sofa.

"Come through but watch your step."

Jack Liffey came to a dead stop in the doorway. Beyond the kitchen the whole downstairs had been hollowed out and most of the floor was a miniature city, like a train layout. Kim lay on his stomach adjusting a long metal gooseneck that depended from a complex grid crisscrossing the room just above head level.

"Downtown L.A., 2099," he said. "Stay over there a bit." He wore bib overalls over a black turtleneck and gave a pleasant oval smile for a moment before going back to tweaking his model. Despite the surfer drawl, he was definitely Asian. He also seemed tall, though it was hard to tell from his position.

"I'm sorry to bother you."

"No trouble. Bruce apologized for giving out the address, but I'm in the book. Of course there's quite a few Kims in the area. Even a few Dae Kims. It could take you a while."

"I'm just looking for Lee Borowsky."

At the name, someone across the room stirred. A thirtysomething head appeared around a stub wall to stare at him. He had shaggy strawberry hair and looked suntanned. This was the true owner of the surfer voice, Jack Liffey thought.

"She hasn't been with us for a while. Hennie here has

taken over for her. You're just in time to see a test. Come around by the L.A. River.''

He joined the assistant behind the stub wall and saw a half-dozen monitors and banks of controls. Dae Kim extricated himself from the model and picked up a joystick hanging from a cable. The apparatus overhead began to whir.

"There's a video camera the size of a peanut on the end of that arm and we can fly it through the model any way we want.''

"You want to tape, Dae?'' the assistant asked. He had a strong South African accent, but the voice was very soft, as if spoken through a foot of cotton wool.

Dae Kim shook his head. "Put it through to A. Bring up the softlights.''

The assistant touched a few keys and bright lights in gauzy boxes came on up in the ceiling. Kim pointed to the biggest monitor. He heard something whir and then the screen lit up and the model world, grown full size, flew past. The camera seemed to swoop and glide between buildings until it came in for a soft landing on a helipad on the roof of a building.

"Bingo.''

"Looked great,'' Jack Liffey said.

"It's not bad.'' Dae Kim hung up the controller on a peg. "Amazing what you can get away with on video. I'm only doing this project for PropellorHeads because I'll end up with the flycam setup for my own use. That makes me halfway to a movie mogul.''

"Can you hear colors?'' Jack Liffey asked casually.

Dae Kim laughed. "Hennie, play something on the Johnson . . . oh . . . Social Impulse.''

The assistant dug through a cardboard carton, discarding tapes left and right, and came up with a fat cassette in some strange format that went into a player in front of him.

"Kill the sound,'' Kim snapped.

An image came up on the monitor, swirling colors that

merged and split, like layers of color being drawn down into a fold of paint in a can.

"Gosh," Jack Liffey said.

Kim laughed again. "Frank Lloyd Wright called television chewing gum for the eyes. Most video art is chewing gum for the brain. Lee loved that damn thing, she'd watch it like a drug. I tried to argue with her. I believe in character and story. Story is the West's contribution to civilization, even when it gets a bit soapy." His mind churned a mile a minute, jumping from thought to thought. "You know the hallmark of a soap opera, don't you? All the dialogue is exactly what any amateur would write, nothing unexpected. For resonance you've got to have the unexpected."

And just then the firebomb came through the back window. The jar broke and spilled a pale blue fire across most of L.A. 2099.

"Out out!" Jack Liffey yelled.

The South African's eyes went wide and he seemed frozen in place and Liffey hurled himself through a corner of the fire, kicked open a French window, and stuffed the assistant outside, then looked back to make sure Kim was going out the front door and stepped out himself into a bed of nasturtiums.

4

ÉPATER LA BOURGEOISIE

HE WAS OUT OF THE NASTURTIUMS AND SPRINTING TOWARD the grapestake fence in back before he realized it. Splinters tore at his palms as he boosted up to see a green Ford Explorer skirr up gravel as it bounced hard out of the alley. He thought he saw dreadlocks on the driver and a sticker on the bumper, green black red.

When he dropped off the fence, Lieutenant Malamud was facing him with a shirttail out and panting a little.

"You look out of shape. It was an Explorer," Jack Liffey said. "Forest green."

"Did you see the driver?"

"Not really."

"Plates?"

"California, that's all."

Faraway they could hear the first wail of a siren. Up the drive, Dae Kim was spraying water in a side window with a hose while Sergeant Flor marched past him with a black water bottle like a cellular phone.

"Who were you calling, Liffey, Evian?"

"I stopped for a drink."

Flor unscrewed the top, sniffed, and then poured out the water.

"I had one of these sports bottle things once," he said. "It broke. Everything breaks."

Flor took out a Swiss Army knife, opened the reamer,

and punctured the bottle a few times before discarding it onto the grass.

The sirens became very loud and then the first one choked off as a pumper pulled up in front, a red sedan squealing in dramatically right behind it. A man came out of the sedan, pulling on a yellow slicker, and sauntered up the drive as if he was on a Sunday stroll. Jack Liffey and the cops watched as he spoke to Kim and waved down to his men, then Lieutenant Malamud tucked in his shirt and walked down to join them.

"You been playing with matches?" Flor said pugnaciously.

Jack Liffey sighed. "I've been helpful, Sergeant. I'll tell you anything I know."

Flor watched with leaden eyes, then glanced at Dae Kim. "How does the slope figure in this?"

He wondered what Flor's problem was. "You know a cop named Quinn?" Jack Liffey had had a lot of trouble with a belligerent Culver City cop named Quinn, and not just over Marlena. It only took about a square foot of the surface of the earth for a man to stand up straight, but you couldn't let anyone take your square foot away or you'd never get it back.

"Buddy of yours?"

"Nah, just a racist cop. Talks about wetbacks a lot."

Flor watched him for a long time without speaking. Down below, the firemen were stringing hose from a hydrant across the street. A ladder truck came up, blocking the whole street. "How does the 'Oriental gentleman' figure in this?"

"Ask him yourself." He started to walk away.

"Liffey! Do you want trouble?"

His vision went red and he turned back and got in Flor's face and noticed the acne scars and the thickened eyebrows and broken nose. He'd probably been a boxer once. After the first few seconds Jack Liffey wasn't half as angry as he pretended, but he could sense they were watching from below and he raised his fists and waved them angrily, saying under his breath, "You're probably a really nice guy. I think I might like you. Of course I don't want trouble. We'll be the best of friends."

He went on for a while, with Flor looking more and more puzzled. It was an old baseball manager's trick so up in the stands it looked like you were cursing an ump to his face, but you weren't really saying anything that he could eject you for. Then he turned abruptly and walked away, past the whole startled group. A canvas hose swelled just as he stepped on it and someone shouted. Someday the cops would figure a way to recruit guys who didn't feel the need to throw their weight around. The shower room at the Olympic Auditorium was probably not the best place to start.

He knew Kim would be tied up for a while now and his car was thoroughly blocked in, so he walked down to Wilshire and Western and found a pay phone near the Metro station and called Lori Bright.

"Hi, this is Jack Liffey. Any news?"

Her breathing was odd at the other end.

"Did I wake you?" he asked. "I'm sorry."

She sighed. "No. I was masturbating and you wrecked the rhythm."

He didn't know how to deal with that. He'd never known a woman who would joke about something like that.

"You want me to call back and start this all over again at some time more convenient?"

"No, that's fine, thanks. No news has flashed past on my ticker."

"Have you ever heard of PropellorHeads?" he asked.

"Huh? No."

"Dae Kim?"

"Is that a Chinese dumpling?"

"Korean. I wouldn't call him a dumpling." He couldn't help wondering if she was using something, or just her hands, and if she was undressed, or was she just teasing him for some reason of her own.

"No."

"Has Lee ever worked directly for her dad or for Monogram Pictures?"

"Lee is fifteen, for heaven's sake."

"Know any Jamaicans?"

"I worked once with the guy from the soft-drink ad with the big ho-ho-ho baritone. I can't remember his name. That was donkey's ages ago."

"Okay."

"Are you going to report in regularly like this, read me the latest clues?"

"Isn't that my job?"

"Something like that."

"Back to work then," he said. "Both of us." He hung up and contemplated Lori Bright sexually, the laugh and the gravelly voice and the bobbing he'd noticed under her blouse and the aura of heat she flung around so recklessly. He didn't know what he felt, but he knew even thinking about it like this put him in over his head. That was one experiment that was definitely excluded.

The news rack had the street edition of the *News*, formerly the *Valley Greensheet*, and the headline screamed that Manson 2 had done in a TV starlet. Through the scratched plastic rack he could read that Kim Barbara Kelly, the bright new secretary from TV's *Friend in Need*, had been found dead in her Silverlake home with OFF THE PIG scrawled in her own blood on the— He wondered when the world got to a point where there wasn't even anything left to copycat. Perhaps it was a good sign that the murder of a celebrity was still shocking.

On a bus bench beside the news rack he saw a Xeroxed flyer, neatly hand-lettered and glued to the backrest. He'd seen them before, from a woman who called herself Saint Becky and plastered her obsessions up and down Wilshire. At the moment she was enraged that "colored people" were stealing million-dollar royalty checks from her mailbox, and to rid herself of the problem she gave explicit directions on getting to the airport—"be sure to 'jot' down the 'directions' and go to any 'bookstore' and find a 'map' and go west on 'Wilshire' to 'Sepulveda' and turn 'left' and in 'case' you have any 'problems' along the 'way' you can call '411.' '' It was apparently their inability to find the airport that kept the blacks from going back to Africa.

He'd seen her by accident once, when he'd been staking out an apartment not far away for the return of a runaway's boyfriend, a stringy blonde in her mid-thirties. She had been flitting from phone pole to bus bench to utility box, plucking flyers from a satchel and gluing them up with a roller of some kind. There hadn't been anything furtive in her movements. She'd seemed perfectly normal, in fact, just intense in a way you couldn't quite put your finger on, like a lightbulb a few moments before it was going to fizz and burn out.

He went into a flyblown diner just off Wilshire and stared dully at the big menu over the counter: world-famous burgers, tacos grandes, pastrami on bun, Armenian pizza, and dim sum, a whole U.N. of ways to combine bread dough and grease. The counterman was Asian and the cook, as usual, looked Latino.

''I'll take a world-famous burger,'' Jack Liffey said.

''No meat.''

''Pardon.''

''No meat. Very sorry.''

''What do you have?''

''No meat.''

''Pastrami?''

''No meat.'' The counterman smiled, with a vague air of embarrassment, and Jack Liffey wondered if there was something he didn't know going on here.

''Armenian pizza?''

The man shook his head sadly. *Politely unhelpful*: he'd taken a whole lot of R&R leaves from 'Nam to places like Singapore and Bangkok, looking for culture rather than whores, and that was Jack Liffey's concept of Asia in a nutshell. Maybe Dae Kim would rectify it.

''Coffee?''

That they had, though he knew it wouldn't be any good.

He sat in a plastic booth to sip dutifully from the foam cup. He looked out a scratched window across an alley at a run-down brick apartment block, the lower windows all kicked in. It was a postnuclear scene, with one old woman hanging sheets dully as if she'd been asleep when the sirens had gone.

He thought of Kathy, and wondered if they'd ever get back together. Things hadn't really gone bad between them until he'd been out of work for a year and was demoralized and drinking. He hadn't had a drink in eighteen months now, no coke in longer than that. No cigarettes for almost a year. On his dresser he kept an ashtray with matches and a loose cigarette, what he called his failure kit. It was to prove to himself he had a right to any good luck that came along, if any ever did. The cigarette was so old, oils were leaching out of the tobacco and soaking through the paper and he was getting tired of looking at it.

The floor shuddered for an instant, then gave one side-ward jolt, as if a giant had swatted the diner lightly. All their eyes met.

''Three-point-eight,'' Jack Liffey said.

The counterman shook his head. ''Four-oh.''

The cook said nothing.

After a moment, with no follow-up, they all stopped anticipating.

He looked at the old building again and thought of Kathy sitting at the vanity mirror, brushing her long brown hair, over and over. It was like an ache. And the high-school teacher she was seeing now. A nice guy, actually. Jack Liffey wanted to drop him off a cliff.

Sergeant Flor had started it off, getting up against him, and he could tell his temper was still frayed. It was a good day to punch someone.

HE found Dae Kim sitting on a stool to contemplate the remains of L.A. 2099. Outside, the fire trucks had gone and the cops were back in their car, looking bored. The South African was squeegeeing up a mud made of balsa-wood ash. The flash fire had made short work of everything west of the Harbor Freeway, L.A.'s "West Bank," and the water had done the rest. A strap of his overalls drooped over Dae Kim's arm, and for the first time Jack Liffey noticed how thin he was. He couldn't have weighed in at much over one hundred.

"Sorry," Jack Liffey said. "It looked really great."

Dae Kim nodded. "We'll have to do it all digital now. I didn't want to. Digital's not really good enough in our price range."

Dae Kim let his eyes drift across the shelves that held old electronic components and meticulously labeled boxes. "It's funny if you're superstitious. Just this morning I was thinking that houses have no memory. All the family dinners that took place right here. The arguments and the making up and kids being disciplined and somebody listening to *The Shadow* on a big, old cathedral radio and somebody hatching plans to go to college, and nervous dates squirming as they wait to meet the parents. It's all gone, just like my model."

"That's the way it's supposed to be."

"How do you mean?" Dae Kim asked.

"Think what would happen if the memories kept piling up and never made room for newer stuff. You couldn't hear yourself talk."

That had engaged the man's notice and he looked at Jack Liffey with new interest.

"You're a strange gumshoe. Did you know the dead have been dying off for half a million years and still they're a minority?"

"I think I heard that. Unfortunately, it's not true if you do the math."

"Okay, but there's lots of folks, right? What always gets me is, where's our Shakespeare and Dante and Rembrandt, and our great statesmen like Metternich and FDR? It doesn't say a lot for the upward spiral of history, does it?"

"It's been a little hard to talk about the upward spiral of history ever since Goethe gave way to Hitler."

He chuckled. "Can I offer you a beer? They're in the icebox there."

"My mom used to say 'icebox,'" Jack Liffey commented. "If you want to know the truth, I think the world tends to make people of stature when it needs them. It seems to be resting right now. What did the cops ask you?"

"If I had any enemies. If anybody was jealous of my work. If I had a lot of insurance."

"Well?"

"No, no, and no, as far as I'm aware. I'll take a beer as long as you're up."

Jack Liffey wasn't up, but he got the two beers anyway, overpriced German bottles with the ceramic-and-spring gizmos for tops. The South African seemed to grow frustrated with the progress of his cleaning-up and stomped out of the house without a word.

Dae Kim watched him go thoughtfully. "He thinks he's seen everything because other people in his country have seen everything, but there's some things you don't get by birthright. Actually he spooks pretty easy."

Jack Liffey fiddled the sprung tops off and handed one of the beers to Dae Kim. "How did you come to have a fifteen-year-old working for you?"

"She said she was eighteen, and the work was just informal. She wanted some experience with art film, and she came and went whenever she felt like it. Mostly weekends and a few evenings."

"Was she special friends with your South African there?"

"Him? I don't think so. He's pretty shy."

"What was she like?"

"Too old for her own good. She was from a film family, but you know that, don't you? Film people are very worldly along a very narrow track, so she'd been exposed to a lot, but she didn't know half of what she pretended to know. Mention a name that a European intellectual ought to know—Lacan, Barthes—and she could give you a little potted summary of what she was supposed to know, but she hadn't actually read very much. The ideas weren't old enough. They weren't inside her. Still, she talked a mile a minute and she was eager to be thought knowing, and that's rather touching. It *is* a kind of respectfulness, after all.'' He stopped to consider something. ''I'd say she usually had an air of rectitude about her, like someone planning to run for higher office.''

''Was she sexually precocious?''

Dae Kim frowned. ''Is that a roundabout way of asking if I was fucking her?'' He looked at Jack Liffey around the bottle as he drank.

''I didn't think it was so roundabout.''

''I'm asexual myself. I'm just not interested.''

''Like Andy Warhol,'' Jack Liffey said.

He grimaced. ''As a rule, I don't like to compare myself. It's not my preferred style of discourse.''

Jack Liffey noticed he was wheezing. Dae Kim stretched his neck back and then brought out an inhaler and hissed it into his mouth. He waited a few moments and did it again.

''Did you know Che Guevara had asthma?'' Dae Kim said after a bit of deep breathing.

''No.''

''With all that marching and hiding in the mountains. What force of will. He said revolutions are made out of love. He was wrong, of course, but it's one of those ideas that ought to be true. Like truth equaling beauty.''

''Or kids ought to have a childhood,'' Jack Liffey said. ''Instead of playing video games.''

''I couldn't agree with you more.''

''Did Lee ever mention Monogram Pictures or her dad?''

''No.''

''Anything at all you can tell me?''

''I think she was keeping a diary. She'd stop what she was doing and hurry off into a corner to write something down. You had the sense she was in serious training to *be* somebody when she grew up.''

''What did she want to be?'' Jack Liffey asked.

"I don't know. But she was a special kid, and I'll tell you how. I got the sense she was trying on personalities, looking for the one that would fit just right when she found it. She's the kind of kid who knows she's responsible for what she's really going to become, not just some cocka-mamie idea of herself."

HE drove up Rossmore, past the tall Ravenswood Building where Mae West had once lived, and past the big walls of the Wilshire Country Club where Louis B. Mayer had fought his way onto the membership list in the 1930s as the first and only Jew, before the Jewish businessmen built their own Hillcrest Club over on Pico and even Groucho gave up and joined a golf club that would have him as a member. Rossmore changed its name to Vine and then he was into the dreary industrial wastes of Hollywood. He'd miscalculated on the address, as everyone always did in that part of town. The downtown, eight miles away, was set on a skew from the rest of the city, and it made the zero point for the addresses drift as you moved north. Rossmore crossed Wilshire at the 4300 block, but two miles due north it crossed Santa Monica at 6300. He turned east again until he found himself in a traffic jam where the shopfronts were all owned by people named Hartounian and the churches were Armenian Orthodox.

Ahead of him a school bus had rammed an old truck that had been stopped illegally to sell vegetables, and two dozen kids in school uniforms were raiding the truck to hurl veg-etables left and right in a gigantic food fight. A zucchini glanced off his windshield and an old woman was berating a girl who was banging together two brilliantly purple egg-plants. Two girls in front of his car dueled with bananas, one of them just beginning to make the transition from lampoon to rage. The old Latino who owned the truck kept trying to shoo children away but it was hopeless.

Glass broke nearby and a young man jumped out of a Jaguar bellowing. Jack Liffey quickly backed and made a U-turn. He did not like to be close to things that were getting quite that ragged. He thought of his own twelve-year-old daughter getting swept up in a riot, and then his imagination saw her hit by a random brick, as his imagination often did, and sweat prickled. The vulnerability of children was unbearable. It was the kind of thought that could taint your whole day.

The address was a small stucco complex built in silent-movie Spanish. The number had a "¾" after it which took him out through a fountained courtyard that had been pretty once but was now a public dump. A small terrier was worrying its way along the edge of the path. Suddenly it squatted and dragged its rear end along the concrete with its forepaws. Worms, Jack Liffey thought, the dog rubbing itself raw against the itch. He wondered what life would be like without hands to scratch an itch.

He found the converted garage on the alley and knocked on the side door. The curtain behind the door window parted to show a face through the glass darkly. The young South African opened the door and beckoned Jack Liffey in without meeting his eyes, then stood with his arms crossed, a body language that said, Don't hit me.

"I'm making tea," he said finally, almost as if apologizing. Not, Would you like some? Or, Could I offer you tea?

"No thanks."

"I'm glad you were there to push me out the window," he said very softly. "I couldn't budge. It's a character flaw."

Jack Liffey looked around quickly for any signs of Lee Borowsky. The room was untidy, but nothing suggested a girl. An envelope on the table with foreign stamps was addressed to Hennie van der Merwe.

The young man fiddled with a teakettle on an electric burner.

"My name is Jack Liffey, in case I didn't say." He couldn't remember if they'd been introduced. Van der Merwe seemed to be hiding deep inside, the sort of kid you never remember much about, though he wasn't really a kid, certainly into his thirties. "Character flaw," Jack Liffey prompted.

Van der Merwe smiled to himself, a furtive smile like a rabbit peeking out of tall grass. "A lot of people think if you're timid, you must be a bloody idiot."

He went back to his tinkering. He seemed to need a prod now and then to keep running.

"But you're not a bloody idiot."

"Lee was working on the timidity. She had a game she called *épater la bourgeoisie*. You know the words?"

"Shock the squares?"

He nodded and ruminated for a while. "She barged into the Eagle Corner Market and asked how many corners there were on an eagle. The point was to keep insisting until they got angry."

"Sounds like a barrel of laughs." He remembered Dae Kim saying the girl was trying on identities, looking for one that fit. "Did you join in?"

He smiled fleetingly, still without looking up. "I suggested she go in the Chinese hand laundry and ask if it was less if you only laundered one finger. She wouldn't. She said it wasn't fair to do it to foreigners."

"Did you ever try to *épater* anyone yourself?"

He shook his head, then poured himself some tea and stared into the cup for a long time.

"You can go home now, you know," Jack said. "If it was the racism you hated."

Hennie van der Merwe shrugged. "One fucked-up country at a time is enough."

Jack Liffey couldn't quite discern his attitude, but that wasn't what he was there for. "What else can you tell me about Lee?"

"Not much."

"What was her relationship to Dae Kim?"

"You don't know the name, do you? Dae Kim is a very well-known video artist. He's got stuff in the Newport Harbor and the County. I'm fortunate he lets me hold his coat."

"Is that what Lee did?"

"Sure."

He sipped at his tea and stood in the middle of the room. A lot of shy people feel compelled to make small talk to keep the ball rolling, but van der Merwe seemed to prefer silence.

"Where would you start looking for her?"

He thought for a while. "You could try this." He handed Jack Liffey a postcard advertising someplace called The Eighth Art. Venue for video artists. New work Tuesday and Thursday nights.

Jack Liffey waited for a while, but nothing else was forthcoming. "Are you going to be a video artist?"

It took him a lot of reflection to come up with his answer. "If I can get over the hurdle of ego. I hate ego."

5

FIVE-POINT-FIVE

HIS CAR STARTED RIGHT AWAY, AND IT WAS LIKE WAKING healthy from a long sickness. A wave of good feeling washed over him, almost made him cocky. He whistled to himself as he accelerated away toward Sunset to head for the Pasadena Freeway. Maybe things would go right for a while.

He stopped at a light behind a black Hyundai with fancy wheels and wide low tires. Jack Liffey was just wondering why anybody would bother putting expensive rims on a Hyundai, when the light changed and he noticed the driver was reading something in the seat beside him. He tapped the horn gently and the guy crammed on his parking brake and jumped out. A wiry-looking young man in cutoff jeans came around and huffed and puffed by his door so he rolled the window down.

"What the fuck you honk at me for?" The man's hands worked asymmetrically and his eyes kept jumping from place to place.

Anger had a bad effect on Jack Liffey. A little hammer in his forehead started thumping and his vision narrowed down. At moments like this he recalled the gang of tough black kids he'd seen go for a puffy hopeless white boy in basic. They knew they were all headed to 'Nam to die and they were getting their last licks in at anything they could humiliate, full of taunt and dare. It was the feel of a baseball bat he remembered, the taped handle in his hand as he had waited for them to come after him next, ready to take a couple down with him, but they hadn't.

"Before we do something here, let's both settle down."

The man glared at the ground and one of his knees was wobbling. He started to rock and Jack Liffey could see he was egging on his own insanity.

"Sorry, man," Jack Liffey said. "I didn't see the way you were."

"You cuntlick!" He wrenched the door open and Jack Liffey came out after it, seeing red. Something sharp hit his shoulder and a woman only a few feet away screamed at the top of her lungs. It sounded like pain and it confused him and made him turn to look. But it was only a heavyset woman watching him, holding her hand to her mouth.

When he looked back, the Hyundai was getting sideways into the cross traffic with smoke off the fat tires, and he stood there in the street wanting badly to feel a baseball bat. He glanced at his shoulder and saw his shirt was torn and blood was spilling out. He wondered if it was a ring or some little palm weapon. He hadn't seen a knife. Ambient sounds came back up and the urge to kill something diminished slowly like a hot fog burning off.

MIKE Lewis and his wife had a rental, shingled bungalow overlooking the Arroyo not far from the Rose Bowl. The wind that funneled up the canyon had found the flagpole on a much bigger house across the street and was banging the metal pulley on the rope and sending a bright Japanese doodad shaped like a carp out over the lawn. The little old Saab wasn't in the drive so Lewis's wife, Siobhann, was still at work. She'd been best friends with his own wife, and when they'd divorced nobody'd felt the need to choose up friends.

Lewis was a social historian who'd been ignored for years until a book on the hidden agendas of L.A.'s elite had gotten hot and now everybody wanted a piece of him, even the elite. When he got out of the car he could hear the manual typewriter going in the front room. Lewis was the last human being to write on a big, black upright L. C. Smith, and it bore the same graffito as Woody Guthrie's guitar, THIS MACHINE KILLS FASCISTS.

The door was unlocked, and he walked right in, holding tight to the rag he'd tied over his shoulder, through the kitchen and then past Lewis. " 'S up, Mike? . . . Use your bathroom.''

"Hi, Jack. Is that blood?''

"Sort of.''

Lewis kept on typing as he went through into the bathroom and took off his blood-soaked shirt. The flow had slowed to an ooze. He found some Band-Aids in the cabinet and made a big X over the slash cut on his bicep, not far above the tattoo, then tied some gauze over that. He knew he should have got stitches, but he didn't get along with needles.

"You know what synesthesia is?'' Jack Liffey called.

"Yup.''

"Do you believe in it?''

"Who knows? I'm not a senses guy, I'm a data guy. In fact, I'm into white knowledge.''

"What's that?'' Still holding his arm, he drifted into the living room where Lewis sat, readjusting a coffee cup on the fold-down desk with great focus, as if getting messages of divination from the damp circles it left.

"Stuff you know without knowing you know it. It's like, every time you get a little shock of recognition from a novel.'' His eye came to rest on Jack Liffey's bare arm, puzzling over the tattoo. "What's 'Good Conduct'?''

"It was an army thing. It's what gets you out of the shit in one piece.''

"Looks like it caught up with you. Don't bleed on the rug, Sergeant. You know, in a deeply ironic sort of way, I was always sorry to miss out on Vietnam, since it was the defining experience of our generation and all that. Just between you and me, of course. I was an SDS organizer.''

"In my case, you missed out on a lot of boredom. I

wasn't on a sergeant track, by the way. Do you know anything about an outfit called PropellorHeads?''

''Software and computer games, taken over last year by an Australian venture capitalist named Nick Dunne, who made his fortune on real estate plus an Aussie beer called Castleton. Installed his own management team. How am I doing?''

''Not bad. Monogram Pictures.''

''Nineteen-forties, they made the Bowery Boys, Charlie Chan, and a lot of Bela Lugosi B-movies. In the sixties, the Roger Corman cheapies made the name Monogram a running gag for any schlock movie studio, but the French liked the spirit of the place so much that Godard's *Breathless* is dedicated to it. On the other hand, the French like Jerry Lewis, so what does that tell you?''

''Today?''

''The current Monogram isn't really a successor. Some Chicago dentists bought the name and the film library, and then Mitsuko bought them, trying to put together a media empire. They're back in business in a different building with a lot of Japanese capital.''

''What do they make now?''

''They have rights to some of the old stuff. And they make TV movies. Disease of the Week. Straight-to-cable horror. Once in a while, like all of us, they try to do better.''

He sipped at his coffee and made a face, then headed for the kitchen. Jack Liffey caught up with him rummaging in a cupboard.

''Do you know any connections between the two?''

''As it happens, yes. PropellorHeads released a computer game called Chan Lives. Might have something to do with Charlie Chan. And it's pretty clever of me to know that because I don't use computers. Hush, I hear leprechauns.''

Jack Liffey listened, wondering what that was supposed to mean. He didn't hear anything but a dog baying until all hell broke loose. The house began to roll and there was a deep rumble like a big jet nosing down, throttles stuck open, about to plow into the front yard. The fridge walked a few steps toward them, and Mike Lewis tried hard to say something, but it blew itself out against the roar, and then Mike was under the kitchen table on his hands and knees. Jack Liffey got into the door frame, clinging to the wall with both arms as the house bucked again. There was a high-pitched crack, like a big tree snapping off, and a panicky kind of dislocation as he attended to images, then sounds, then touch, checking in on his senses by turns, not knowing which one would turn out to be the key. After what was probably only ten or fifteen seconds, things began to settle and the noise was just gone. He wondered if the noise had existed at all or was just his imagination supplying a sound equivalent to the terrible rolling thrust.

"My my," Mike Lewis said. "That was over five."

"Amazing how well trained we are," Jack Liffey said, referring to their taking shelter.

"It's like riding a bicycle. You never forget how to fall off."

"We know enough not to run outside and get killed by a falling chimney."

"Door frames are passé, Jack. They talk about getting under tables now."

Jack Liffey looked at the sturdy table. Mike Lewis was sitting up under it, peering around the kitchen. Funny they hadn't heard the dishware breaking. There was a lot of it on the floor.

"That would save you a nice coffin-size space if the house collapsed."

Jack Liffey stepped outside and saw the air was filled with dust. Every car alarm in the universe was going off and there was a queer electricity in the air, like a promise of something more. He tried to will the seething inside himself to settle. There was nothing quite like the earth moving under you to hit you deep, where something in you needed things not to move. A siren started up, and a woman in an apron stood in her yard up the slope. She waved shyly across the ice plant and bougainvillea.

"You okay?" she called.

"Sure."

"Can you see a gray cat? It looks Siamese."

He looked around, but he knew none of the missing pets would show up for days. He shook his head and she waved once and walked away. The house had a hairline crack diagonally up a patch of stucco on the add-on room in back, but it might have been there before.

Inside he heard the TV come on. He was surprised there was still power. When all was said and done, after the terror receded, there was always something a little too cozy about an earthquake. It wiped away every kind of failure and started everybody even.

Mike Lewis sat in a lotus in front of the little TV. The announcer wore an open-neck sport shirt, harried and pissed off, as if he'd been dragged away from something more interesting. He was on a cell phone, trying to drag the real dope out of a geologist, like a police reporter trying to make a felon confess.

"It's just an earthquake, Mike. They won't know a thing yet."

"You realize this and football are the only live TV we ever see?"

"Do you know any serious bones of contention between PropellorHeads and Monogram?"

His interest gathered slowly, like a comedian doing a slow burn. His gaze came around. "Should there be?"

"Maybe." Hidden agendas and corporate feuds were the air Mike Lewis lived on.

"Give me a day."

Jack Liffey called his answering machine and amazingly enough got through. There was an old message, halting and breathless, to visit Lori Bright, which did funny things to his respiration that he did not want to think about.

He thought of his dog, Loco, probably burrowed under his bed and howling. Long ago he'd left Marlena Cruz his door key.

"It's a five-point-five," Lewis called out. "Epicenter in the Valley near Tarzana."

"Marlena, this is Jack. How are you?"

"Hello, Jack, it's wonderful to hear your voice." Emotions banging into each other in her voice. They had unfinished business and he didn't know what he felt about it.

"Your shop okay?"

"There's stuff all over, and Dan's window broke out at the Bean. Nothing too bad. Are you okay?"

"I'm fine, but I'm worried about my dog. You've got my key, you know, in the pencil box." She'd also once had a little throwaway pistol of his for safekeeping.

"Sure, I know."

"Could you send your nephew down to see about the dog? Tell him to be careful, it's half coyote and tends to flip out in strange ways. I just don't want him left alone in there if he's hurt. If the dog's okay, Rogelio can just put out some of the dog food from the pantry."

"Rogelio's not around. I'll go myself, Jack. Right away."

"Thanks a lot."

"Will I see you later?"

She was never shy about pressing an advantage. "If I can get back. Thanks a lot. Bye, Marlena."

He stared at the small black cordless phone for a moment. She was a good friend and she loved dogs. But she'd fallen in with an asshole like Quinn for a while and that pissed him off somewhere deep, as if it reflected on him. He tried Lori Bright's number, his heart doing funny things again, but a strange-sounding busy signal started up even before he finished dialing and he guessed that was the end of phone service for a while.

"You're not going to try to drive?"

"I'll stay off the freeways."

"And stay out of any big cracks."

"And you watch out for Jamaicans."

"How come?"

"If there is a feud here, it seems to run via Jamaica."

Mike Lewis's eyebrows went up comically. He spoke slowly, judiciously, "Remember last time, when you got mixed up with the hired guns? Mon, I can tune you into the vicissitudes of history, but I can't protect you from them.''

JUST down the street from Mike's, a young Asian in a tiger suit was guarding the front of a mini-market with an AK-47 across his chest. It might have seemed an acid flashback to 'Nam, but he had seen so little combat that the guy reminded him instead of the bad old bomb-shelter days of the 1950s, when the government pamphlets told you to shoot your neighbors rather than let them crowd in. Past the mini-market a bungalow was off its foundation, broken-backed, with a few sad people trying to prop up one wall with a big post. It looked like about a third of the chimneys in the area were down.

It was a tough trip from the Arroyo to the Hollywood Hills without the freeways—down Figueroa, he figured, then skirting Elysian Park and taking anything west that was going. In fact, by the time he got there, the police had blocked off the old Fig bridge over the L.A. River and they wouldn't let anyone on until it was inspected. One alternate route ended in a fallen peppertree, and farther south, cars were gridlocked against some other obstacle. He finally went north and got across at Fletcher and wound down through the Silver Lake hills. People were already setting up camps in open fields and parks, mostly recent immigrants. Central Americans had long memories for earth-quakes.

Then he came around a corner by the lake and had to stop fast. A dozen horses were spooked and rearing, each held by a wrangler. Beyond them the street was a prairie of some strange angular rubbish, like a beach after a hurricane. People were digging through the rubbish with a sense of urgency, hurling things aside, and most of them were dressed as hussars or grenadiers or something like that. A hussar at the center of the scene shouted and pointed and others congregated with a kind of rapt fury.

He got out and traversed what turned out to be a moraine of lath and canvas and plaster chips toward the busy group.

One slab of castellated fortress still stood, and he saw that it had all been a false-front film set. What remained was painted so crudely he was surprised it would even fool a camera. Perhaps it had been a movie about a movie.

"Denny! Get a fucking crane!"

"Sorry, man. We wrapped the crane this morning."

A man in a devil suit struggled to lift a long two-by-four still attached to a lot of rubble.

"Somebody who isn't a junkie give me a hand here!"

Jack Liffey wedged his shoulder under the two-by-four. A grenadier slipped in beside them, and the plume of a brass helmet waved in Jack Liffey's face, smelling for some reason like beef bouillon.

"Heave. One-two-three, *heave.*"

"Put some emotional investment in it. Lift!"

Something ripped audibly and the plank rose a foot.

"Annie, look for us!"

A stunning-looking redhead with a clipboard hurried up and tucked her head under the canvas.

"Nobody home, dudes."

"Down on one."

They released the plank and it crashed with a big billow of dust.

"Who are we looking for?" Jack Liffey asked.

"Bobby Rafferty," the grenadier said.

"Not only the biggest child star since Macaulay Culkin—" the devil started in.

"But *bankable.*" the grenadier finished for him. "Worth millions. Cute as a button."

"Nasty little drugged-up aggressive brat."

"But bankable."

"Nice little ass on him, too."

The devil and the grenadier shook hands. "I'm really glad we had this little talk."

Jack Liffey followed the redhead toward another commotion. Two more grenadiers were prying up another rag of the castle and a man in a business suit was down on his knees talking into the space beneath. The redhead offered a water bottle to one of the grenadiers, who shook his head. Jack Liffey threw his weight into the lift and the flap peeled up all at once to reveal a man in a cardinal's hat lying on his back. He wore white brocade robes that were covered now by dust and clutched a pastoral staff at his side, exactly as if laid out in state.

Sun hit him square in the face and he blinked twice. "The Lord giveth and the Lord taketh away," the cardinal intoned. "And if that's not a square deal, I'll kiss your ass."

They hoisted him out, and Jack Liffey walked away. It was the frame of reference that was missing. He'd made a minor science out of staying in touch with the real, and now he was trying hard to touch something real. It was all unnerving him. The earthquake, the strange frustrating journey, and now the film crew with all their weird confidence and irony. It was a bubble in the world. Little by little the make-believe and the glamour and grace had to blind you, he thought. Everything becomes easy, fun, everything reinforcing your ego. And not far away on Hollywood Boulevard runaway girls with acne and almost no inner resources were turned out as cheap hookers by seventeen-year-old pimps with even worse acne. It was a cinch Lee Borowsky would never leave the bubble and never end up down there.

Of course, it was Lori Bright that he was thinking about.

Two ambulances raced past him as he drove across Los Feliz. As usual for an earthquake, there was a lot more to-do than actual damage. Relatives would be calling from Michigan after the networks culled the worst damage, assuming their nieces' homes had been leveled, but the only serious damage he saw was an old masonry five-story with a wall fallen away to expose several rooms. The beds and closets and toilets were open to the air in that unbearable intimacy of catastrophe.

He stood on the brakes as a huge snake crossed the street in a hurry, hardly believing his eyes. Everything seemed to have shaken loose and the denizens of nightmares had come up for an airing.

6

ALWAYS INSULT WHAT CAN HURT YOU

PART OF A RETAINING WALL HAD GIVEN WAY ON ONE SIDE OF the steep road, forcing him to go slow and jeep over rubble. The wall was made of flat, broken-up chunks of concrete with ice plant in the niches. He wondered if anyone else made ugly walls like that or if it was just an L.A. phenomenon, because there was so much broken concrete around from tearing everything down once a generation.

Her house at the top end of Bluebird looked unharmed, and he realized he was back for the third time in two days. As he wedged the wheels he heard Lori Bright's voice in his head and was ambushed by emotions he did not want to deal with. Something was making him a bit spacey and confused and in more of a hurry than he had reason to be. He remembered a famous calendar shot of her in net stockings with her knee crooked up in one of those artificial dancer poses. It was as vivid as Sophia Loren in the wet shirt for *Boy on a Dolphin*.

A small fountain he hadn't noticed before was a lion's head against the wall spitting softly into a basin. He stopped to let the playing water do what it could for him. Mold grew on the shadowed wall where the water splashed, the lion looked smug and triumphant, and cool seemed to radiate off the surface. He wondered what it was deep in the psyche about splashing water that soothed. If anything, it should suggest the wearing away of everything, oceans that would burnish the earth smooth as a Ping-Pong ball to erase the works of humankind.

The chimes rang deep in the house somewhere and the suspicious-looking maid opened almost immediately and looked disappointed. "Come, please."

"Expecting Ramon Novarro?"

"He's passed away."

He realized that she had probably ushered dozens of famous actors in that door, maybe even Ramon Novarro himself, and their names would not be a joke to her. He wondered what it might have been like to blow smoke at Steve McQueen. He was crossing some spooky threshold into another universe, and he could feel his psyche touch gingerly on whatever it was that was disturbing him. No matter how many times you told yourself it didn't matter that she was a movie star, it did. He wondered if he'd been happier in life, maybe it wouldn't be hitting him so hard.

"The señora is meditating."

That brought up a picture of Lori Bright sitting in a lotus in front of a plaster Buddha. He wasn't sure it was something he wanted to see. The maid led him through the living room, where something made of blue glass had broken on the tile and been swept into a pile, then past an open library door where he saw a lot of books on the floor.

"You got hit pretty hard."

"Yes, sir," she said, noncommittally.

"Any structural damage?"

"Do you believe in God?"

He frowned as she glanced back at him magisterially. "Would it change the amount of structural damage?"

"A large fish tank fall over where I was sitting only a few seconds early. Señora Bright call me, but I was lazy and stayed sitting and then God tole me get up. It was just the right time. God saved my life."

"Good for Him." That particular drift of argument had always annoyed him. "Too bad He didn't take the time to warn the old guys in the Sylmar Veterans' Home that collapsed last time."

She scowled and opened a door for him.

"He here, señora."

It was hard to figure out what sort of room it was. There were a lot of trophy cases, and a tiny desk and a beat-up Swedish walking machine. Lori Bright seemed to be behind a translucent Japanese screen that blocked off one corner.

"Please give me a few moments," he heard in that husky voice that gave his crotch a shiver. The maid shut the door and he was left with rustlings behind the screen and a faint hum of fluorescents.

He strolled along the trophy case. There was no Oscar, but there were a lot of others, four big garish Golden Globes and lots of plaques. His eye lingered on a Cannes award for best actress, in *Lit à Colonnes,* which he thought meant "The Four-Poster." There was a photo of her, much younger, beside Jean-Luc Godard and somebody else in huge spectacles. Her eyes were demurely on the ground and Godard was about to speak.

"Best actress at Cannes," he said aloud. "I didn't remember you'd got that. That's really something."

"You're looking at my awards." Her voice sounded gently amused, as if he'd told her he collected matchbook covers as a hobby. "Don't you think getting worked up about awards is a little like worshiping the barometer for the weather? The real satisfaction is in the making."

"Awards really don't mean anything to you?"

"Every year I'm amazed that the whole world watches film people give each other those things. Can you imagine tuning in to watch a banquet for the best supporting real-estate salesman, in the under two-hundred-and-fifty-thousand-dollar category?"

"I wonder why I'm having trouble with sincerity here. Maybe it's all these display cases and, you know, the little lights pointing out the bigger trophies."

She fell silent and he allowed himself a little grin. He bent down to read a plaque, a humanitarian award from some Methodist society.

"My husband made the cases for me," she said mildly.

Her throaty voice stroked the words, like making love to them. "My husband at the time. It's been so long since anyone's been insolent to me, I forgot how to respond for a minute."

The grin was still with him and he liked it. It almost got him caught up. "It's kind of a point of honor with me, always insulting what can hurt you."

"Not a point that's well appreciated in Hollywood. But I like the concept."

On top of one of the display cases he found a copy of *Peterson's Field Guide to Western Birds,* tented open, and he picked it up to see the color plate for "Buteos or Buzzard Hawks." Beside the book was a pair of twenty-by-fifty binoculars.

"You're a bird fancier?"

"It's been an enthusiasm."

He hefted the big binoculars. "These are too powerful. You can't handhold twenty power," he said. "The military quits at seven."

"Actors learn stillness. Every year a red-tailed hawk nests in a big Jeffrey pine down the hillside. I started watching her fourteen years ago, though it's probably her daughter or granddaughter by now."

He rested his elbows on the deep sill and pointed the binoculars out the window, startling himself with the eye-filling profile of a policeman's head. He refocused and saw the embroidered emblem of Rosewood Security on the man's shoulder. He looked about twenty, carried a holstered revolver, and strolled along the edge of the yard, looking out at the view.

"Did you order up the rent-a-cop?"

"Lee's father did."

" 'Stop or I'll shoot . . . maybe,' " he joked.

"Actually Lionel wants to talk to you. He's on location about two hundred miles away and he can't tear himself away from his *big epic*." She gave the last two words a nasty twist. "At least for anything as trivial as his daughter.

Could you drive up there and see him? It'll be on expenses."

"I might have to rent a car. Mine doesn't like to get very far from home."

"Suit yourself, Jack."

Jack. He liked his name in her mouth, and it did something to him deep under his belt.

For an instant he took a step back from himself, saw himself standing there listening to the gravelly voice emanating from behind the screen. It was ridiculous, something a screenwriter would have concocted in the fifties. In the Cary Grant film, it was a bubble bath. In Godard, she'd be reading Horkheimer aloud. In a Peckinpah, she'd be torturing a small animal to death back there. He remembered a Western where she'd unbuttoned a blue work shirt facing William Holden, who was holding a six-gun but looking nonplussed, and she'd turned away at the critical moment to let Holden look but not the camera. *The Johnson County War.* He remembered now that he wanted to ask her what she'd been wearing underneath.

He strode across to the translucent rice-paper screen.

"Enough of this," he said as he pushed the screen aside. *"Jesus fucking Christ,"* he added.

"I thought you'd never peek."

She lay on her back on a kind of raised-leather doctor's examination table, with a dozen acupuncture needles sticking out of her nude body, one or two in the tenderer spots. She had wide hips and her large breasts were flattened into pools. With great concentration, she touched a needle that emanated from the large brown aureola of one nipple and made a little cringe of pleasure.

"Vibrate a couple of these, will you?"

"It doesn't hurt?"

"The touch of a needle can be sensuous. You ought to try it."

"Is this something you do when life gets boring?"

"Oh, don't be *dull.*" She cranked her neck around to look at him. "Are you intimidated?"

"I usually get to be good friends before I twiddle some-body's needles."

She began plucking out the needles, a little flinch now and then. "I'll make it easier to get to be friends, then." She raised herself on one arm, a few remaining needles bobbing and swaying under the laws of gravity.

"Mama, send lawyers, guns, and money. I'm in over my head."

"Warren Zevon," she said, laughing, and that made him suddenly less nervous. She wrapped a rubber band around the bundle of needles and tossed it onto a wooden side-board. "Why don't you start by coming a little closer. You're not one of those men who need to woo by candle-light are you?"

"It's a definite plus." His eye kept going to other things in the room, the coffered wainscoting, a display case of Japanese dolls in kimonos. Somewhere inside he expected a blackmailing photographer in a fedora to leap out and snap a shot with a big Speed Graphic and a real flashbulb.

"A lot of men have wanted this body," she suggested.

"Oh, including this one, believe me."

"Then stop standing off with that schoolboy rectitude and let me unzip your pants."

Something was all wrong, but he let her.

HE lay alone in her big tangled bed, trying to touch bottom. The sheets felt silky and he could tell his whole body smelled strongly of her. She had gone off, whistling, to bathe or primp or something, and he should have been elated. She claimed it was some Far Eastern discipline that had taught her to get in touch with her body, so she had come right away, just from his touching her nipples, and then a couple more times as they did other things. It made him feel potent, as if he could point his finger and cause explosions. Of course, she might have been acting. How could you tell?

It was like falling through suddenly into a subterranean province where you didn't belong. Had she slept with Mitchum? Had she been to dinner parties with Dore Schary and Sam Goldwyn? If he moved in with her (imagination works fast), would the old crowd sneer about it? Would everyone think of *Sunset Boulevard* and the doomed William Holden?

Glamour—it was just something the media threw at you to convince you that you were missing out, but if you acted quick, you could hop into the limo and be strong and loved, you could be there, too, posed by the pool with the cocktail if only you bought the Calvin Klein underwear. Futures endlessly and subliminally deferred when they failed, one after another. There was some kind of dissonance now between this silk bedroom and all the rest of his life and he had no idea how to deal with it. Mike Lewis had once done a magazine piece about some street kid elevated to celebrity artist overnight and the epigraph had been: ''Don't fuck with fame; it'll bite you on the ass.''

But Lori Bright was real in her own way and she was sure a lot of fun. He couldn't help seeing himself squiring her to an Academy banquet, the surprise escort, arm in arm past the cameras and some latter-day Walter Winchell blathering away about the mystery escort, with Kathy and Maeve goggling in stupefaction at their TV.

He heard her whistling as she approached and he found he was trembling a little. She came in wrapped in a fluffy towel, and it was just too much like a movie to bear. He shut his eyes.

''Feeling okay about this?'' she asked.

''Thanks for asking.''

''You feel like you're not attached to the earth. You're watching everything from a great distance.''

He felt the bed shift, then opened his eyes and saw she was brushing out her wet hair. ''I'm okay.''

She glanced at him with a faintly skeptical smile. ''Please don't reduce it to the ridiculous just because it feels strange to you. I don't like men fucking my image.''

A wave of annoyance swept over him. ''*Men*. That puts me back in the cheap seats.''

"I want to see you again." She took his hand, and the annoyance evaporated all at once. "Jack, I'm only a girl from a small town in Indiana who got too much too fast and never recovered from it. Please just take in life's rich pageant here with me. And if it gets too much for you, get off the merry-go-round in peace."

It was the best offer he'd had all day.

THE remote on the old answering machine in his office wasn't working, as usual, so he had to schlepp all the way across town to get his messages. He wanted to check on Loco, anyway.

He still carried the strange aura with him as the Concord finally coughed to life in second as he coasted down Bluebird. He'd thought he would just step back across the threshold into the world he knew, but things didn't work that way. What you did changed you, he thought. Nothing was ever provisional. Now he didn't quite know who he was.

There was less earthquake damage when he crossed La Brea, which was pretty much the border between the Westside and Old L.A. A broken plate-glass window, a few chimneys on lawns. A man was up on his roof trying to heave a tall TV antenna upright.

He tried to imagine himself eating out at some posh place with Lori Bright and couldn't do it. He turned on the radio for a while, but his tuner was stuck and he only got the all-news station, which left him with a shrill voice screeching about Manson 2 and how he was bound to be a mama's boy who'd been coddled by liberal teachers and a society gone spare of rod. He turned the radio off so he could go on thinking about Lori Bright.

It was probably the infatuation that made him careless. The green Explorer had to have been parked down there, maybe even in front of the boarded-up window of the Coffee Bean. Coming up the cement steps to his office, he hadn't even spotted the jimmied door. He did, however, spot the clumsy Webley-Fosbery revolver, big as a toaster in the big Jamaican's big hand. His dreadlocks were tucked up in a red, green, and black knit cap and it looked like he had searched the office and left everything tossed around.

"Hey!"

"Hush you mouf, an tek you hans up."

"I'm not armed."

"I-an'-I a suss dat out." He patted Jack Liffey down expertly, then forced him to kneel and handcuffed him to the leg of his desk.

"You not a penetrate what inna man heart till you see inna man *wallet*," he said brightly.

The Jamaican went through the cards from the wallet and looked them over carefully, then pocketed about forty dollars. He sat on the edge of the desk, looming over Jack Liffey.

He seemed to ruminate for a moment before speaking. "I get a job, go fe tek my business an' dere you be. Mr. Butt-in. Man say, Go kick dem ass, dem be wicked, and dis time, I-an'-I boun fe harm de wicked and dere you be agin, really an' truly. Don' it seem funny to you, mon? Like we got we a commonness."

"I'm looking for a missing girl," Jack Liffey said evenly. "If you're not into kidnapping, we don't have a beef."

The Jamaican seemed to see something interesting across the room and made a beeline for a plastic relief map up on the wall. It was the L.A. basin, given him by Maeve for his birthday.

"Dis de true riddim of de city."

He looked it up and down, tracing the exaggerated relief of the Hollywood Hills with his finger. Ominously, the finger lingered just about where Lori Bright lived. Jack Liffey noticed for the first time that there was a lumpy blue gym bag in the middle of the room. It wasn't his and he wondered what it contained.

"Now my views on de ting. Firs ting, you in de way here. You hang wit de PropellahHeads, an' day a substantial problem for I."

The Jamaican sidled up on the gym bag as if something living in it had to be approached with caution. He grabbed quickly and snatched out a portable tape player.

"Hello dere."

His eyes lit up as if he'd met an old friend and he set the player on a chair and punched it on. Immediately a reggae rhythm spilled out, everything about the infectious music in a hurry except the beat itself, that throb that lagged back in its own hypnotic lope. He cranked the volume up ominously.

"Righteous, righteous."

"Listen, I'll tell you anything I know. I was looking for a girl who used to work for the PropellorHeads. Lee Borowsky."

The Jamaican looked skeptical. "You jus' numbah-two son." He smiled. "Firs ting, you tell me now wa gwane wit you."

"Man, I wish I knew what's going on. I really do."

"Den, I-an'-I got to downpress you, you no see it?"

He reached into his blue bag again and came out with a bottle of Jamaican ginger beer. Jack Liffey relaxed a little. He'd been expecting a weapon, a knife or a sap. The Jamaican shook the bottle hard and banged it on the desk a few times.

Jack Liffey's knees hurt on the hard floor and he was readjusting his posture, a grimace closing his eyes, when the arm went around his neck. He could smell the man, strong and earthy, and a rough palm clapped over his mouth. The Jamaican knocked the cap off the bottle with one practiced swipe against the edge of the desk and then the bottle swept up against Jack Liffey's nose. A bomb went off inside his head. He fought blindly against the arm, but it was too powerful and he had no leverage. Fire burned through his sinuses, down his windpipe. He was drowning.

"You be one weepy baldhead, mon."

The Jamaican put his thumb over the bottleneck and shook it up again.

"Get ready fe tek some blows."

Jack Liffey heaved with all his strength as the bottle came around and only part of the spray blast went up his nose. Still, it destroyed his resistance instantly and left him retching and coughing. Another blast would drown him as surely as cement boots.

"Oh-oh."

He could hear a siren in the distance and then a woman's voice, shouting. "The police are coming! I can see them!" It was Marlena and her voice had never sounded better.

"Babylon come fe tek me. I-an'-I forward now. I did warn you, mon. Don' you be blow past all de trees in I yard."

He picked up the tape player and sauntered out the door. Jack Liffey lay full-length, coughing and racking and spitting, every atom of his sympathetic nervous system trying to clear the horrible burning ginger out of his windpipe.

Still nobody came. The retching slowed to a spasmodic cough. He lay there wondering what the Jamaican knew and didn't know. The man didn't seem to have anything to do with the kidnapping, hadn't even been interested in it.

Finally a shadow filled the door. "I'll be damned. Not again."

Jack Liffey thought he knew the voice, but he didn't have the strength to lift his head.

"This is the guy, all right, spends his life steppin' inna shit. Every time I come up here, his place is like a bunch of warring raccoons came to visit."

It was Quinn, the only man in L.A. he could see himself killing on a dark night.

"Bet he don't even want to file a report."

"Yes, I do."

A second cop came in, Quinn's black partner, whose name he couldn't remember. Black—that was the name. How could he forget? He had seemed decent enough.

"So it's going to be good cop, bad cop." Jack Liffey sighed.

"What the fuck's a good cop?" Quinn said.

"The guy was Jamaican. I was there when he firebombed

a house over in Koreatown yesterday. You might tell a Hollywood Division cop named Lieutenant Malamud.''

''You sure about the nationality?'' Black asked as he helped Jack Liffey sit up. His wrist was still cuffed to the leg of the desk.

''If he wasn't from the West Indies, he's really gone and OD'ed on a lot of reggae.''

Quinn prowled around, poking through the flotsam of the office, while Black took down the report on a small leather notepad.

''Son of a bitch,'' Quinn said all of a sudden. ''A *clue.*'' He was holding up a small ceramic bowl in the Desert Rose pattern. It was the last survivor of Jack Liffey's mother's dinnerware and he'd kept bent paper clips in it. ''We got us a discrepancy in the landscape.''

Nobody said anything. He had a terrible headache, throbbing and banging.

''I can't count the times I walk into some tough guy's place and find fine china on the desk.''

Jack Liffey was expecting him to break it casually. It was his style. But he seemed to be off his game and he just set it down. ''You're such a swell fellow, Liffey, we won't do any more of this today.''

The two cops lifted the desk so Jack Liffey could get the handcuff free. It was better than nothing. As they were getting ready to go, Black gave Jack Liffey a little look that seemed to be apologizing for his partner. ''You sure you don't need an EMS?''

''I'm okay. They're probably not much good with ginger ale, anyway.''

''Say hi to the big M broad,'' Quinn said at the door. ''She really knows how to do tricks.''

Jack Liffey almost lost it where he sat. ''It was stoneware, shithead. Not fine china. It was the most famous stoneware pattern ever made in L.A.''

''No shit, Sherlock. I'll make a note of that.'' Black dragged him out the door before they could get into it any more.

Jack Liffey's vision slowly cleared from the pink buzzing. He stared at the delicate little bowl with its wild roses. He saw it on his mother's Formica kitchen table, holding stewed prunes, or sitting in the back of the old Coldspot fridge with leftover macaroni and cheese. It had been made by the Franciscan works up in Glendale, he thought. Until they'd polluted the land so heavily with lead, they had to be put out of business and the buildings torn down and the earth scoured through sifters, and the pattern was bought by Wedgwood over in England, who still made it. There was a moral there somewhere.

After a discreet interval Marlena Cruz peeked in the door.

"Oh, Jackie." She hurried in and knelt beside him in the middle of the mess.

He found himself staring at the sheen of stocking on her big thighs where she squatted, her two knees thrust together, and she wriggled so the black skirt rose another few inches. She leaned awkwardly and hugged his head to her bosom.

"Jack, this is *awful*."

"I'll be okay. Really."

But she wouldn't stop pawing his hair down, over and over. He hoped to hell he didn't smell of Lori Bright.

"Jackie, poor Jackie." She didn't say a word about Quinn.

You jus' numbah-two son, the Jamaican had said. It couldn't mean anything. It had to be some prank of a joker god that Monogram Pictures had made the Charlie Chan movies.

7

EVERYTHING EXTREME IS VANITY

THE RADIO HAD TAKEN TO CALLING IT THE BIG TARZANA AF-
tershock, and apologizing that it had been downgraded to
a 5.4. Apparently the Big Tarzana Aftershock had dropped
trees on half the cars in the city because there were no
rental cars going except the exotics and he didn't feel like
trying to justify a Ferrari Berlinetta to Lori Bright on an
expense sheet at four hundred dollars per.

Maybe there'd be something tomorrow morning. He
thought of flogging the old Concord 250 miles up the eastern spine of the state to the film location and 250 back, but
he always ended up with a vivid mental picture of the shuddering old Wisconsin-built orphan, the last of the AMC
line, with 235,000 miles on the clock, blowing steam and
coming to a stubborn halt somewhere on the Sierra Highway.

"Whoa, boy."

Loco was gnarring softly back in the depths of the walk-
in closet, eyes like red coals among the shirts. The dog food
in the kitchen had gone untouched. Rather than risk a serious incident, he tossed in a pound of ground chuck and
left the dog to nurse its coyote soul by itself.

Then he called Mike Lewis but got Siobhann in one of
her pissy protective moods.

"I can't, Jack. He's typing and he gets cross if I so much
as poke my nose in."

"Come off it, Shiv. He feeds on interruption."

"We're just about off for a meeting of that group that's trying to green up the L.A. River."

"Now there's a concept. Put him on please."

"Two ticks, then. I can tell when the rhythm suggests he's about to hit a thinking place." Her voice was husky and intimate and something suggested she looked on delaying him as a kind of moral victory. He wondered if she was getting even in some way for Kathy. He'd never noticed her choosing up sides before. "How's Kathy anyway?" she asked out of the blue.

"Now, how would I know, Siobhann? You've probably seen her since I have."

"My money's on you two getting back together. You've beat the demon rum, and you two were always a loving couple."

He liked Siobhann, but for just one red moment he wanted to come down the line and make her eat the telephone receiver. He could sense her will on the other end, unswerving, and her motives impenetrable. "Thanks for the reminder. Have we perhaps fallen into a thoughtful conjuncture, yet?"

"Ever so sorry. Here he comes. It's Jack, Mike."

"Thanks."

"Health to you, Jack," she concluded.

"Something similar back." There was a clatter where she dropped the telephone on a hard surface, then Mike was tutting on the line. "Jack, do you know how they test to see if jet engines can survive bird strikes? They bolt them on a test bed, start them up, and hurl chickens into them. Thawed frozen chickens. They even built a compressed-air cannon that shoots the chickens into the engine."

"That's a pretty thought."

"Imagine a fine rain of emulsified fowl coming out the business end. Actually I'm using the fact as a kind of epigraph to a chapter on the aerospace industry."

"It's nice to know the old values aren't dead. Did you learn anything on Monogram?"

"Indeed I did. Siobhann is making signals at me. We have to run, so here it is in a nutshell. Solly Winer, who was bought away from Columbia by Mitsuko Inc. to run the studio and bring it back from the dead, has a real hard-on for PropellorHeads. Something about them cheating him. I don't know the whole story, but he hired the Hollywood fixer G. Dan Hunt to handle it. Hunt is from the old school. He's worked on payoffs and a couple of palimony cases and I think he kept the Heidi Fleiss address book out of the public domain. The kind of guy you tell to go clean up a mess and you don't want to know how."

"He use Jamaicans?"

"Not that I know of."

"This is sounding more and more like something that happened in 1948."

"Everything happened first in 1948," Mike Lewis concluded. "You need a new line of work, Jack."

As he passed a small derelict grocery, a bronze-skinned man dressed like a Zouave with a scimitar in his waist paced the parking lot, making hard turns at each corner and shouting commands to himself. He might have been preparing for a movie, or just listening to faraway voices. It was good, he thought, that there were things in life you would never understand. It suggested a kind of exemption from accountability.

The tense and angry commute traffic was already dying away to its ordinary sullen press. The evening darkened and took on its impersonal menace as he headed up to West Hollywood. He wore the frayed old bomber jacket that he'd got on R&R, swapped by a Zoomie for a full case of Budweiser. The name tape still said KELLEHER, but he'd taken off the big round unit emblem with the grinning cartoon bomber. He wondered if the jacket would make him more conspicuous at the The Eighth Art, or less.

• • •

"**HEY**, my dad was an immortal.''

"So was mine, but he was only immortal till I was about sixteen.''

Jack Liffey waited patiently by the crowded counter to get his coffee, keeping one eye out for blacks with Jamaican hats or dreadlocks. There was a lot of black around, all right, but the kids were wearing it—black shirts buttoned to the neck, black pants, and girls in black turtlenecks. One young man hammered at a laptop at a round table, but mostly the people sat restlessly on threadbare sofas and folding chairs, facing down a deep and narrow storefront at a big, blank TV screen.

He got his coffee in an absurdly oversize cup and sat at a table across from an uneasy-looking young woman in a pink sari who had one of those Indian colored spots on her forehead, though she didn't look the least Indian. She was overweight but had a hard line of a jaw, as if she'd had surgery on it.

"Do you know when the videos start?'' she asked.

He didn't, and almost immediately she was telling him about her unhappy marriage to an Indian who hadn't turned out to be the wealthy businessman he'd said and then had moved his mother and two sisters into their tiny two-bedroom in Palms. The whole family spent most of the day criticizing her housekeeping and telling her how they'd most likely be lighting her on fire to get rid of her if they were home in Ahmadabad.

The place was beginning to fill up, the kids straying in in groups of five or six, all looking like refugees from art college, except for one table where they had brush cuts and two of them wore camouflage fatigues.

The girl in the sari went on talking about her life going to shit. Some days he hated being the kindly gramps, but it could be useful. He showed her the photograph of Lee Borowsky, and when she didn't recognize it, it was time to move on.

He bought an overpriced Italian cookie at the counter and

a woman almost his own age sought him out.

"Are you here to show?" she asked. She clutched a copy of Maugham's *The Razor's Edge* and wore a denim mini-skirt that looked out of place, or out of time.

"Not this time," he said.

"I just love narrative evening. I'm not a big fan of the abstract videos."

"Me, too," he said.

"There's supposed to be one tonight on religion. I love things of the spirit." She said it with the kind of intensity that made you wonder if she'd just had her medication adjusted. "I used to think we were into the Last Days, but I'm not a Christian anymore. Not since the solstice."

"That's interesting."

She leaned into him, and he noticed she had a faint unpleasant aroma. She whispered: "I know it sounds crazy, but I'm getting into a new religion that's based on the random exchange of apparel."

She held a fist secretively between them and opened it up as if to offer a counterfeit Rolex. It was a pair of black panties.

"Trade me a sock," she insisted.

"I'm sorry, I'm an agnostic," he said.

She made a soft baaaing noise and blinked several times, and he wondered if he was beginning to have trouble with reality again. He hadn't had anything stronger than coffee in over a year. He got her to look at Lee's photograph, but it meant nothing to her and then, luckily, a heavyset man with a bad complexion whistled for attention as the lights came down and the show began without preface. He found a folding chair against the wall.

Like most projection videos, the picture was not very good. A small group near him cheered good-naturedly at the title, which was *Art Show,* and then he saw a slow dolly around a sculptural form that appeared to be in a museum. It was squat and bronze and for a moment he thought it was a big scarab and then it was just a flattened blob of metal with what might have been a seam around the middle.

The camera retreated toward a wall and a bell rang on the soundtrack. Suddenly the light changed and there were people wandering past the blob.

They hummed and frowned and scowled as the scene jumped from one set of gawkers to the next. Soon the groups were explaining the sculpture to one another.

"... dismantling the naturalist traditions ..."

"... makes the space it inhabits vibrate with light ..."

"... a new dynamic relationship between object and observer ..."

"... questions the enigma of visibility itself ..."

When the audience had all had just about enough of stuff like that, the gallery cleared out and stayed empty until a couple of flower children wandered in and patted the sculpture familiarly. They were about to wander off when the boy did a take and broke into a grin: "Ellie, look, it's two turtles fucking."

The coffeehouse erupted in cheers and Jack Liffey found himself smiling.

The second short was about a Chicano boy who looked about nine and was being ordered around by an abusive and alcoholic father, then ignored by his mother and taunted by older siblings. This one was hard for Jack Liffey to watch—any abuse of children really pulled his chain—but he stayed with it. The boy's stoicism went on and on and eventually you started hearing a strange noise under everything else. At first you guessed a train in the distance, or a car hammering over a wood bridge, and then it got louder and seemed to be machinery pounding away on sheet metal. It grew so loud that you couldn't hear anything else and the camera moved in slowly on the frozen angry face of the boy, and then abruptly a teenager was pounding a speedbag in a gym.

Again the audience burst into applause, with one table hitting it harder than the rest. Jack Liffey noticed that the guy on the speedbag was bellied back from the table, grinning, and it started coming clear that it was mainly the cast and crew of the videos who made up the audience. When

the next video was announced, the baton of fervent applause passed to another table.

He lost interest in the videos but not in the crowd. He
looked around at the vaguely self-important, not unhappy
kids and wondered, if things had turned out a bit differ-
ently, if he'd ever have ended up in a place like this, taken
some arts course at UCLA, fallen in with the high-button
crowd, and sat up late talking fiercely about the enigma of
visibility. It probably wasn't as bad as it sounded. He might
have ended up lashing together some sense of vocation that
felt like it justified his life. He didn't usually indulge what-
ifs, but he found he wanted to like these kids for some
reason.

He saw a skinny boy at a table with his shoe off and his
foot obviously far up under the skirt of a girl who was
giving dreamy looks at the wall. He remembered what an
idiot he'd been in college, wasting all that opportunity on
one drunken party after another, chasing the wrong women,
and taking the easiest classes. Back when life was still provisional and still could go this way as well as that. He felt
a profound sense of loss for just a moment, and then he
chased the whole thing away.

The heavyset man announced the main course, an hour-
long documentary on the SHARPs, which he explained in
a bellowy voice stood for Skin Heads Against Racial Prejudice, and the table with the short hair and fatigues whistled
and clapped. Jack Liffey remembered the Nazi leaflet in the
girl's coat pocket, and he settled back to watch the virtuous
lads applauding themselves. He guessed there were two
sorts at the table, the young men in camouflage who were
the SHARPS in person, and the artier-looking kids who
were probably the filmmakers.

The show was mainly grainy heads talking about their
lives as the camera moved restlessly around them, and after
ten minutes he found his mind drifting away. He wondered
what they would make of the old guy behind them in the
SAC jacket, and he realized all of a sudden that he was just
about the only person in the place who'd seen *Ozzie and*

Harriet when it wasn't yet high camp and Vietnam was still a real place to Americans, with real pain. On the wall only a few inches from his cheek was a poster of Leonard Nimoy as Spock making his four-finger V gesture. It seemed an odd emblem for the sophisticates at the Eighth Art, but he supposed it suited the TV generation. He leaned away to read the talk balloon someone had written on it: *Jim, TV is information severed from all lived experience.* And another hand had added in tiny letters: *The true problem lies in the scale of what must be destroyed before anything can be renewed.*

One of the SHARPs waved a hand high in the air all of a sudden, as if asking permission to go to the bathroom. The sleeve was rolled up enough to show ring after ring of barbed wire tattooed around the biceps. The video seemed to be winding down into a chaos of testosterone—swaggering black and white gangsters who barged arm in arm through startled shoppers, a strange dissonance between angry bellows and words of brotherhood. The SHARP table whistled and pounded their fists over the credits and others applauded politely.

When the lights went up, Jack Liffey made his way to their table.

"Congratulations," he said.

The eyes of one of the SHARPs lifted to him, trying to look hard and mocking. He had a sinister little goatee.

"For what?"

"The movie."

"I was in it. I didn't make it." The second SHARP was fat and looked even more like a biker. The other three at the table wore plain dress shirts buttoned up to the neck and looked a bit sheepish.

"*They* made it."

"Congratulations to them, too." He brought his eyes back to the first SHARP. Dogs were said to go into attack mode if you stared at them long enough, but if you could back them down you had them in your pocket forever.

"I'm happy you found a way to be civil in an uncivil world."

"You mean cause we like blacks? Man, they ain't nothing civil *in it.* They're cool dudes, that's all. I grew up south of Slauson."

Jack Liffey didn't break eye contact. "My name's Jack Liffey. I find missing children."

He fished out the photo and set it on their table.

"What would Nietzsche say about that?" one of the filmmakers asked.

"He'd say life is a lot of bullshit with people trying to take people off," the first SHARP said. He finally allowed himself to look away from Jack Liffey long enough to glance at the photograph. He showed no recognition.

The music came on all of a sudden, right in the middle of some techno-dance number, like a door opening on a busy factory.

One of the filmmakers leaned in to look at the photograph.

"It's Lee," Jack Liffey heard, and he lost interest in the SHARPs.

"You know her?" The filmmaker looked about eighteen and nervous, just barely able to grow the blond mustache.

"Sure. She was a real pest. She and her pal have been working on a documentary on our local Nazis. We crossed paths some."

"Tell me about her pal."

"Looked a bit like a Samoan, huge as a house, but I think he was white. He ran the camera and she was producing. They wanted some comments from Christopher and Samuel." He meant the SHARPs, and he used the first names gingerly, as if he just might not have permission.

"When did you last see them?"

"I don't know. Greg?"

"Three weeks? A month? What's that weird smell?"

"Man, don't you know grass?"

"That's not dope," the thin SHARP said.

''It's patchouli oil,'' Jack Liffey said. ''Somebody around here's wearing it.''

''You musta been a hippie, guy.''

''All of us were hippies back then. How would I find Lee or her big friend?''

''Don't remember his name. He never talked. You could try her school. I think she goes to that ritzy school in Hancock Park.''

''No good. What else?''

He shrugged. ''Follow the subject. She was going down to get something on that cocksucker in San Diego County, you know, the guy with the shortwave radio show that the militias all listen to.''

One of the SHARPs cackled. ''Heh-heh-heh, you said 'cocksucker.' ''

''Shut up, Beavis.''

There was a commotion across the room. The boy who'd had his foot up his girlfriend's skirt was standing up, holding a nude foldout picture of her over his head, showing it off to the room, and the woman in question was snatching angrily at it.

''Another country heard from,'' one of the filmmakers said.

He talked to them for a while more, but they didn't know anything else.

''Good night, gents. Keep up the good fight.''

''Fuck the good fight,'' SHARP number one said.

''As Nietzsche would say,'' one of the filmmakers added.

Jack Liffey smiled. ''Nietzsche said that everything ordinary is habit, and everything extreme is vanity.''

He let them chew on that as he walked away in a solemn processional step.

8

NOTHING IS WHAT IT SEEMS

HE HAD ANOTHER COFFEE AT THE EIGHTH ART, FRENCH ROAST and good and strong, and he chewed over his situation for a while, all the oddball things that had been plopping down on his plate and how crowded the plate was getting. There was a missing willful girlchild, a movie star whose image in his head gave him the willies so thoroughly his mind shied away, a summons to see the girl's father, who was shooting an action movie two hundred miles away, a Jamaican tough guy who kept popping into frame like a Punch-and-Judy puppet, a penny-ante movie studio caught up in a feud with an obscure little start-up CD-ROM company, and now, just so he didn't get bored with it all, a radar blip of neo-Nazis coming in low. None of it made any sense and it wasn't getting any better when he thought about it, so he went home.

It was past ten-thirty but she must have had sensors planted, because the bell rang ten minutes after he got in. He was still filing away the bills and discarding the catalogs for shirts with little animals on the pocket and he hadn't even tried to deal with Loco yet.

Marlena waited sheepishly in the doorway. He'd guessed who it was and he half expected to find her there, wearing a coat with nothing underneath, but a little too much water had gone under the bridge for her to try that on again.

"Hi, Jack. Can I come on in?"

Her eyes looked inexpressibly vulnerable. Something about her always seemed too holy to hurt.

"Of course, of course. You can get yourself a drink, too. Pour me a ginger ale, would you?"

"That's wonderful." She was into the kitchen before he thought of Loco.

"Hold on. You're good with dogs, right?"

"My Fidel thinks so."

"I've got an earthquake-crazy dog in the closet."

"I don' know about that, Jack. Loco's not really no dog, he's one crazy border wolf. He can take off your face with one bite."

"We're two big intelligent creatures. We ought to be able to deal with a little dog."

"I don' know."

It was a double closet door and he'd left both sides ajar just in case the dog decided to come out on its own, but it hadn't. The red eyes were right where they'd been five hours earlier, and just as crazy. It wasn't even the call of the wild inhabiting the eyes, it was just fear clotted up so close to the surface that there seemed no depth at all behind the pupils. Jack Liffey opened the doors slowly and sat on his haunches facing the dog, cooing softly.

"It's okay, boy, it's okay."

Marlena brought a saucepan of water and two drinks. She set the pan down and gingerly settled beside him.

"What you gonna do now?" she asked.

"I don't know, but I'm not giving him the closet to keep."

The package of hamburger he'd thrown in was untouched and starting to drip juices. They sipped their drinks, and Loco gnarred softly.

Jack Liffey nudged the saucepan of water toward the dog. "I wish I had some dilaudid to throw in the water."

"I think you want a dart gun, like the guys in game parks."

He sipped the ginger ale and, not for the first time, questioned his decision to give up booze. He wasn't really an alcoholic, just prone to hiding himself away in ordinary pleasures, and he'd decided to deny himself all of them— tobacco, Scotch, drugs, even Raymond Chandler books, and not necessarily in that order. It had something to do with proving his general worth to himself, but a Scotch would have been pretty good right then.

As if it had little significance, she rested her hand on his knee. He liked the heat of her touch, and he was amazed all over again by the fact that getting excited by one woman did not prevent getting excited by another.

"I'm sorry you saw me with that policeman," she said softly.

"You have a right to be with anyone you want. It's just it was that shit Quinn."

"He hit me up, you know. I tole him to go 'way."

"So you said."

"He was like some guys I knew. . . . I had a rotten time, Jack. Back some time."

"I want you to tell me about it, but we need to take care of Loco first."

"Sure."

"Easy, boy, easy. It's going to be okay." He inched closer to the dog and the growl ratcheted up a bit. "You're certainly no judge of the Richter scale, boyo. That was only a crummy little aftershock. You're just wrapped too tight. Think of all your compatriots that put up with the real thing out there near the epicenter in the Valley. Miserable little terriers bearing up with grace under pressure, flop-eared cockers, even poodles." He didn't add lapdogs, in deference to Marlena's Fidel, a squeaky-trembly hairless rodent dog. He murmured on for a while and then slowly pointed his finger straight at the dog's face, like Death in a Swedish movie. The dog recoiled a few inches and gave a strangled cry. He let his hand drift closer and closer.

"Careful, Jack."

"It's okay. I'm the boss. I think I saw some life in his eye."

He touched lightly under Loco's chin, then pressed the

flat of his hand up against the dog's chest, right between the wobbly forelegs. The dog mewed once and collapsed like a deer caught by one expert rifle shot. Exhausted, it went straight into a comalike sleep.

"Sleep it off, boy."

Marlena's hands were on his back. "Your touch is magic."

"Mmmm."

Her arms went around him from behind and her large breasts pressed into him.

"I didn't ask for bad luck, but it came looking for me again, Jack. I'm glad you're always nice to me. I had a real bad childhood, you know."

"But you turned out fine."

She kissed the back of his neck and one hand slid under his shirt and played with his nipple. "You want things all figured out and over with, don't you? You got to pay attention to the in-betweens, Jack, and respect where people are coming from."

"Tell me about it."

Before they made love, she told him what she'd always avoided telling, about growing up in a family of Protestant evangelicals in Montebello, a ratty house in a ratty flat street even more east than East L.A. She had been allowed no TV, no movies, no boyfriends, no makeup, no telephone calls. Her father had taken an irrational dislike to her and made her do all the housework while her younger sisters got to play, and she'd finally run away with an Anglo biker at fifteen, just to get out of the place, but the biker had passed her around the Devil Jokers in Fullerton and her father wouldn't have her back when she showed up, locking the door and shouting out the window that she was spoiled now. She'd returned to north Orange County and settled in as the bikers' property, which was about what she thought she deserved for messing up her life. She got so used to it all that she developed a kind of loyalty to her misery, the sense that that was where she really belonged, and she began to find even her despair soothing.

"Jesus, Mar, I'm going to start crying here."

One day they'd all got doped up and decided to punish her for some fault by driving a half ton of Harley over her dog, hooting and mocking her tears and singing a horrible boozing song called "Lupe, the Hot-Fucking Mexican Whore." That had torn it. She'd thrown herself on the mercy of a cousin whose family were Catholics. They took her in and she converted on the spot. She went to school with her cousin, in Duarte. A year later her cousin was killed in a drive-by, but the family kept her on and she finished out high school.

"You don't want to hear about my first husband, the big tuck-and-roll specialist at the body shop." She shuddered. "After him, I married an old widow man from Sonora who was sweet to me. I didn't love him much, but he didn't mind I wasn't no virgin and he left me the money for Mailboxes-R-Us. He couldn't have no kids, but I got no gripes against Salvador. He was a kind man."

The story reinforced his intuition of holiness, and he wondered if it would interfere with lovemaking, but he needn't have worried. All the abuse hadn't dimmed her enjoyment of her body and hadn't left her shy about it either. The only thing that seemed to bother her was getting caught up in all the straps, her slip and bra half off and tangled, almost weeping with the urgency. Quickly he helped.

"Go on, Mr. Detective, go on go on, you do Brown Betty *like that.*"

"LIFFEY, this is Sergeant Tomas Flor. Be downtown Thursday at ten. We got some gentlemen of the Jamaican persuasion here we want you to take a gander at. Don't be late, you know what's good for you. This judge we know loves to issue bench warrants for material witnesses and we love to serve 'em. *Hasta la vista, esse.*"

"Oy, you're all heart, Flor," he said to the ether.

Why, he wondered as he pressed the reset, did so many cops feel they had to throw their weight around? He had no problem with cops in theory. They filled a function in the world. But too many of them just liked to let you know they were in the fraternity and you weren't.

A dozen black teenagers were lined up like a medieval gauntlet on the walk outside his condo and they murmured vaguely threatening noises and wore what must have been the latest rage—dark sunglasses with holograms of eyeballs that seemed to swivel as you passed. It was like being challenged by a dozen black Marty Feldmans and he burst out laughing.

"You stepping up to us, man?"

"Oh, dear, no." It was curious how sharing the walled complex defused any real challenges and made them all neighbors in some old-fashioned way. Some good came of walls, indeed, Mr. Frost, he thought. "Where do you buy them?"

"Eye-Eye Sir in the mall," one of them grudgingly offered.

"I'll get a pair for my daughter."

It was one of those glorious early winter mornings with the sky like a bowl carved out of iridescent blue jade and by the time he hit the Valley there was still only a little smog. Marlena had loaned him her near-new Nissan Sentra. Something about the angle or the depth of Japanese seats always cramped up his legs, but he was in no position to be picky.

The freeway was closed at Devonshire and they detoured him onto Sepulveda. The overpass of the Simi-Ronald Reagan Freeway was apparently suspect after the aftershock and they had attached huge weights to it and were ramming it over and over with a giant machine that set up heavy vibrations he could feel in the car seat. He half hoped it would fall. L.A. had more than one ex-freeway named for an ex-president. The short Marina Freeway had once been the Richard M. Nixon, and for a lot of people it had been touch-and-go if this one would lose its name, too, after the

THE rent-a-cop told him they were shooting right where the Temple of Kali had stood in *Gunga Din,* but he'd seen the movie too long ago to recognize anything. The Alabama Hills back of Lone Pine were all rounded, weathered rock, like the rubble of a small city kicked into heaps by an angry giant. He'd been flagged down by the rent-a-cop a half mile back and told to park, and he had walked up the box canyon toward the pall of dust that hovered over a semicircular pocket in the hills.

"Have you ever acted in a wildlife short?" a man at the table of box lunches was asking a beautiful young girl with a long braid.

"Not so's I'd notice."

"I was a zebra, I swear to God. They had to pad the film out."

Only a half-dozen people seemed to be released to eat, and they were peering into the cardboard boxes, as if searching for *just* the right turkey sandwich. A row of hovels had been built against the cliff ahead and a lot of the actors wore loincloths and looked curiously white of skin, like Finns in the middle of winter. Many of the too-white people were waiting curiously by a Land Rover with some contraption on the roof that reminded him of his mom's Electrolux vacuum. Perhaps they were making *The Far Planet of the Dustballs,* he speculated.

He found a young woman with a clipboard and told her Lionel Borowsky had asked him to come out.

She pointed. "They'll break in a minute."

A cluster of men sat on beach chairs under a canopy. He couldn't see a camera, but there were a lot of lampstands and platforms and big black suitcases scattered around. A pile of bloodied severed limbs waited to one side.

"What's the movie?"

"*The Makers.* It's a lost story by Philip K. Dick—*you* know, the *Blade Runner* guy."

"How can it be lost?"

"Well, *you* know. It was *found,* for cripes sake. It's about a bunch of androids who run off to live in Tibet and forget they're androids. Over time they build up a bunch of myths about the Makers who made them and then one day these two down-and-out Brooklyn guys stumble into their valley. Sort of *The Man Who Would Be King* meets *The Terminator*.''

A couple of actors he vaguely recognized emerged from the Electrolux Land Rover and walked among the too-white people and then he noticed the cameraman with the Steadicam following them, like a man strapped into a big drill press. When you lived in L.A., you knew about all the latest film gimmicks.

''I said no fucking giggling!'' The wail curled up unnaturally from the canopy, electronically amplified, and bounced off the cliff. ''If it happens once more, I'm calling the union and you're all off the picture! Take lunch, you sick grifters, and calm down.''

''That's Jerry Tuck, the first AD.''

''Uh-huh. Can I go over, now?''

The shoal of too-white folks drifted toward the box lunches, and the cameraman started unstrapping himself.

There was no question which man under the canopy was Lionel Borowsky. Everything in the valley was turned just perceptibly toward him, as if waiting on his whims. He was heavyset and balding and he had almost managed to straighten his body into a line by stretching his legs forward in the aluminum chair and letting his head dangle back with his eyes closed. A much older man with dead flat eyes sat beside him, glaring out at the AD, who was chasing after the too-white folks, waving a little battery megaphone. Two men in polo shirts stood behind the awning, rocking now and then like backing vocalists.

''Mr. Borowsky, I'm Jack Liffey, the man who's looking for your daughter.''

The eyes came open and found him with sleepy menace. He watched Jack Liffey for a while.

''Mr. B,'' someone said, ''we still got the stand-ins waiting off there.''

He waved it away. Jack Liffey noticed that the old man

was rolling a quarter across his knuckles without looking, like George Raft.

"Are you an ex-cop?"

Jack Liffey shook his head.

"What makes you think you can find her?"

"It's what I do."

"And take women's money, a lot of which is my money."

Jack Liffey's vision went pink. "You didn't ask me all the way up here just so we could wave our dicks at each other, did you?"

The backing vocalists went very still, and even the quarter faltered in mid-knuckle. Suddenly Lionel Borowsky sat up and grinned. "Dennis, write that down. I know just the place for it, right after the buzzard scene. Somebody get Jack Liffey a chair."

He put out his hand to shake and a folding chair materialized.

"Mr. Liffey, welcome to my set. This is my father, the famous blacklisted director."

"I don't remember any Borowskys on the blacklist."

"Irwin Cohen."

"Oh, of course. My privilege."

He shook the old man's leathery hand.

"Eh." It was a Jewish sort of shrugging noise.

"I may as well explain the names," Lionel Borowsky offered. "I went back in the record and found out what was going on at Ellis Island while a third of Eastern Europe was fleeing the pogroms into North America. The schmucks who ran Immigration couldn't deal with all those Polish consonants so they counted down the lines of these bedraggled pilgrims just off the boat"—he counted off those surrounding him—"Levy, Cohen, Stein, Levy, Cohen, Stein. Pure *goyisheh kop*. Long ago I went back and found that granddad was Yusul Borowsky, not Joseph Cohen, but dad is too stubborn to change back."

"I already monogrammed my shirts." He rolled his eyes. "This is a sign of going mad, taking yourself so seriously."

Jack Liffey sat.

"Coming from the man who went to prison rather than open his yap." He waggled a thumb at his father. "He wasn't even a Red. He just did it because Hammett did."

Jack Liffey admired that kind of bullheadedness, but he let it sit there.

"Mr. B, David is objecting to doing his scenes out of sequence. Says his emotions will all end up with clear black lines around them." The AD shuffled his feet uncomfortably.

Lionel Borowsky grimaced. "Tell him I don't want emotions. I want him to deliver the lines I wrote. Coach him until he remembers the lines." He glanced at his father and added softly, "And then we'll change them on him."

"Getting a Performance out of a Schlemiel 101, four units," the old man said.

The AD deposited a shopping bag full of box lunches and wandered away with the two backing singers, arguing about the afternoon schedule, leaving only father and son and visitor. The director dealt out the lunches. "Have one, Mr. Liffey. You may as well get something out of this trip."

"I had an idea that you wanted to see me."

"Oh, I did, and I've seen you."

The old man frowned into his box and then tossed it aside.

"What did you see?"

"A guy who's either schtupping my ex-wife or soon will be."

Jack Liffey decided to let it go some more and see what happened. "Why would that matter to you?" In his box was a turkey on wheat in a clear plastic tub, a big red apple, a brown cello bag that said HAWAIIAN POTATO CHIPS—NOT FOR RESALE, and a rolled-up napkin with plastic silverware sticking out. He'd heard that Hollywood catering was high end, but it certainly wasn't true on the set of *The Makers*.

"See?" Lionel Borowsky said to his father.

"Okay, what can I do? Once again, you're right. A great

intellect, my son, a mensch, a guy who's lived the examined life.''

Lionel Borowsky started to eat and then spoke unashamedly with his mouth full. ''Don't mistake me, Mr. Liffey. I don't care what you do with Lori. She has a fertile imagination for boy-girl stuff and you're consenting adults. I needed to gauge how your loyalties might have become clouded. Beware of her. She may not be quite what you think. She is entirely capable of . . . oh, just about anything. She could, just for instance, stage a kidnapping for some nefarious purpose of her own. The only thing keeping me from suspecting that is the paltry ransom. Fifty thousand dollars is not a lot of money in her circles, or in mine.''

Jack Liffey remembered her saying something of the sort. ''In my circles, it'll do, but I'll take your word for it. What else would she gain by staging a kidnapping?''

''That's another thought.'' He nodded as he appeared to mull it over. ''But in eighteen years of directing movies and forcing underfed, overimportant, and oversexed kids from the midwest to reveal their inner feelings, I've learned that I don't know a goddamm thing about their feelings. The only sure touchstone is believing whatever anybody tells you is absolutely not what they're feeling.''

The old man snorted. ''Hang on, I got to write that down.''

''Can I ask you a question?'' Jack Liffey asked.

''Sure.''

''Do you know a company called PropellorHeads?''

He seemed to think it over for a moment. ''They're a little game outfit that licensed a single use of one of Monogram's old movies from the forties for next to nothing, and then they made about five games out of it. I even know the Aussie that runs it. He's a very, very small land shark. Between him and the old boys who run Monogram, I wouldn't bet a lot of money on Australia.''

''Did you know your daughter did some work for them?''

He looked genuinely surprised. ''She's just a kid.''

"A kid who's into movies." He liked the idea that they finally conceded he might know things they didn't know.

Just then a young woman wandered past with very large breasts struggling against a bright blue halter top. Some of her spilled out and some was rosy and firm and she laughed at something in her head with the kind of voice you heard on telephones when you got the wrong area code. It aroused him and made him think of Lori Bright and he was surprised by the urgency of his desire. What a disorderly set of emotions he had developed, he thought.

"Is she in tight with the flakes at PropellorHeads?" Lionel Borowsky asked.

"I don't think so. Do you know any Jamaicans?"

"I met Bob Marley once. Kept thumping a big Bible and I couldn't understand a word he said."

"Any living ones?"

Something clouded in his eyes, but he wasn't going to share it. "Nope."

"I'll keep you informed, then. Can you hear colors?" he added as he stood up.

They looked at him as if he was crazy.

"I'll track her down for you, if I'm not too busy fucking your wife."

The old man roared with laughter.

9

HE WAS DUE BACK FOR THE POLICE LINEUP AT TEN, SO HE had to rouse himself in the motel bed at about five to be safe. He'd never had trouble running on half sleep; in fact he rather liked the buzz of stoic rectitude it gave him.

He showered and got on the road so fast it was still dark. The two-lane highway ahead of him was dead straight, with truck lights hanging out there for a long time and then exploding past with a gust that rocked the Nissan. A bit of moon was dying out and the half-light under the hills filled the desert with hallucination, a lot of ghosts he didn't want to see. Eventually he watched a bloodless sun come up over the barren Argus range to the east. To the west the first light hit the snow-powdered crests atop the long wall of the Sierras, and before long, morning light was hanging above the dark desert floor like a gas.

The desert had a stark kind of virtue. It reminded him of the last time he'd had his body in tip-top shape, and a good morning run would leave him tingling with chaste satisfaction. A kind of rejuvenating cleanliness waited out there, broadcasting a kind of hope out of all the emptiness. It was where visionaries and prophets came from. And samurai, defenders of the weak.

He knew he was straying further and further from the easygoing technical writer he had once been, the family man and homeowner who avoided anything new and unusual. That life was like a dream he'd had, a pleasant-enough dream, but evaporated, long gone. A big hand had descended from somewhere, and had as if casually, indifferent to his hopes, overturned everything.

WIRE PALADIN, SAN FRANCISCO. He saw the calling card with the silhouette chesspiece from his TV youth. He didn't even have Richard Boone's fancy hotel room to return to, no faithful Chinese servant to set out his clothes. He grinned at himself: as a boy, he had misread the calling card that opened the show. He'd thought Wire was the character's first name.

THE place didn't look much like it always did on the cop shows. It wasn't shabby at all and it wasn't cramped. There were two rows of plush theater seats on his side of the one-way window, like a private screening room for the moneymen at Fox. Lieutenant Malamud was there, standing up by the big window, and Flor sat at the end of the aisle. Dai Kim was there, too, sitting glumly in a tidy suit. For some reason, a chimpanzee in a tutu was handcuffed to a seat arm at the back, and once in a while the animal tugged at the cuffs and made a little scree, but it seemed pretty resigned.

"I can't wait to resolve the OMB thing," Flor said.

"I tell you, I never saw the guy," Dae Kim complained.

Malamud shrugged. "Maybe you seen him elsewhere. Maybe he's been stalking you."

He tapped a little squawk box on the wall and spoke into it. "Let's rock-and-roll, folks."

A door on the other side of the window came open and a reggae band trooped in languorously and lined up under the big black numbers. They all had dreadlocks and bright shirts, and one of them bobbed regularly as if singing to himself, but Jack Liffey could see immediately that his Jamaican was not among them.

"He's not there," Jack Liffey said.

"Take a good look, Liffey," Sargent Flor said. "It wasn't easy to dig up a bunch of Jamaicans at this hour."

"I said he's not there. I can see them."

"Take a really good look. Stare at them for a minute. I'd like to be sure you got highly motivated."

He wondered if Flor had been talking to Quinn over in Culver City. He had it in for him for some reason and it was going to end badly.

"I'm motivated. I drove all the way back here from Lone Pine this morning."

"What a shame. We thought you'd help us clear up our OMB business. Just give us five minutes, okay? What about number one?"

"Sure, what about number one? Have him step forward."

Malamud punched the box. "One, step forward."

The first Jamaican wriggled two steps closer to the one-way window and rubbed his side as if he'd slept on it wrong.

"Now have him sing the chorus from 'I Shot the Sheriff,' " Jack Liffey said.

Malamud suppressed a laugh, but Flor turned and glared. "You think that's funny?"

"Anybody want to explain the chimp to me?" Jack Liffey said.

"Not particularly, asshole."

"Flor." Liffey stood up and Flor did, too, twenty feet away. They locked eyes and moved a step toward one another.

They glared for a long time until Malamud rang a buzzer. "Liffey, over here. You're pretty lively for this time of morning."

He turned and waited for whatever it was.

"Be cool. I told you once this is a big war we got here. We're watching over it. You know who we are? We're the moral order. We sit up on Olympus, and when something gets a little out of line, we reach down and straighten it out so the sides fight fair. Now, you may not think so, but this is a big responsibility. It weighs heavy on us."

He noticed Dae Kim slipping out the door.

"Now, anytime we want we can take disability from all the stress of dealing with guys like you, move to Idaho or Nebraska or wherever with Mark Fuhrman. They say it's nice out there. You got your seasons, you know, a hundred and twenty in the summer and a hundred and twenty below in the winter. But we choose to stay here and keep watch over the world and we like a little respect."

"I offered you a fair break the first day," Jack Liffey said. "I've been straight as I can be and all I get out of your partner is attitude. I don't care if all this being a prick makes him feel powerful, I just don't give a shit."

"Get out of here, Liffey. You don't have a notion."

The chimp chirped and screeched as he went out the door. In the hall Dae Kim caught up with him.

"They don't like you very much."

"I was beginning to figure that out."

"In case it matters to you, I heard them talking. OMB means the Old Movie Bitch."

THE anger smoldered out as he stood in front of the glass wall of Parker Center and started to feel lonely and confused again. People like Flor focused him, but it was a false kind of focus that didn't last, like a bickering household that only pulled together to shout at an outsider.

He walked the six blocks to the Bradbury Building on Broadway and rode the open-grillwork New Orleans elevator in the atrium up to seven. He always got a kick out of the big eye they'd painted on the frosted-glass door. Their home office in Cincinnati had been famous for strike-breaking since the turn of the century, but the L.A. office had spent the forties protecting the illegal gambling ships off Santa Monica and Long Beach and later ferrying cash back and forth to Vegas. Now they claimed to be legit and the sign inside the door offered services like Debugging, Embezzlement Detection, Executive Protection, Inventory Shortages, and the like.

"Is Art Castro in?" he asked.

It was a new receptionist. The old one had taken a serious

dislike to him for having cheap shoes and a Timex. It must have been something they taught in receptionist school. This one actually smiled at him and wasn't looking at his feet or his wrist, so he figured he got to start with a clean slate.

"Could I tell him who . . ."

"Jack Liffey. I'm a friend."

"He's with a client," she said, "but I'll put your name up on his screen." She typed something into her keyboard.

"I guess technology is just new ways to be rude," he said.

She shrugged a little with her eyebrows. "But it's subtler. It's sort of Zen rudeness."

"I'll have to meditate on that."

He took a seat as far as possible from an immensely fat man who took up at least two places along the plastic bench seats. He was sweating as if he had just jogged there and his hands worked on the seat beside him.

The nearest magazine was something thick and glossy called *Loss*. He picked it up idly, opened somewhere, and read, . . . *no longer the person you once were inside, all the feelings and the children you might have had and even the ones you did have. I wake every day facing the inescapable fear that even less will be left than the day before*. He saw a photograph of a man sitting cross-legged in a park. It looked vaguely like himself.

He turned quickly to the back to a photograph of a man missing both legs, his trunk propped up on a little roller platform like a skateboard. The man held up a drawing he seemed to have done of himself, grinning maniacally.

When he looked up, the fat man was staring fiercely at him and he glanced down again at the page to see a photograph of a wrecked station wagon with a caption about a wife at the wheel and all the children asleep in the back. He wondered who on earth would want to read this thing, if it was a way people soothed themselves if they only experienced small losses.

"Jack."

Castro was in the hallway, immaculate in his tidy flat mustache and linen suit.

"Come on back."

For an instant they tussled at a sixties handshake, ending in a fumble and an exchange of wry smiles. They'd met first in a brief passage through Vietnam Veterans Against the War in the early 1970s.

Halfway down the hall, Jack Liffey said, "That one liked me a lot better than your old receptionist."

"Don't get settled. She won't be here long."

"I won't ask why."

"Nothing sinister. She's just a temp."

"We're all temps, Art, with a sufficiently broad perspective on life."

The man smiled coolly and nodded Jack Liffey into the office. It was a two-window office with a pretty good view out to the south. Things looked okay from up here, but really it was a waste of decaying mid-rises that housed swap meets and Spanish movie houses. One insurance company that had banked on the Anglo city spreading south from the Civic Center had lost big when the palefaces built their New York–scale high-rises out to the west instead, and now this lone skyscraper was marooned down on Twelfth Street in a vast sea of Latin America. It only took a few blocks in L.A. to take you irretrievably across a border.

"How did that thing turn out?" Art Castro asked. "With the envelope."

Art Castro was holding some evidence for him as insurance, but it was the kind of insurance that you wanted to have around for a long long time.

"Okay so far. Don't go peeking."

He laughed. "Sooner or later an envelope like that's gonna want some rent."

"I throw you business, Art."

"Just kidding. But the day Rosewood Agency actually needs your referrals things are getting really fucked up, I can tell you. I helped you out of love."

Jack Liffey shrugged. "Then it's the thought that counts. I've got a question about one of your competitors, G. Dan Hunt."

For a few moments Art Castro rearranged things on his desk, swapped an ashtray for a stapler, and squared off the blotter. Finally he nodded. "Sure. You mixed up with him?"

"Just curious."

"He's not really a competitor of ours. 'Course, no one is. His dad was an L.A. fixer, you know—it's the 1950s and Louis Mayer hears some reporter out on the margins is going to do a piece saying Rock Hudson is a fairy so G. Dan is sent to talk to the reporter. The city used to work that way when the press was mostly a gentleman, but now it's mostly not. I hear he tried to cover up that strange business with Begelman kiting Cliff Robertson's checks. You can see it doesn't work anymore. The tidy world those Jewish glove merchants ran is gone. . . ." He tailed off.

"So," Jack Liffey said. "Like, if I asked if there was anything more serious he's involved in these days, would you go around rearranging your desk again?"

He smiled. "He was rumored to be involved in the Hundred Committee. That was those Cuban thugs down in Florida that Nixon used to run."

"Are you telling me he bumped off Bobby Kennedy?"

"No. Absolutely not. But that *kind* of thing, maybe."

"So he deals in funny moral areas," Jack Liffey said.

"I guess that depends on your sense of humor. I liked Bobby Kennedy."

"Cubans, huh? I think what I really want to know is if he ever employs Jamaicans."

Art Castro thought about it, as if he might be deciding whether to hold something back. "The eighties was the era of the Jamaican posses. They ran dope and stuff in some parts of town, but now they're all going to junior college and starting small businesses. You know, it's a funny thing, your basic American black doesn't like your Jamaican much, thinks he's uppity and too close to whitey. Me, I love the sound of the accent.''

"This wasn't, like, an abstract question, Arturo.''

"Okay, sure. I think he's got a Trenchtown lad he uses.''

"Green four-wheeler?''

"I wouldn't know, but I can find out.''

"You do that. Please. And let me worry about Sociology 102 and whether the Mexicans like the Costa Ricans and Peruvians. I love everybody. What would we do for food without immigrants?''

"Around here, you're the immigrant, *esse*.''

"Sure thing. And you natives are welcome to all the hamburgers you want.''

HE let the Nissan idle smoothly at the bottom of the hill, unable to decide whether to drive it across town and give it back, or summon the nerve to drive up the hill to see *her*. Two police helicopters circled and circled out over Hollywood, buzzards waiting for something to die. There was no denying it, she had him in a sweat. It was something he remembered from his teenage years when he was drawn to things he knew were bad for him, but he was going to do them anyway. How could any human being watch movies all his life and not want to be up there with one of those forty-foot-tall presences? To leverage his own ordinary-scale existence up into Magicville.

He stopped the car and found a phone box.

"Mike, tell me, why is looking at a movie star so weird?''

"Weird?''

"You know, in the flesh. It's like a spot in a mirror that you can't get a focus on.''

"Mm-hmm.''

"So, what is it?''

"This isn't a joke? I thought you were calling to *tell* me,'' Mike Lewis said evenly.

"It's a question. It's a matter of life and death.''

"Oh, life and death. I'd better be serious, then. When

you think of a normal friend of yours, like me for instance, your referent is all the things that have happened between us, the words we've exchanged and the things we've done together. Okay?''

''Sure.''

''When you think about a movie star, what you've got instead is all those movies you saw with the passive part of your brain, and worse, part of you was up there being somebody else. The referent is daydreams.''

''So?''

''That isn't weird enough for you? Gotta go, Jack. Whatever you're thinking about, don't do it. It's going to be really bad news.''

''Thanks a lot.''

Mike Lewis hung up. He knew Mike was right, but he'd given up so much, he couldn't find a way to deny himself this, too.

SHE was sitting on a bench in back with her binoculars, looking out over one of the ravines. She wore a silky silver blouse that was unbuttoned pretty far, so something red peeked out of the depths, and she seemed to break into a genuine smile when she saw him.

''Jack, it's good to see you.'' That voice like water over rocks. His heart thumped and he felt a little dizzy.

''You look good enough to eat,'' he heard himself say.

''That could be arranged.''

She held out one hand, and he didn't know what she was asking. He took it and she reeled him in gently and kissed him on the cheek. She patted the bench beside her and he sat. The security guard was still there, pacing slowly along the rim of the yard as if deep in thought.

''Did you see Lionel?''

''Mm-hmm.'' He remembered Lionel Borowsky's warning: this woman wasn't what she seemed, this woman was capable of anything. He seemed to be floating an inch or so off the bench.

''What did he want?''

He hesitated and then made a decision, he wasn't sure why. Maybe just because she was his client. "He warned me obliquely that you might be behind the kidnapping."

She laughed and passed the back of her hand gently across his lap, as if inadvertently, showing that she noticed he had an erection. "Is that all? Do you think I am?"

"Frankly, it would make me really pissed off if you were. No matter what you're paying."

"But do you think so?"

"No."

"Why not?" She cocked her head to look at him and he felt like a faintly interesting butterfly waiting for the ether jar.

"Do you always know why you believe people?"

"Oh, yes. But I'm pleased I have your vote of confidence, even if it's irrational. Even if it's sexual."

"There's that. Hows about you let me take you to lunch? You don't get out much, do you?"

"What do you mean?"

"You know, grab a bite at the McDonald's, shop at the Ralph's?"

She laughed. "Most of what I need comes to me."

"That's what I mean. Come slumming with me. I'll take you someplace I promise nobody knows your name. Or would that hurt too much?"

He was pleased with himself. She was a bit off balance and maybe he could establish some kind of equality after all.

"I'm not so vain to think I'm recognized that often anymore."

"No, but if you keep going to Spago and calling ahead for reservations, you can stretch it out, can't you?"

She let that go. "What if the kidnappers call?"

"You don't have a cell phone?"

"Okay," she said. "Drag me to Sherwood Forest with the peasants, if that's your game."

"My game is getting you down where the air's thicker. It's too thin up here in cloud-cuckoo-land for me."

He was glad he still had the serviceable Nissan. He cringed to think of opening the door for Lori Bright onto the shredding seats of the Concord, watching her step daintily into the two inches of effluvium on the floor. Even in the pristine Nissan she sat uneasily, as if she'd never been in anything more proletarian than a stretch, and he drove down to the ragged east end of Hollywood Boulevard that was now little Armenia. Pibul's place was wedged between a liquor store and a shop called Plato's Household that specialized in extremely ornate china plates and doodads. All the other stores on the block had Armenian script over the doors, like a dozen ways of drawing a rounded chair.

Phuket Thai didn't look like much outside, but inside it looked worse. "It's pronounced fuckit, more or less," he said as they drove around to the lot in back. "You've got to be careful, though. You might make it even worse. Thai's a tonal language. The single syllable *khao* can mean 'they,' 'badly,' 'rice,' 'white,' 'old,' or 'news,' depending on your tone."

"You speak Thai?"

"No. Hi, Pibul."

"Hello, Mr. Liffey." The distinguished-looking Thai bowed slightly to Lori Bright, but without recognition. There was an old man at a corner table who looked grizzled and homeless, drinking tea from a glass, and a young couple were eating shrimp as far away from the homeless man as possible. On closer inspection, the grizzled man was playing chess on a little board with pegged pieces. Every once in a while he made a move and expressed some emotion at his invisible opponent, fury or satisfaction or bewildered awe, and then he would rotate the board and express the opposite.

"Pibul, did you ever see *A Week in Palm Springs? Enough Is Never Enough*?"

"Are those movies? No, I don't think so." His forehead wrinkled up, as if his ignorance might displease them.

"Great. Two Singhas."

He retreated through a bead curtain that clacked and swayed.

"You were in Thailand, I take it."

"A military outpost in the northeast, not far from Laos. I watched radar screens by day and read books at night. It was a whole lot better than getting shot at."

The owner brought two large amber beers. "Would you like to order?"

"Let's have a nuah yong for starters and we'll split one of your drunkard's pastas." It wasn't on the menu, but it used to be, a melange of chili and mint and pork and flat pasta that Pibul Phanomyong himself had invented.

He nodded and withdrew.

Lori Bright glanced at the photo of the king on a little shelf like a shrine. "I always wanted to do *Anna and the King of Siam.* To come up against that stuffed shirt and win him over and get him to stop lining up those kids."

"I bet you did. Did you make your own kid line up?"

A chill descended with breathtaking effect. "Are you being philosophical or inquisitory?"

"I get hints that she's unhappy."

"She's a teenager. It's an occupational disease. It's the time of ghastly loneliness when every boyfriend who moseys away is an irredeemable loss. And all adults are put in the world to deny you things."

"So you didn't get along."

"I didn't beat her with a coat hanger. Why are you obsessing on this?"

All of a sudden he knew exactly why. The missing girl must have represented his own daughter, the black hole that marked the spot where his life had been sucked away. And just like that, the grief that he thought he'd conquered flooded back in. That very weekend he remembered Kathy was going to relent and let him see Maeve again, even if he couldn't pay the child support. He held himself very rigid, pretending nothing hurt. "She's my job, isn't she? Finding her."

"You're a strange man," she said, watching him carefully. "You'd never make a movie star because your personality isn't static enough."

"And here I thought it was my looks."

The plate of nuah yong arrived and she watched him dip the thin steak into the garlic chili sauce with chopsticks, then followed suit. She was good with the sticks, and she showed off her admiration for the burst of flavor with a big Groucho lift of her eyebrows.

"That's what we brought to the screen, you know. The thing that mere actors couldn't do, no matter how good they were. Whoever Jimmy Stewart played, he carried with him that bemused small-town righteousness that you loved and trusted. And Marilyn, she always had that deep devious sensuality that's only given to the pure of heart."

"And you?" He heard Mike's words about celebrity and daydreams on the phone and wondered just where he was. He was in a seedy restaurant in Hollywood, all right, but he was also sitting opposite lips that had once kissed Marlon Brando. Hair that always caught the backlight no matter which way she turned.

Words evaporated away as they talked, like the mist over ice in the sun. And she was watching him as if she was about to eat him alive.

"What do you think *I* projected in all those films?" she said.

"You were sly and knowing."

She nodded slightly, as if it was a half-bright try. "I've paid my dues in the big bad world and I know more than I'm ever going to let on. Somewhere sometime I made a stand for the right thing and I lost badly for it. Now I'm a stoic failure, but I have a bigger soul than all these successes around me."

"Jesus, sort of a younger Rita Hayworth," he said.

"Thanks for the *younger*. What are you doing this afternoon?"

"I've got to see some Nazis about your daughter."

That stopped her for a moment, which was the point. She'd already adjusted to the Phuket as if she'd been coming there for years. You had to get up damned early to stay ahead of this woman, he thought.

"Come back to me tonight. Please."

"I wouldn't call it the impossible dream."

And then she jumped six inches as if someone had stuck her with a needle.

10

A MORAL REFERENCE POINT

HER HAND WAS CLAPPED AGAINST HER BREAST, AGAINST WHAT looked like a slim silver pen but turned out to be one of the new pagers that got your attention by shuddering away in your pocket like a rat in a straitjacket. It was letting her know that her cell phone, set to mute in her purse, was ringing. She dug the phone out, more agitated than he'd ever seen her, and listened with a frown.

"When? *Okay*. How?"

She turned the cell phone off, moving very deliberately now, and stared at the tiny instrument as if it might turn into something quite different.

"That was the call," she said at last.

"How long have we got?"

"An hour, to get home and get the money—I have it ready. And get to Forest Lawn in Glendale."

"Pibul," he called. The cook stuck his head through the bead curtain. "Do us a favor."

OUT front they waved cheerfully, arm in arm, as Pibul drove off in the Nissan, then they ducked back inside. He wasn't certain, but he thought it was Malamud and Flor in the white Caprice parked on the red zone down the block. No one had ever bought that car but cops, what the kids in his condo called a real P-ride. Five minutes later Pibul Phanomyong had the car idling in the garbage-smelling alley in back.

Jack Liffey gave him two twenties. "Thanks, my friend. Find someone to give your drunkard's pasta, maybe the chesshead."

Pibul wrinkled up his forehead. "No good. Jailbird chess, all impulse."

"That doesn't disqualify him from eating."

He didn't see anybody following them up the hill. He dropped her off and then punished Marlena's Nissan fast along Los Feliz to beat Lori to the cemetery. He cut down a side street, nearly losing it to the strange understeer of front-wheel drive, and caught a glint in the street ahead. It was one of those unexpected sights that his eye had trouble resolving, and when he did he was standing on the brake.

Fifty homeless scavengers had chosen the middle of this street for a meeting, and they pushed their shopping carts along, filling the roadway from curb to curb. The carts brimmed with cans, cardboard, plastic Coke bottles. The whole moving shoal trended eastward, dot-dashing with light through the arching Chinese elms, but not fast enough for him. He backed into a driveway and headed for another shortcut.

Then he was turning off at the grand iron gates into the parklike cemetery. It was not the usual graveyard. There were no headstones, no real reminders of death to ruffle the moral stillness, no rue allowed. The founder of the place had long ago decreed that death was an upbeat occurrence and only the soothing and sunny were permitted in his cemetery. He headed up the hillside through the scattered pines and sycamores to the little walled courts along the ridgeline.

He had trouble finding the Court of David. He followed the signs but still couldn't find it and then he parked and got out and discovered the plinth where the giant sculpture should have been but where there was an apology on a little plaque instead. For the third time a reproduction of the David had been toppled by an earthquake and a new reproduction was at that moment being carved out of Carrara marble by one of the world's most acclaimed contemporary artisans.

He seemed to have beaten them and he took up a discreet watch in the next courtyard over, the Court of the Mystery of Life. There was some complex sculpture group posing along the wall, but no humans were in the court. He had a good view down the slope where a fat man was planting a small Confederate flag, and a woman not far from him was sitting cross-legged on the grass, reading a book out loud to one of the markers set below grass level. A gardener was far away with a posthole digger, and nobody else was in sight. He plucked a wilted rose out of a bronze urn to give his hand something to do.

Partially screened by cypresses, he could see to his right the plinth where David should have stood and straight ahead he could see miles across the smoggy Valley. He wasn't invisible and he decided he'd better look busy, so he turned to the big sculpture group next to him, twenty figures emoting in various ways around a couple of marble doves who were kissing. He couldn't help thinking of the two turtles at the Eighth Art.

Then he noticed a plaque at the side, with a lot of text keyed to the figures.

1. A boy who is astonished at the miracle that has happened in his hand—one moment, an unbroken egg; the next moment, a chick, teeming with life. "Why?" he asked. "How did it happen? What is the answer to the mystery of life?" he questioned.

Fucking A, Jack Liffey thought. His eye went down the plaque.

The happy family group, not greatly perturbed by the mystery, although even they seem to ask: "Why do the doves mate?"

There was a powerful thumping as a helicopter passed overhead and skimmed out over the Valley.

Gentle Reader, what is your interpretation? Do you see yourself in one of the characters here portrayed? Forest Lawn has found the answer to the Mystery of Life. Have you found it? Or are you still in anxiety of doubt?

He felt a shiver—the daffy earnestness had distracted him for too long, and when he glanced back at the road, a Volvo station wagon was coming up the long slow ascent. He drew back deeper into the court, but he soon saw that the Volvo was full to the gills with a serious-faced African-American family and the car muttered past.

His eye went to another plaque beside a bronze door in the wall at the side of the court. The plaque told him that Death was nothing more than a simple door in a garden wall and not to be feared at all. The hair rose on his neck and he broke into a sweat. *There* was the door. Uh-unh, *later*, he thought. It was a damn strange neighborhood he had wandered into. Wind picked up and a few errant brown leaves skittered across the flagstones.

A black Mercedes convertible with the top up was climbing fast. He couldn't see into the smoked windows and he knelt as if he were offering up the wilted rose. The car stopped right in front of the Court of David and the door came open. Lori Bright emerged with a small flight bag in her hand and strode to David's plinth. She hadn't had any trouble finding it. Perhaps she'd been to Hollywood funerals here.

She noticed him kneeling on the lawn but did a good job of concealing it. Down the slope the woman was showing off pictures in her book to the grave site. The man with the Confederate flag was standing with his hand on his breast, reciting something that was blown away by the wind. Lori Bright paced the Court of David for a minute, and he could see how tense she had become. She kicked at a pebble and it skipped away into a flower bed.

A funeral went past far below, Lincoln after Lincoln. They stopped at a set of blue folding chairs that faced an open grave. He watched it for anything unusual, but everything seemed normal. It was time to move. He'd be conspicuous if he stayed there any longer, and he started slowly down the hillside toward the Confederate supporter, who seemed to have finished his recitation. He heard the elec-

tronic brrr of a telephone and held up as he heard Lori
Bright murmuring behind him. Discipline kept him from
looking back.

"Jack!" her voice came sharply. There was such anguish
that he turned back after all. She stood there with the bag
at her feet and the cell phone in one hand. She was staring
forlornly at a piece of paper in her other hand. "Help me."

He trudged back up and she handed him a Polaroid photograph. It showed a thin sad-looking girl with short dark
hair holding that morning's *L.A. Times* under her chin. JET
FIGHTER CRASHES OFF VIRGINIA BEACH.

"They said they'd changed their minds about making the
swap today. They'll let me know." She seemed really
wrung out. "Bastards."

"Where was the picture?"

"Over there in a plastic bag."

He looked fiercely out over the whole scene. The Confederate was dwindling down the hill, the woman with the
book was lying flat to sun herself, and the funeral party
were taking up their seats. Was that a glint of binoculars
from the faraway trees? The wind was picking up.

"Will you come back tonight?" she asked forlornly. "I
need you." It was a strange time to be thinking of that.

"I'll come back."

"Now they'll probably raise the price," she said.

"Now they've had a good look at *me*," he said.

It was the same cool wind blowing in out of left field and
Jack Liffey made himself thin to work down the row to the
empty seat beside Art Castro.

Art offered the cardboard tray and Jack Liffey took a
Dodger Dog wrapped in foil.

"Man, you know just what I like," Jack Liffey said.
"Watching a bunch of grown-ups in pajamas running
around on grass." He squinted at the uniforms on the out-
fielders. "What's that P for? Pasadena? Paris?"

"I can't figure out your prejudice, Jack. This is manly
stuff."

''You've been around a war. How can you stand all this spurious loyalty? Man, those players don't come from L.A., even the owners don't.''

A big man in a blue parka was starting to look oddly at them.

''That makes it purer, *esse*. It's about watching guys who are the best at what they do, do it. It's like ballet with muscles.''

The batter hit a long ball into center and the whole stands gasped and then sighed in disappointment as it was caught, and the fielders zinged the ball around a bit.

''I don't like ballet much either. It's too much like baseball.''

''Didn't you play as a kid?''

''I liked a game with more possibility to cheat.''

Art Castro laughed and the big man in the blue parka glared and stood up. For a moment Jack Liffey thought the man was going to try to get seriously in his face, but he met his eyes and something the man saw there changed his mind and he slid down the row.

''*Hombre*,'' Art Castro said, ''someday you'll get in trouble like that.''

Jack Liffey held up the ticket stub. ''This is my space, right? You paid for it.''

He shrugged. ''My company did.''

''You can't let anybody take your space. You'll never get it back.''

''That's some profound shit, Jack. You take that philosophy out into East Los and you can get yourself dead three times a day.''

Now Jack Liffey grinned. ''Okay, you win. I've got a hot date. I'd like to hear what you found out.''

There was a sharp crack and twenty thousand necks craned upward at a towering pop fly. Two fielders nearly ran into each other, but at the last moment one dived unceremoniously out of the way. The catch ended the inning, and a screechy sound system started to rasp out Queen's ''We Are the Champions.'' He had no idea at all why sports fans went nuts for a dead homosexual pop singer from Zanzibar.

"G. Dan uses a Jamaican all right. His name is Tyrone Pennycooke. His street name is Terror. They're not really working for the local boys at Monogram Pictures. They were hired direct by whoever came over from Mitsuko. Those Japanese companies are so used to using yakuza to clear up their little problems they did the next best thing over here. Somebody must have thought dreadlocks and tropical shirts were better protective coloration in L.A. than ninja jumpsuits." He contemplated for a moment. The man in the blue parka came back with a big paper cup of beer, but he kept his eyes averted. Jack Liffey thought about ginger ale for a moment.

"Jack, these guys may be into some kind of vendetta, but unless I'm way off base, they aren't involved in a kidnapping."

"Yeah, it doesn't make much sense to me, either. If I needed to get in touch with G. Dan, where would I go?"

"I happen to know he lunches at Musso and Frank's every day. They keep a booth for him on the left side toward the front."

For some strange reason, he felt intensely alive all of a sudden, almost elated. The horrible music had stopped. The cold breeze gusted through people's hair, the high stadium lights cut cones out of the dark, and voices made a susurrus that rose and fell all around as the infield worked a ball around with a distinct popping. Lori Bright and anticipation, that was probably it. He wondered what Art Castro would say if he told him he was about to drive up into the Hollywood Hills to fuck a famous movie star. He wondered if women ever had ignoble thoughts like that.

"Thanks, Art." He got up.

"Jeez, Angelenos are famous for trying to beat the traffic, but the top of the third is really pushing it some."

He was tired of disliking baseball, so he just waved and wormed his way down the row to an aisleway. The crowd roared as he went out the portal. From the lot he looked back at the unnaturally lit structure in Chavez Ravine. The Ravine had held a Latino village up to the fifties, already being torn down for new integrated and subsidized housing, and then the *L.A. Times* and real-estate interests had combined to throw out the progressive mayor who had been behind it all. He wondered what that picturesque high valley in the hills would look like now with a big integrated housing project instead of the baseball palace. To be honest, he thought, the tenants would probably have torn the place up pretty badly by now. There were no jobs going, and when people didn't have jobs, they got demoralized. He knew all about that.

Before he could get into the car a bedraggled skinny girl appeared from behind a battered old Ford van, her hair tangled as if she'd slept in the weeds. She looked about fourteen and wore a sparkly bandeau where breasts might show up someday soon. ''Blow you for two bucks,'' she said dully. She made pumping motions with one hand and formed an *O* with her tiny red mouth. He gave her two bucks and shooed her away. It would go for crack, but what could you do?

Descending from the Ravine, he looked out over the famous shimmering lights of L.A., a billion acres of yellow-lit distress. His elation was ebbing fast. He still felt alive, but not quite clean anymore: he'd grasped that odd sensation of vitality up there without paying for it in some way.

STEAM billowed up his nose and made him sneeze. He was in a big, low bathtub made out of mirror tiles that reflected more mirror tiles on the bathroom walls beyond until you couldn't tell what was what, like being trapped in an experiment in optics.

He'd liked her better anxious, distraught about the ransom call, but a few drinks and the swooshing water jets had finally seen to that. He could barely see her through the fog and bubbles, but he could locate her as a haunted presence at the core of a big clot of froth that spilled over the tub edge to obscure yet another point of reference. And sonar helped: she was humming something to herself, a lullaby.

An arm appeared out of the bubble bath and did something over against the wall. Miles Davis came up, playing "In a Silent Way" from an unseen speaker, and she scatted a bit with the music, and he went with it and hunted with his foot until he settled it into her crotch like a bicycle seat.

"Mmmm."

She tugged his foot against her with one hand and rocked as the foam slowly cleared. Her eyes were closed. He could see her hand fumble on the soap shelf for the remains of a joint. She discovered it had gone out and ate it.

"It's good to be with someone new. It's getting harder and harder to find a new perspective. Move like that. Yes. Another J?"

"Nah." He hadn't had any of the first one.

"Puritan. You going to turn down experimental sex, too?"

"Did the white rats survive?"

She sat forward, smiling into his eyes. "I'll bet there are things you've never tried."

"Does that mean *you've* tried them all?"

"Name something and I'll tell you."

His mind was silently going bananas.

"What's your wildest fantasy?" she insisted, running a finger around one of her own nipples that was still lathered with the evaporating bubble bath. "I've done it." She leaned and touched his lips with a finger. "Shh. Yes, I've done *that*." When she withdrew, she pretended he was going to speak again, though he wasn't, and then touched his lips again. "Aha. I've done that, too."

"Wow," he said. "Me, I'll never forget the day I got my hand up Jeannie Dankov's bra in the eighth grade."

She took his erection with one hand under the water and then reached for a small wicker box he hadn't noticed on the edge of the tub. "I can feel you trembling."

"I'm just a poor kid from the sticks. I'm doing the best I can."

She tipped something out of the box into her palm and bounced it a little, like jacks. Part of him was getting pretty worked up, but another part was standing back a bit wondering if he was about to learn what Catherine Deneuve had had in that little box in *Belle de Jour* that left a spot of blood and a big smile on her face.

She supported her left breast on her palm and clipped a gold ring through a piercing he hadn't noticed in the nipple.

"I thought you had to leave those in," he said, as nonchalantly as he could.

"Is that what the lab rat told you?" She placed her finger on his lips again. "There's more."

"Oh, I never doubted it."

She stuck out her tongue and used both hands to locate the hole for a round gold stud that went through about a half inch back from the tip. "You'll like this one."

She climbed out gracefully and flexed in the mist like a dancer. Something in the bright, fixed look in her eyes worried him. "Come."

He followed her into the bedroom with its big bed and gray silk sheets reflected in even more mirrors on a soffit overhead. For the next ten minutes or so he did his best to keep up with her expectations, but a cinnamon-flavored oil got in his eyes and he started sneezing uncontrollably. She reached under the bed and brought out a Polaroid camera.

"You're so lugubrious," she said as she pointed the camera at him.

"Don't do that," he said sharply, angered all of a sudden by the tears streaming down his cheeks. When he cleared his eyes, the camera was still pointed at him.

"I'll do what I like in my own bedroom." Something very hard had entered her voice.

"I'm asking you."

"So what?"

"Please, then."

The flash went off in his face, and he got off the edge of the bed. Their eyes locked, and neither of them looked away as they listened to Mr. Land's invention whir between them and eject its instant print. He reached out and put his hand on the camera. The strap was tight around her wrist and the only way he could have gotten it from her would have been to hurt her.

"Do you want to be hurt? Is that the point?"

"If you hurt me, I'll kill you," she said evenly.

He hadn't got this angry at a woman since Kathy, and he forced his rage to back off, just crushed it deep into the white space at the center of him. Hers was still there, brewing up off her will. It was like standing in the street looking at a house that was perfectly normal except for the one chink in the curtains where you saw the fire going within.

"You do what I want in my house."

Fame will bite you on the ass. The demigod had gone and left something else entirely.

"Uh-huh, sure," he said with all the generosity he could muster. It would be what he gave her. He was still struggling for a moral reference point when she started to demonstrate what the stud through her tongue was for.

HE SAT IN THE CONCORD AT THE TURNOUT INTO CASPERS Regional Park, where ten years back a mountain lion had killed a small child and set off a frantic shooting expedition across all the inland mountain ranges of southern Orange County. The air smelled of sage and Jeffrey pine, plus a hint of sweet rot, maybe garbage at the campground or a skunk a week dead somewhere. He watched an empty stretch of the Ortega Highway, trying to come up with something he could do to reestablish a coherent ethical landscape, instead of the confused and ineffectual mess that surrounded him now. Not so long ago he'd felt he had his life honed down to a fairly simple code: do the best you can, avoid self-pity, and quietly hold on to what's yours. But his path had become lined with all manner of things that were not accounted for in that code, things that were inexpressibly more complicated. Even the trespasses had become more complicated. In some way he could not put his finger on, what he was doing with Lori Bright was leaching away whatever merit he'd thought he had saved up for a rainy day. And he knew he would be going back for more. Even now, forty miles away from her, thinking about her dark energy made him tumescent.

He'd driven home that morning and fed Loco, as back to normal as the beast ever got, returned the car to Marlena, and got into an argument when she asked where he'd been all night, and then he'd called Kathy and miraculously she was still letting him have Maeve for the weekend. Thus he had completed all his cosmic assignments, and there was one decent and ordinary thing to look forward to. He thought involuntarily of twelve-year-old sharp and inquisitive Maeve crossing paths with Lori Bright, and shuddered. He drew a heavy line: two separate worlds.

A station wagon full of kids driven by a young woman swung past on the highway, but it wasn't what he waited for. Somewhere up that road in the Cleveland National Forest, roughly where Orange County gave way to Riverside County, he'd been told there was an unmarked dirt turnout where an unmarked trail led up to what was called, in some circles, the Hermann Goering Shooting Range. It was just a clearing in a high canyon, where the neo-Nazis and militias practiced with their weapons, licit and illicit. It was all probably illegal, but nobody official seemed to care very much, and the boyos themselves wouldn't go to any of the official rifle ranges because government spies took down your name and the U.N.'s black helicopters might drop out of the skies at any moment to arrest you.

He'd been half expecting a Humvee or a Jeep painted up in camouflage, but it was just a battered old pickup with a yellow rope tying down the hood, a rifle rack in the window and a couple of duffel bags in back. He waited a minute and then followed, checking each turnoff he passed. Within five minutes he saw the pickup again on a dirt pad off the high side of the road. The duffel bags were gone and it was parked beside a beat-up VW squareback with a bumper sticker that said F**K CLINTON AND HER HUSBAND. Right-wing wit took a little getting used to, he thought.

For protective coloration as much as anything, he strapped on the canvas holster that held his .45 pistol, a cheap Argentine copy of the U.S. Army service M1911-A1, and he followed the obvious path up the canyon past a live oak and clumps of deep green sumac, the pistol banging away at his hip like a maul. All of a sudden he heard gunfire ahead, a few spaced bangs in a heavy caliber and then a burst on full auto, tinnier, probably one of the little nine-millimeter spray guns that the NRA had fought so hard to protect so gangbangers could shoot up each other's little sisters from passing cars. After a few moments of silence there was a very loud double blast, sawed-off shotgun, he guessed.

For some reason, he did not feel much fear, just a tingle of anticipation as he came around the spur of a hill and saw the clearing. There was a shrill whistle as he hove into view and the firing stopped. Three young men turned to stare. What the hell are *you* staring at? he thought.

A skinny young man in fatigues and a black beret stood at a card table loaded with weapons. He held what looked like an M-16 on his shoulder. He'd expected that, but he hadn't expected to see two other men in strap undershirts and a lot of tattoos posing side by side, their legs bowed out like sumo wrestlers. They were heavyset, like weight lifters, and each held his arms hooked in front of himself as if he was about to bash his fists together.

"Heil," Jack Liffey said, to warm them up.

"Yeah, truly," one of the wrestlers said. This one's tattoos looked Asian, continuous fields of blue tracery that implied dragons and fire. The other had spirals of zigzags all the way down his arms. They gave up whatever pose they'd been striking and straightened up. He had to remind himself that even goofs could be dangerous.

"Steak and eggs," the one in fatigues seemed to say. Jack Liffey wondered if he'd misheard or if it was a password challenge.

"What you doin here?" one of the sumo wrestlers asked.

"Same as you. I come to practice."

"You look like a fed to me."

He walked nonchalantly to the weapons table. "Don't sweat it. If I was a fed, there'd be helicopters all over the place."

He let them wait while he looked over the weapons. There was another M-16 with an M-70 grenade tube under the barrel so dented it would never be used again, a couple of bolt-action deer rifles, an old British Sten that looked like it would blow up in your hands, a wooden presentation box that probably held some sort of target pistol, and he'd guessed right about the sawed-off. "I'm a friend of Tom Metzger down in San Diego and I come here all the time."

He saw a full-length poster they had propped up against a hill as a target, and he had to bite his tongue. It was Martin Luther King, Jr., smiling with his remarkable grace. He already had a number of holes in him.

"Been to any encampments?" the one in fatigues asked.

"I'm a poison toad. I don't ask who you're with, right?" He looked at the two wrestlers. "And you don't ask me."

"Sure, man. Long as you're standing up for the race."

In the next few minutes all three of them said "nigger" as many times as they could, and he was forced to say it a few times, too, which started to work at his temper. He had a feeling things weren't going to turn out very well for somebody. The skinny one in fatigues took off his beret to reveal a blond brush cut, and there was an extraordinary stillness that came over the kid, not much more than twenty, when he wasn't talking, as if he had come from a colder, more austere world. He was too young to have had Ranger training, but he wanted you to think he had.

"Hey, Mr. Toad, you ever seen Atua Hau?" It was the gaudier sumo wrestler. "You got a treat."

They took up their bowlegged posture again and they reached overhead in unison as if to grasp a chin-up bar.

"It's like tai chi but more martial," the one in fatigues explained.

Suddenly, without cue, they shouted out a cry that made his neck hair stand on end. Together, they pulled the chin bar down, stomped one foot, then the other, turned their heads to the left, and stuck out their tongues as far as they would go, then turned the other way. They picked up a chant as they worked out the ritual movements, matching each other word for word and gaining in intensity, barking out the phrases as they pummeled and yanked on the air around them.

He could only make out snatches:

"... A proud white Aryan ..."

"... Behold the fate of our race ..."

"... Protect the blood of our family, our culture, our folk ..."

"... The mad dog is the first shot ..."

"... The sly dog is the last suspected ..."

He wasn't sure he'd heard the last axioms right. If he'd come upon either of them drilling singly, the effect might have been comic, but together it was eerie and stately, like a well-rehearsed line dance for schizophrenics. He had no idea where white supremacists had come up with some debased Maori warrior dance, but it was worth the price of admission. Eventually they ran down with a bellow about Ruby Ridge and free-free-freedom and then they toweled off and came to the card table to claim weapons.

"Super-duper," he said.

"Ain't it."

Jack Liffey opened the presentation box on the table to see a silver .44 auto-magnum that probably cost close to a thousand dollars. It was a strange-looking pistol, all odd angles and reflections on polished stainless steel so it looked as if it had been carved out of ice, and it sat in a velvet cutout that just fit.

"Quite a gun, ain't it?" the kid said.

"A gun is a piece of field ordnance with a high muzzle velocity and low trajectory," Jack Liffey said amiably, quoting his DI from Bragg. "This is a pistol."

"There's only three hundred and eighty-eight in the world," the kid said, trying to recover. "High Standard ain't made them since the eighties."

He picked up the auto-mag and ejected the magazine, noticed the tip of a jacketed .44 and felt the weight that said it was chock full, and then slid it back home. The weapon was ridiculously heavy and all that stainless steel glinted like a homing beacon, but the balance was good. He put it back down and looked over the other weapons. Mostly they were junk. The Sten belonged in the trash be-

fore somebody got hurt with it. He took a closer look at
the assault rifle the blond carried and saw it was a Colt
Sporter, the civilian model of the M-16. From the factory
it came as only a semiautomatic, but that wasn't fixed and
fated.

"You convert that?" Jack Liffey asked.

He nodded. "I bought the sear kit mail order. It's a bitch.
I'll show you."

The big one with the Asian tattoos chose one of the bolt
rifles, and the one with the barbed-wire tattoos loaded up
the sawed-off that had once been a box-lock dove gun. It
had been cut so short that you could see the red cardboard
of the shells peeking at you an inch or two down the two
barrels. That would be a hell of a persuader for a bank
teller, Jack Liffey thought. The one with zigzag tattoos
backed off to the side with the shotgun, still keeping a
weather eye on the interloper. Jack Liffey could see he
hadn't won their trust.

The blond lowered his assault rifle and suddenly the canyon was full of sound, like one continuous roar of an un-
muffled dragster, spent brass arcing away from the rifle.
Martin Luther King's left leg sprouted holes, but then Jack
Liffey heard a little zinging sound in his ears and went for
the ground. The Aryans fired away, too rapt to notice the
ricochets coming back.

No discipline but plenty of firepower, he thought. It was
the American condition.

"Oh, *bitch*in'."

"Get some, mother*fucker*. Man, I can't get *enough* of
that."

When the magazine ran out, Jack Liffey stood up and
dusted off his hands. "You might want to move the target
a bit," he said evenly. "There's some solid granite back in
there."

"Huh?"

"That little singing sound is lead coming back this
way."

"Bull*shit*. I didn't hear nothing." The one with the Asian

tattoos looked sheepish, but the blond was trying to tough it out.

"Have it your way." He took out the photograph of Lee Borowsky. He might as well get everything he could before they killed themselves off. "Has this girl been bugging you?"

"How come you're asking?"

"She's been bothering friends of mine and I want to have a little talk with her."

They craned their necks. "I remember that cunt," Asian Tattoos said. "She was hanging out at the roadhouse with a big guy with a camera. They was looking for skins who was into Hitler parapher."

Jack Liffey gave him a fish eye. "You're not? You into *Stalin*?"

"Hey, each his own thing, man. We're into pure white *American* blood. Maybe Hitler was cool for Germany, but that was a long time ago."

He started going into a story about some African-American girl they had humiliated in high school, and Jack Liffey's skin was starting to crawl, when the man with the zigzag tattoos brought the sawed-off around and spoke for the first time. "Okay, mister. Here's the way it is. It's time you tell us your game."

Jack Liffey met his eyes and they played dogs for a while. He could see the red of the cartridges without looking directly at the sawed-off. Nobody moved.

"You're too fuckin' curious for me."

Jack Liffey smiled without breaking eye contact, and Zigzag started to look worried.

"I can drop you where you stand."

"Your first mistake," Jack Liffey said evenly, "was choosing a weapon that would blow away all three of us over here."

They could see right away he was right, and like the untrained hooligans they were, they were so swiftly demoralized by the mistake that they had no idea how to put things right quickly enough. In that space Jack Liffey picked up the auto-mag. He took a step toward Barbed-wire and grasped the barrel of the sawed-off. He tilted it straight up with his left hand and yanked hard, the man's finger still on the triggers. Both barrels let off a terrible roar into the blue sky.

"Jezuz ka-beezus!"

The young man's jaw hung open and Jack Liffey used the barrel of the auto-mag to tap the lower jaw open a few inches more, then he rested the barrel on the lower incisors. He wasn't sure this one was the top dog, but it seemed to be working out that way.

"Close your mouth on the pistol. You make any sudden move, I'll notice."

The man let his lip descend gently.

"Teeth. I want to feel teeth. You understand nobody is to fuck around."

"Umm."

"You guys can't go around pointing weapons at people. It gets people pissed off. Now, I'm just asking a question, that's all. When did you see the girl? Anybody can answer."

"A couple weeks ago," Asian Tattoos said.

"Be precise. It matters."

"A week ago Tuesday. We was up there visiting a sick friend Tuesday."

Just before the kidnapping, he thought. "Was she getting chummy with anybody?"

"Some guys from WASP." The blond took over. Jack Liffey's eye searched him out, and he went on quickly. "Okay, it means White Aryan Skinhead Psychos."

"That sounds redundant."

"Huh?"

"Where would I meet these folk?"

"They hang out up Bouquet Canyon. A roadhouse called the Big Oak."

He'd passed only a mile or two from there on his way up to the Owens Valley. It would be in one of those scrubby canyon passes of Canyon Country that ran from the very north end of the San Fernando Valley out to the High Desert. Where the rednecks and cops lie down in amity, plus gold prospectors, junk collectors, dog breeders, and gun-toting Baptists with "Keep Out" signs on their gates. It was the outer rim of white flight, all the refugees from the twentieth century.

He could feel a tremor pass up the pistol. "Did you want to speak?"

The young man made a noise in his throat and Jack Liffey adjusted the pistol long enough for him to speak.

"We don't mean you no harm," he said contritely.

"Then you'll find I have a warm and sympathetic nature. You two sit down. Your pal is going to walk me to the road. Heil Hitler, folks. You, keep your teeth on the barrel, and back up the path."

He looked worried.

"You can do it."

It was ungainly and slow, but he kept Zigzag entertained with the story of Brer Rabbit and the Tar-baby plus a little history about Joel Chandler Harris and *The Atlanta Constitution*. Zigzag backed up with his hands on his hips and his elbows thrust out, his back bent forward a bit to cushion the pistol. Every once in a while he bobbed a little as he stumbled and extended his arms for balance.

At the road Jack Liffey took the young man's car keys and made him sit a few yards down the low side of the highway. "I'll leave the keys and the auto-mag at the first turn."

Barbed-wire watched the ground sullenly.

"We don't want any more trouble with each other, do we?"

"I know where the bitch is, man, but you can shoot me and I won't tell you shit."

Jack Liffey considered threatening him, but the boy was right, there was nothing he could do if he wasn't prepared to shoot.

The fact that he'd known something all along and hadn't given it up brought the boy up in his estimation a bit. It was something, a particle of honor. In another universe, he would have lectured the overgrown child about the roots of the American republic in the Enlightenment, and the contributions of blacks and Jews to American culture, and about the fragility of justice and honor, and everything would have been changed between them. But that was another universe.

"Get another racket, son. I was never much of a soldier, and you couldn't even handle me."

"**OH**, Dad, you should *see* her! It's so pathetic."

She stopped laughing to take another bite out of her Pink's hot dog. He always let her have a Pink's hot dog, though Kathy disapproved. They sat at the plastic table at the back of the patio, the very one where Bruce Willis had proposed to Demi Moore, surrounded by dozens of people who kept looking around at each other to see if any of them were movie stars. He drank coffee out of a foam cup. He had a lot of weaknesses, but Pink's hot dogs were not among them.

After a bite, she giggled again. "She had the flu for three days, way, way bad. Then she thought she was better and she got up in the morning and it was like the right side of her face had collapsed. Like it was a hillside of mud and it just, you know, *slumped*." She covered her mouth to kill the laugh.

Maeve wore a bit of makeup and her breasts had started to grow since he'd last been allowed a look at her. It was hard to disapprove of that, but it made him anxious. Too many things could happen to girls, *far too many*. She slurped on the straw.

"What's wrong with her?"

"The doctor said it's called Bell's palsy. The flu germ jumps into this nerve that goes through a hole in your skull and the nerve swells up until it hits the bone and then it just goes on strike, so nothing works on one side of your face. Mom *drools*." Maeve giggled. "It's so *weird*. The right side of her face is fine, so half of her goes on smiling or frowning or blinking and the other half is just dead as a dognail.''

"Doornail.''

"What's a doornail?''

"Beats me. It's just an idiom. Is the palsy permanent?''

"Naw. They said it would go away pretty soon, but Mom is in hiding until it does. That's why she wouldn't come to the door, she's not mad at you.''

"She has every right to be mad,'' he said. "I made three hundred and forty dollars last month. Which is half my bare mortgage, not counting condo fees, so I didn't have a lot left over for essentials like supporting you.''

"Is it that bad?'' She glanced down at the remains of the hot dog, as if she'd just thoughtlessly eaten his inheritance.

"It's better now. I've got a rich client for a while.'' He showed off the cellular phone that Lori Bright had insisted he carry.

"Cool! You've got a cell phone.''

So, the word 'cool' was back. "And I've got a lovely date.''

She blushed.

"Who has paint all over her face.''

"Oh, Daddy, please please don't object.''

She hadn't had it on when she came to the door at Kathy's, but ten minutes later she'd pleaded to go to the bathroom at a Chevron and she'd come out with it on. She wasn't quite twelve, but he didn't have the heart to make her wash it off. That was one of the problems of being an intermittent father. He wasn't that worried about it, though. She was too levelheaded to end up obsessing for long about makeup or clothes.

"Got any oddities for me?'' he asked.

"Jody showed me one! C'mon, let's go.'' She wolfed down the fag end of the hot dog.

"You are what you eat,'' he said.

"Woof,'' she said, and he laughed. She was a great kid.

They reclaimed the Concord and he headed down La Brea at her direction.

"Go right on Wilshire. Now pull in there. Look across the street."

With the car idling, he stared across six lanes of light traffic at a big oval bank building in smoked glass. It was ugly, but not ugly enough to stand out much in L.A.

"Uh-huh."

"Look close."

"John Wayne on a horse."

"Look at the horse, Dad. You're not very observant."

She was right. He started laughing right away when he made himself look. There was John Wayne and his chaps and six-gun and his mouth open a bit as if he needed to move his lips to read the street signs. Nothing too strange until you looked at the horse and noticed that it was far too small. Maybe it was an attempt to aggrandize the Duke, and maybe it was just clumsy sculpting. The equestrian sculpture gave the impression of a man sitting on an over-size Saint Bernard.

They crossed the road on foot to get a closer look, and he noticed right away that it was definitely not a mare the Duke was riding, and it was very well hung for a little horse. He didn't mention that to Maeve. He'd never drive down Wilshire again without laughing. It was like someone pointing out to you that Steve McQueen was always up-staging his costars by tugging on his earlobe and fiddling with his hat, and you could never look at *The Magnificent Seven* the same way again.

"Okay, doll, you get a point for that one. Who's ahead?"

"We're even. Twenty-two apiece."

"Then I'm going to blow you out of the water with this one, but it's not a funny one. It's a nice one."

"We'll see."

You only got points by convincing your opponent the oddity was worth it, and there were no rules. He picked up Crescent Heights and headed north to the hills. Just after it became Laurel Canyon he made a hard left. "Bet you didn't even know there was a Hollywood Boulevard up here." Up here it was just a winding two-lane hill road, with a few of the usual stilt houses on the sides. He handed her the emergency necktie from his glove compartment. "Blindfold yourself. You've got to see this all at once."

She was restless with excitement, and tied the old striped tie over her eyes. He wondered what a prowl car would think, if one happened by, or even the woman in the Volvo turbo who slitted her eyes and glared at him as she went past.

He found a wide spot about where he wanted and stopped.

"Blindfold off, punkin, and tell me where we are."

She ripped the tie over her head without loosening it. She blinked theatrically and then goggled at the sight of pleasantly rolling hills staked out with grapevines just off what appeared a country road. Beside the vines was a stone Tudor cottage with a twisty chimney, and there was a Tudor farmhouse farther back.

"Wow. France, I guess. This is outtasight. You get a point."

Just then the cell phone *brrred*, and a chill went through him. Kathy would kill him if Maeve got involved in any way with his business.

"This is Jack."

"Jack, they called. They want the fifty thousand plus my small Utrillo and I've got twenty-five minutes to get there. They want me at the *other* Forest Lawn, the one in Burbank. At the foot of the Lincoln sculpture."

"They haven't seen this car. I'll be there. Bye."

His mind was ticking over as he swung the car around. If he went like a bat out of hell over Laurel Canyon and down the Ventura Freeway, he could just make it. But there was no time to do anything with Maeve. He considered and abandoned one idea after another.

"What a lovely voice. Who was that?"

Daddy's new lover, punkin, the famous movie star. Uh-huh. "My client. A rich lady."

"Why is she taking money to Forest Lawn?"

He sighed. "Will you please promise to stay in the car?"

12

STRAINING UP THE STEEP BIT OF LAUREL CANYON NEAR MUL-
holland, the car offered up its little shudder, something to
do with the carburetor, and he held his breath in a rage,
thinking that he'd get out his .45 and put a round straight
through the hood into the damn carburetor if it chose this
moment to die. Maeve sensed his intensity and retracted a
bit into herself, squeezing the tips of her fingers, one after
another, the way she did.

"Honey, I shouldn't be doing this with you along, but I
can't just dump you off by the road, I'm sorry."

"Are you gonna be in danger?"

He shook his head. "They haven't seen this car, so they
won't know who I am. Would you grab the Thomas Bros.
out of the glove compartment and double-check my navi-
gation."

He could see her fumbling in the corner of his eye and
then he was preoccupied with making a reckless pass on
the wrong side of an old Toyota. He cut back in, the heavy
car wallowing in the swerve.

"Oh, Jesus, give me that."

She was staring down at the .45 in her lap, still in its
canvas holster, frowning at the automatic as if it were some
refractory science-fair project. His big hand took it gently
off her lap and tucked it under his seat. This was starting
to spin out of control and his mind's eye taunted him with

a number of unpleasant possibilities. Gosh, Mom, guess what Daddy had in his car . . . !

"I put it in there yesterday for something down in Orange County. . . ." That wasn't helping much. "Try page twenty-four. Tell me where to get off the Ventura, the closest ramp to the cemetery."

When he got a chance to glance over, she seemed to be all right, biting her upper lip as she thumbed the frayed map pages.

"You okay, sweetie?"

"You're going awful fast, Daddy."

"I know."

"What page did you say?"

"Twenty-four, I think."

"Buena Vista is right across from the entrance. No—you're on the wrong side of the river. You got to go to Forest Lawn Drive and come back a ways."

"Thanks."

He looked for cross traffic as he came off the hill and then gunned across a red light at Moorpark. The freeway was just ahead and he cut off a shiny new Lexus for the on-ramp and then he was cramming into traffic with the old Concord floored, slewing across the path of an eighteen-wheeler that smoked its brakes.

"*Wooo,*" she said. "It's a good thing I trust you, Daddy."

He changed lanes left and right to go around the slower cars and gain a few seconds. He wasn't thinking quite straight and the road signs nearly panicked him into ducking down the ramp onto the Hollywood Freeway where it took over the designation 101, but he remembered at the last instant and cut back on in front of a pickup with a bewildered-looking rube in a straw hat. He glanced once and saw that Maeve sat with her eyes closed and her hand clutching the armrest.

He swung off the freeway ramp and slowed dramatically to loop back along the base of the hills, past Mount Sinai, the Jewish twin of Forest Lawn, and then he turned in past the mullioned Tudor mortuary building.

"It's okay, punkin."

He didn't have time to stop and ask where Honest Abe stood, but he guessed at a big monument up the hill where he saw a black Mercedes SL that looked like Lori Bright's. He climbed slowly and let his car mutter past the Mercedes. Miraculously, he had ten minutes to spare.

He parked about fifty yards past and got out. "*Stay,* no matter what," he said sharply.

He strolled out onto the grass across the road from the giant pensive Abraham Lincoln and pretended to read the plaques set at grass level, as if looking for a particular one. They were all in Armenian characters and had little etched portraits of balding men with mustaches. Due east of him there was an elderly couple who held hands as they stared mournfully at the ground. Improbably, he wore deep green lederhosen and she wore a dirndl. No one else was around. Down below in the smog of Burbank was the postmodern Disney animation building like a dropped box of Legos, with ANIMATION written across the roof in huge letters in case you really needed to know.

He heard the door of the Mercedes open and shut. It would have looked strange if he hadn't been curious, and he let himself glance at her. Lori Bright strode toward the big Abe with a bright blue airplane carry-on bag. He checked his watch, glanced at the car, and seemed to concentrate on something in the middle distance. She set the bag at Abe's feet, rubbed her forehead, and started back. He looked away. He guessed they would come zooming up the road in a car, and someone would sprint to the statue. He wished she'd told him more about the arrangements for the transfer.

A light plane came over the hill, *brrring* on the air like a sense memory of Vietnam, a spotter for the artillery that was coming, and it passed straight out toward Burbank airport. When it was gone he could hear traffic off the freeway and intermittent wind on the dry brush a little farther up the hillside where a wall marked the boundary of the un-natural greenery and the beginning of Southern California's natural yellow. Peaceful as a graveyard. The elderly couple knelt and in the corner of his eye the spot of bright blue still rested at Lincoln's feet. Lori Bright reached her car and the door slammed weakly.

Wind had played in her hair, a picture he held on to, and he thought idly of the feel of running his hand over it, twisting it around a finger. He realized that she wore it a lot longer than most women her age. Kathy had gradually trimmed her hair back to a kind of whipped-cream helmet. He wondered if that represented a reining in at some key passage in a woman's life, a passage that Lori Bright had emphatically declined. The Mercedes drove up the last leg of the loop road and then slowly down toward the exit.

Worry crept up again. Maeve was there, only a few yards away, but her head was as motionless as an extra headrest in the car. He couldn't stand there exposed forever and he headed slowly back to the beat-up Concord. A glance told him the polka dancers were still kneeling in prayer. A heavyset gardener putted up the hill on a Cushman three-wheeler. Jack Liffey stiffened when the go-cart stopped near Abe and the gardener dismounted with a big rake. He hoped to hell the man wasn't about to tidy up the abandoned flight bag, but that seemed exactly his purpose.

Jack Liffey reached the Concord and waited. The big gardener rested his rake on the steps and picked up the bag, hefting it gently as if weighing it. Then all at once he was sprinting straight uphill with the bag, toward a gap in the low wall that gave onto the weeds and live oak. Jack Liffey was in the Concord immediately and by some miracle it started on the first crank. Maeve shrank back into the seat, knowing enough not to ask him anything just then. The car rammed right over the shallow curb and headed toward the sprinter. A small part of him hoped he wasn't doing too much damage to the grass, but most of his attention was focused on the back of the sprinter, the overalls and a blue work shirt. The big man had dark hair and broad square shoulders. He was making good time with an unusual reaching run, pushing off harder with his right at each step.

The Concord banged its underside, faltered, and then stalled unexpectedly in a shallow depression in the grass. He was out immediately, not more than twenty yards behind the man, praying all of a sudden that the kidnapper wasn't armed. He'd left his pistol in the car.

The gardener made a strange flying lurch out the gap in the wall onto a clay path and Jack Liffey saw that he was gaining. He was just cranking up to full throttle as he left the grassy expanse himself and then he felt a sharp burn in his shins and the earth went haywire. Blue sky was where it shouldn't have been and his arms windmilled. A ragged crop of granite was coming up on his face and he twisted away. There was a jolt and a sharp pain in his cheek. He tumbled sideways once more and then the world stabilized, leaving him with his nose in the dirt. He could feel he was badly dazed, but he managed to lift his upper body off the ground a bit before crying out with a bright pink blaze of pain.

He heard sparrows twittering. A rustle somewhere. His own heart thundered. Then he realized he was lying on his side just beyond a gate in a stone wall, his shoulder in a gritty pile of exfoliated granite. He was not quite sure where he was or why. When he sat up he could see his Concord on the grass below with both doors open. Something was wrong with that. He was having trouble deciding what it was doing there, but he knew that wasn't the only thing that was wrong, and the other was much worse.

A little girl in a thin pink sweater bolted right past him out of the grassy park and a chill of panic took him from head to toe.

"No!"

The girl had been carrying his .45 as she ran, clinging to the heavy automatic with both hands.

"Maeve!" he shouted, and passed out.

.   .   .

THERE was blood in his mouth. He knew that. Something warm rested against his forehead and his closed eyes burned yellow with sunlight. He opened them to see a concerned face against the sky. A familiar face, beautiful face, but without a name. He'd lost his memory to concussions twice before, and still had recurring nightmares about it. Once in sixth grade he'd waited on deck too close to the cleanup batter, who'd caught him with a full swing to center, and once in the showers in basic he'd slipped on a bar of soap and gone down hard on the back of his head. It was mostly the short-term memory that went, leaving a profound sense of frustration, and it came back soon. He knew that, but this time something else was wrong, he just didn't know what it was.

"Jack, what's my name?"

"Mary? Lucy? You're a movie star, aren't you? What is it that's so terribly wrong? It's like a *death*."

"What time of day is it?"

"I don't know." He looked around. Grass one way, weeds the other, a smudge of smog far down below. His whole body tingled with the awareness of tragedy.

"You're going to have a terrible shiner." She touched his temple and he winced.

He wanted to lie back and sleep and let the terrible confusion pass, but adrenaline was still working. There was something he had to do. By pure will he fought with his obstinate memory, like climbing up a dark well by the dug-in tips of his fingers. He was Jack Liffey, he lived in Torrance, he was a tech writer at TRW—no. He *had been*. He lived in Culver City.

"You look like Lori Bright. You were in *Ancient Parapets*. God you were sexy in that negligee."

"Thanks."

"You could almost see your breasts in the backlight."

"You've seen my breasts, Jack. In nothing."

That confused him anew. And then he cried out. The guilt had slipped in under the radar.

"Something is wrong. I know it."

"Who was the little girl?" she asked.

Every hair on his body stood on end. He had a mental picture of Maeve scampering past him carrying his .45. What appalling circumstance had led him even to *imagine* he had seen that? He was on his knees, with pain shooting through his head, gasped with it once, and then he was shaking off Lori Bright's clinging hands and on his feet.

"That was my *daughter*."

He broke free and ran up the trail through yellow, knee-high weeds. He wasn't thinking, his gaze just firing left and right.

"Jack, be careful."

"Maeve! *Maeve!*"

Trails ran left and right up to the ridgeline that was almost within reach, just *there*. The widest trail looked as if it had been worn by weed sledders on their cardboard rides. He thundered up that one, ignoring the way his brain shifted inside his skull with each step. He came over the shallow ridge and saw a fire road just ahead, and not far down the road there was a chain-link gate hanging off its hinges where the fire road turned to a real, paved one. A girl came trudging around a curve in the road, carrying something the size of a book wrapped in a pink sweater in her hands.

"Maeve!"

He fell to his knees and nearly fainted with relief. Lori Bright was beside him, steadying him. It was coming back now, and he had a vivid sense of how fabulously, unbelievably lucky he was to have his daughter safe and healthy. Lori Bright could go to hell, the kidnappers could go to hell, the rest of the earth could go to hell, as long as Maeve came back okay.

She scrambled the last few yards and flung her arms around him, banging him on the back with something hard.

"Oh, honey, honey, why did you take the gun?"

"I saw the little guy trip you . . . I don't know, I thought you'd need it. And then I sort of forgot I had it. Did I do wrong?"

He just laughed in relief. All their hands were on him

now, trying to hold him up, but he got dizzy and sat hard.

"You've got a real goose egg, and you're going to have a black eye."

"Maeve, I want you to meet my client. This is Mrs. Bright."

"Hi, Mrs. Bright."

Stiffly the woman shook hands with the girl, as if afraid she might break her bones.

"Two-MDD576," Maeve said suddenly, proudly. "Mildly Disabled Dog, that's how I remembered it."

It took a moment before he realized she was giving him a license number. He laughed and patted her knee.

"What did the car look like?"

"You know I don't know cars. It was gray and old, like something an old man would drive to go to the store once a week."

"Good work, punkin. What's this about a little guy tripping me?"

"He was hiding behind the wall there. It looked like he swung a big stick at your ankles, then he ran."

That would explain the peculiar behavior of the earth, he thought, upending all of a sudden. He was getting a lot of it back. He got up and steadied himself against the woman, but every time he moved his head, his brain objected savagely and he had to clamp his eyes shut.

"You've got to have that head looked at."

"Lucky I didn't get hit somewhere vulnerable." He struggled to the wall where Maeve's little man must have waited. Weeds were crushed down, but he was no Indian tracker. Out in a clump of weed he saw a flash of color and picked his way across to it. He plucked the crushed bright paper up by a corner, smoothed it a little, and then stuck it into his pocket.

When he got back Maeve was playing grown-up, talking to Lori Bright in that stiff dispassionate voice that she thought adults all used. He collected the gun wrapped in her sweater and they helped him back to his car. Miraculously no one from the mortuary office had been summoned to shoo them off the grass or have them arrested.

"Jack, I can't let you go like this. I know a doctor who'll look at your head right away. Fifteen minutes."

He put Maeve in the car and then asked Lori Bright quietly about her own daughter. She said the man on the phone had promised to release the girl in the morning, and she could only trust them.

The instant he sat in the Concord, he nearly passed out when someone started sawing into the side of his skull and she got her way about the doctor. She moved the car off the grass for him and then drove them all to a clinic in a nondescript building without a nameplate right on the border of Beverly Hills and West Hollywood.

"This is where the studios used to take their starlets for D-and-Cs."

Information he'd rather not have had bandied before Maeve, but she probably knew about things like that already. If she didn't, she would soon enough. "Annie, hey, do you know what's a DNC?"

It turned out to be the kind of clinic where the corridors had carpets and nearly first-rate original prints on the walls and the examining rooms played Mozart very, very softly. They X-rayed his head and gave him painkillers and told him to call back if he started hearing voices.

He didn't hear any voices, but it hurt like a bastard when he moved his head, and when he shut his eyes just for a moment on the way to the car, he woke up on Lori's sofa.

LORI and Maeve were playing cards on a small Greene and Greene table, under a hanging stained-glass-and-redwood lamp that could only have been designed by Frank Lloyd Wright. They sat hunched forward on Mission ottomans, for all the world like sorority sisters. Maeve giggled and the picture made him nervous for some reason, as if he'd sold his daughter into white slavery.

Lori Bright said something mirthful and that whiskey voice reinforced whatever dark fears he felt, like the richest Scotch flowing over warm rocks. Surely Maeve would sense too many cigarettes, too much drink, too many men coming up the backstairs.

He heard the snapping of cards for a few moments and then Lori Bright's voice poured richly through the room again: "Are you sure I can't play a jack on that?"

"No, the rules change every four turns. That's the way the game works."

"I think you're making this up to keep me in my place."

"Ladies, what time is it?"

"Another country heard from." Lori Bright looked over at him genially.

Maeve ran across to him. "Daddy, are you okay?"

"Sure, honey. I think we'd better get home."

"Mrs. Bright's made up beds for us here. The doctor said you had to rest." Very softly, she added, "She's really nice," as if validating his choice in girlfriends.

Oh dear, oh dear, he thought.

Lori Bright stood. "I'll get us all some camomile tea." And she drifted out of the room. Jack Liffey felt like the subject of a prearrangement, left alone with Maeve for the imparting of some deep secret.

"Is she a movie star?" Maeve asked breathlessly. "This house is brutally cool."

"What makes you think she's a movie star?"

"I saw a picture of her in another room with a man I think was Jack Nicholson."

"She was in movies in the 1960s and 1970s. She had a small part in *Teacher's Pet* with Nicholson." He rubbed his forehead. And how did he know that? Oh, Daddy, have you been reading up on her credits? Renting her old movies? Oh, Daddy, what's happening to you?

"I think she likes you, Daddy."

Maeve's starstruck twitter was like a footnote to his own darker lunacy, and it was too late to shield her from the whole shadowy fugue.

"Punkin, I'd like to ask you not to tell Mommy about this."

"Why? She always says she'd be happy if you're seeing someone."

"I'd like to stay friends with your mommy and I just have a feeling this would interfere. Just for now. Please."

"Sure."

And probably not tell Marlena, for good measure.

He could turn his own daughter into a liar for him. The first sidestep into this new world of portable ethics. No, not the first.

Mike had warned him that fame would bite him on the ass. And Art Castro had told him more than once that Trouble was what you got when you let your dick lead you around. But this was way beyond those warnings, deep into some kind of darkness that only came over you when you violated a thing at the core of who you were.

Lori Bright came back in with a tray of tea, smiling like Lady Bountiful, but it wasn't tea he was starting to want. Then he saw the glitter in her eyes and realized it wasn't tea she'd had on the way.

"WANT to do a line?"

He shook his head. "Believe it or not I don't like feeling my heart pounding like a jackhammer."

"That's not the organ I was thinking of going to work on." She snuffled the powder off a hand mirror with the kind of red mini-straw that they put in bar drinks. "And you could do with a little pounding down here."

She wiped her nose against his penis, which gave his penis a cool rush, but then she subsided into thoughtfulness and sank back into the gray satin. His penis went to ice and began to swell as if it had a mind of its own and he was getting more and more nervous knowing Maeve was in a guest bed down the hall, sleeping in a borrowed nightie made of French silk.

"What a sweet kid she is. The way every emotion shows on her face, even the little guile she can muster."

"I think we were all like that."

"Innocence. It's just sitting there as we grow up. It's

like a big rock in the front yard and all the urgencies and the other stuff pile up around it like silt and the top of the rock gets smaller and smaller and then it's buried. Just gone.''

"I'm not sure it's innocence you should be mourning. I believe in the benefit of understanding how things work. I bet there's mature kinds of integrity, too.''

She grinned and perked up. "Your innocence still sticks out of the silt a bit. Let's see what we can do with it. Ever been tied up? Feeling helpless is a real rush.''

As usual she wouldn't accede to anyone else's wishes, and it was about a half hour later, his wrists and ankles tied to the corners of the bed by the kinds of padded restraints they used in hospitals, and he was beginning to regret just about everything in his life, and Lori Bright had just said, "I like to *give* hurt a little, too.'' And then the wall cracked all of a sudden with a sound like a gunshot and the bed heaved and rolled.

"*Do* it, *do* it,'' Lori Bright called furiously to the moving earth with a druggy fire in her eyes, as if mass destruction would validate some deep need in her.

"Daddy!'' Maeve cried in the hall.

13

A SERIOUS CRUNCH MODE

JUST ANOTHER AFTERSHOCK, BUT IT HAD BROUGHT WHAT WAS left of his code of honor down in ruins. Maeve had cried out from the other side of the bedroom door, but even in her panicky Daddy-calling, she knew enough not to open Pandora's door, and he'd had to leave the day-saving to Lori Bright, who had gathered herself back from somewhere far away, her eyes unglazing, then moistening and softening. She had tugged on a bathrobe and slipped out to comfort Maeve as he lay there like a trussed roast.

And whatever it was clutching at him, breathing heavy in his ears, it was still there promising the erotic brass ring on the merry-go-round.

A few years back, when he'd finally given up the drink and drugs, he'd sworn a mighty oath that control was the one thing he'd never lose again. Never get smug, he thought. You could always be blindsided by what you didn't understand. Celebrity, and tales of the Polo Lounge, and familiar faces huge on movie screens, and all that erotic catnip, and the spooky grappling with a woman who had something dark and something soft and something needy warring inside her, like a child inside a woman inside a child.

There was no high road to be found that night.

• • •

SOMEWHERE deep in the night, Lori woke him from a woozy slumber and handed him her cell phone.

"Liffey?" a voice said darkly. The voice seemed familiar.

"Who is this?"

"This is Lieutenant Malamud." There was a long pause and a heavy breath. If he'd been more awake, he might have said something about the breathing. "You can look for the girl. It's your job, we understand that, but stay away from G. Dan Hunt. That's something else, and I assure you he has nothing to do with the girl."

Jack Liffey cleared his throat, but it didn't do anything for the horrible throbbing in his head. "Malamud, I wish I knew your edge in this thing."

"No, you don't."

He looked at the phone for a moment after it went dead, then handed it back to Lori Bright. "Cops. They've got it all their own way and that makes them think they're smart."

He wondered who'd told the cops he was looking for Hunt. Could it have been Art Castro? Or did they know something about the Jamaican?

She wet the tip of her finger and touched it to his penis, but there was nothing doing there.

BY morning, his headache was letting up and Maeve and Lori both made fun of the giant black eye that was claiming the left side of his face. Maeve jabbered away about Spanish Revival architecture as they reclaimed the car and he drove her home. He was so relieved that Maeve's purity and cheer seemed to have survived that his spirits soared with gratitude. He drove past toppled chimneys and retaining walls and a few blown-out picture windows. L.A. had both riots and earthquakes, he thought irreverently, and the only real difference was that, after the riots, more poor people ended up with good TVs.

"I forgot to get her autograph!"

"Don't worry, punkin. I'll get it for you."

"She's your girlfriend, isn't she?"

Oh-oh. "I'm not sure you'd put it just that way." For one thing, Lori Bright was a bit old to be called a girl.

"You didn't sleep in that blue room beside mine."

"Another detective in training." He tried to make light of it. "I'm fifty-two, Hon. I'm allowed to sleep where I want."

"Don't worry. I know you don't want Mom to know about Lori right now."

In a slightly better world, he would have said: Hon, I was wrong to ask you to keep your mom in the dark. I don't want you ever to lie. You can tell her whatever you like. But it wasn't a slightly better world, and she'd already seemed to reconcile herself so easily to the accommodation.

"Coo-uhl." The word had several syllables, and she smiled happily. "We'll let it stay a secret liaison."

He wondered if she'd started reading the Victorians, or if the expression was just from some cheap romance with a torn bodice on the cover.

He had to slow to a crawl to weave between cars that were double-parked all over the street, and they both looked at a big vacant lot where a score of Latino families were still setting up camp in makeshift tents of black plastic and cardboard to escape the aftershocks of the aftershock. Squat brown women carried buckets of water and the children lugged cardboard boxes of belongings. In this part of mid-town they were mostly Central Americans.

"They come up here for a better life and all we offer is spiteful laws, the lousiest jobs, and earthquakes."

"Mommy says half her fourth grade is Guatemalan kids this year."

"Do you have any in your class?"

She shook her head. "My best friend is Armenian," she said proudly. "Eremy. She's really smart and she eats this funny pizza with, like, a spicy meat paste on it."

"Lahmajune," he said dryly.

She was startled. "How did you know?"

"I know a lot, punkin. I know the value of pi to nine

places. I know how to find runaway girls. I know that the Cretaceous comes *after* the Jurassic. But I don't know the first thing about the human heart.''

"Huh?''

"HELLO, Bobo. It's Slack Jack.''

"Not *the* Slack Jack.''

"The very.''

Beau Creighton had been his best friend in basic and then at the army's E-tech school, a southern boy from a Birmingham steelworker family who'd gone straight from the University of Alabama into Peace Corps training to learn how to build wells in African villages. He'd trained for three months at a disused summer camp in Louisiana, learning an obscure Bantu language with three tongue-wrenching clicks in it, and playing peace songs on his twelve-string guitar for his new friends every evening. A few hours before the plane could take off for London, Nairobi, and its final stop in Gaborone, Botswana, the army had drafted him. He was still playing the twelve-string at Bragg, sitting disconsolately on a bunk, when Jack Liffey walked in and asked if he could tune it down and play ''The Bells of Rhymney.'' Beau Creighton had looked up with red eyes, and Jack Liffey had taken a bet with himself that in the next ten seconds this tall, skinny Fucking New Guy filling out their intake was either going to weep or laugh hysterically.

"I will never surrender of my own free will,'' Detective Sergeant Bobo Creighton called into the phone in a peculiar emotionless staccato. It had been on a poster over their bunk, part of the Soldier's Creed, and they had made endless jokes about it. To this day Jack Liffey did not know how Bobo had gone from redneck to peacenik to soldier-technician to cop, but he was the only friend he had in the police force, even if it was Denver. ''I don't see you much no more, boy.''

They chatted for a while, but they both knew Jack Liffey wanted something.

"They got a new system here, Bobo. Ever since some creep got the address of a starlet from the DMV and then stalked her home and killed her, you want a name or address from Motor Vehicles, you got to be somebody with access. You've got to know the code for the day."

"I heard about that, pardner. Rebecca Schaeffer it was, from the sitcoms. My girls were crazy about her."

"How 'bout you call up some cop liaison number and get that code of the day for me. You know I'm no stalker."

There was a long pause. "What do you *do* these days, Jack?"

"I find runaway kids. Honestly, Bobo. We're on the same side."

"Where you at now?"

Jack Liffey gave him his number.

"If you don't hear from me in twenty minutes, I got a bad case of second thoughts."

But he heard in ten, and got what he needed.

"HI, this is Sergeant Flor in Rampart Division," Jack Liffey said over the phone. He was wobbling in and out of a nasty José Jimenez accent. "Couple things I wan' choo ta do for me."

"What's the password?" The clerk had a throaty voice, but dead bored, like a hooker asking if you wanted to go around again.

"Oh, yeah. I got the word here somewhere. I writ it down. Here we go: evening notion."

"Go ahead."

"Tell me what you can about California 2MDD576."

He heard the computer keys clacking away at the other end.

"That's a tan Oldsmobile registered to a Danny Firestack." She gave him an address in Saugus. That was Canyon Country all right.

"And what have you got registered to Tyrone Pennycooke?"

That took even less time. " 'Ninety-three Ford Explorer,

green.'' An address in Windsor Hills, not far from him. Windsor Hills was an island of county land in the hills north of Inglewood, some of the choicest black middle-class homes in the United States.

''Now, Liffey, Jack. What does he drive?''

''Nineteen seventy-nine AMC Concord, white.''

''What idiot would drive *that*?'' He hung up.

HE swung over Slauson to have a peek at Windsor Hills. Most of the houses north of Slauson were 1950s and later, those split-level ranch numbers with scalloped eaves and big decorative birdhouses over the garage. But Ridge Glen was older, Tudor and Norman and Spanish places, probably built where they'd torn down the 1932 Olympic village. He parked a half block from the big beige bungalow where a green Explorer sat in the drive. A ''For Sale'' gallows was planted on the lawn, with a little plastic leaflet box that said TAKE ONE. He sauntered up the block past the house, took a leaflet, checked out the Explorer, and continued on.

The green-black-red bumper sticker said IRIE across it, which he figured was some kind of dread talk. He read the leaflet as he strolled: the house had four bedrooms, two and a half baths, a den, a remodeled kitchen, and it gave good curb appeal: $209,000. About half what it would be worth a few miles northwest in a white area, curb appeal or no.

He wondered whether Terror Pennycooke was the seller or just a tenant. There was a broad shady porch with a big glide on it like something out of Bedford Falls. At the corner he touched the rough bark of a liquidambar tree like tagging home and turned back.

Two African-American boys about ten came out of no-where carrying model airplanes. They made rat-a-tat noises and swooped the planes at one another. It was like stumbling into a photo negative of his own childhood. His best friend Kenny Orcot had flown a control-line Stuka against his Spitfire with its balky .049 gas engine, but Kenny's mom had moved away when she divorced. It had been the only divorce in the whole neighborhood. What a strange aberrant moment in American history the fifties had been, he thought, a blink of white middle-class daydream caught fast between the Nazis and crack cocaine.

He didn't see anyone else and he got into the Concord and headed north, wondering if the name Ridge Glen wasn't an oxymoron.

JACK Liffey took a shortcut up Veteran and stopped for a minute to watch the Crockery Man at work. He was up on his scaffold, a squat Mediterranean-looking man covering his house from ground to roofline with colorful fragments of plates and saucers and cups set into plaster. He'd pretty much finished the lower half, but it would take years of neighborhood protests and injunctions for him to finish the rest. Buckets on pulleys waited on the front lawn full of more building material. He waved, but the man didn't see him.

He and Maeve had awarded it the first point in their contest of L.A. oddities.

THE receptionist was on her knees trying to scoop runaway Skittles off the plum carpeting.

"Remember me?"

She looked up, scowling, then seemed to remember him. "I must look totally geeked out." She stood and showed him a handful of the candies. "I switched from M&M's when they put in those awful blue ones. You want Brucie?"

"Sure."

"Watch your step."

She tapped a key on her keyboard. "Bruce, that cop guy was here before wants some face time."

"Thanks, Bambi."

The receptionist went down on her knees again and crawled toward him. It was disconcerting, like being prayed to.

"A whole bunch of red ones. Jeez."

Bruce Parfit opened the double door and hung in it with

a distracted air. "You catch us in a serious crunch mode, mate. Perhaps another time."

"I know who burned up Dae Kim's."

The man's manner changed instantly. The long ponytail bobbed, then he seemed to notice his receptionist grubbing under the desk and shrugged helplessly before beckoning Jack Liffey inside.

"Last time we had a little chin wag it nearly lost us our best filmmaker."

"It was you they were after, not me."

Bruce Parfit led him along the corridor past a homemade banner that said, YOU ARE IN A MAZE OF TWISTY LITTLE PASSAGES, ALL ALIKE. A young man stood along the wall straining at something in his hands. As they passed, Jack Liffey could see that his index fingers were deep into an old-fashioned straw finger trap. He hadn't seen one of those in years.

A woman in a work shirt and overalls stood at a whiteboard in a small bay off the hall writing up numbers in fluorescent colors. She noticed them passing. "Bruce, I tell you, you just can't comb a hairy ball smooth."

"We'll still give it a go, Joanie."

Bruce Parfit sealed them into his big corner office, cutting off the fast beat of techno-dance music from somewhere. Out the floor-to-ceiling window, the digital display on the big billboard was still counting up smoking deaths. "So . . ."

"I'm going to take your side," Jack Liffey said. "I'm not sure why. Monogram may have a legitimate grievance, I don't know about that, but they got me pissed off. Wasn't it Chairman Mao who said my enemy's enemy is my friend?"

Bruce Parfit smiled gently as he sat behind the big clean desk. "Me and my mates used to think the Great Helmsman was the ridgy-didge."

"Pardon?"

"That's Australian for the bee's knees. These days I

think the world can get on pretty well without him and all he wrought.''

"If we start adding up what the world can get on without," Jack Liffey observed, "there's no telling where we're going to end up."

"Mate, ask not what I can do for you. Ask what you can do for me."

"Monogram's not really your problem. Your problem's in Japan, with Mitsuko. They're a big *zaibatsu* cartel that owns Monogram the way they own pocket change and geishas and a few blocks of downtown Sydney. You don't mean much to them until you become an irritant."

"I know Mitsuko. They bought up a lot of mining rights back home."

"I have a friend who knows Mitsuko, too." This had come from Mike Lewis. "During the war they used Chinese and Korean slave labor. They worked them to death and after the war two of their executives were brought before the war-crimes tribunal in Tokyo. Actually they were given life sentences, but there was an unpleasant deal to let them go. There always is.

"Anyway, they play rough. In Japan, if a zaibatsu feels somebody beat them unfairly, they use yakuza to get even. All the *zaibatsu* have ties to the gangsters. So over here they did the next best thing, they used a strong-arm agency Monogram Pictures has had on retainer for decades."

He thought of Terror Pennycooke and could almost taste ginger ale.

Jack Liffey paused a moment. He definitely had the man's attention. "I'll take care of the local talent because it's become personal, but I thought you might want a chance to get even with the home office across the seas."

The Australian's eyes widened slightly. "That's a flaming big fish to grill, mate."

"Have you got any first-rate hackers? I know one, but he's out of action for the moment." He smiled, thinking of poor Chris Johnson forced to work on an old 486 computer without a modem, pacing back and forth through the tangle of unusable electronics in his living room and having to go to the pay phone at the corner to call out. No phone line was a condition of parole.

Bruce Parfit looked at the ceiling for a moment, leaning back in his chair, then out the window at the layer on layer of smog, squarish mid-rises like upended Kleenex boxes, and tall teetery palms. "A test match of electronic aggro."

He sat up straight and punched a single key on his computer. "Michael, is Ad in with you?"

"Sure, Brucie. We're all on wall time."

"Row on in here."

"Can it wait?"

"Now."

In a moment the door came open, held by a very young Asian, while a skinny black kid on polio crutches lurched in and sat hard on a leather bench. He was far too young to have had polio, and he wasn't very good with the crutches, so Jack Liffey guessed he'd only been crippled a few years. The Asian shut the door softly and sat on the front edge of a purple sling chair.

"This is Jack Liffey, a friend of ours. Michael Chen, Admiral Wicks."

They barely acknowledged him. It took a moment to realize that the last bit was the black kid's name, not an honorific. There were a lot of African-American Generals and Admirals for some reason.

"I hope this is important, Brucie," Michael Chen said. "We were in a killer run of code."

"It's important."

"Well, bazz fazz and rowrbazzle," Admiral Wicks said.

"You're too young to know Pogo," Jack Liffey interjected.

"We read reprints." His remarkable chocolaty-brown eyes came around, fixed and flat enough to hide behind, and he finally gave Jack Liffey a moment of hostile study. "I just want to establish that you're old enough to have read the original, and you feel sufficiently bad about being old."

"I feel sufficiently bad, thank you."

He nodded at his crutches. "You know, the thing that challenges you can become an interesting new way of looking at the world. You want to find a challenge for everyone."

"I've got my own problems, thanks. One thing about this little tech war we're going to talk about, I'd like you to plan it out but put it on ice until I give you the go-ahead. I want to see if there's any chance of a peace treaty first."

14

WAVING A DEAD CHICKEN AT THE PROBLEM

DOWN CRENSHAW AT VERNON AND ELEVENTH THERE WAS A twenty-foot doughnut propped up against the sky. Beneath it was an L-shaped streamline eatery with some fading signs for doughnuts at yesterday's prices and a promise that they were the city's best. He parked in the lot that Continental Doughnuts shared with a repair shop, and a dozen eyes in a group of loungers followed him idly as he went inside. This was an African-American area and there probably weren't a dozen Anglos a day who sat down in the red plastic booths.

He didn't sit down either. He nodded to Josette, who worked the counter three days a week, and then inclined his head toward the other angle of the L. "Josette. Ivan in back?"

"He getting ready for his taxes." She waggled a finger to beckon him in closer and he leaned on one of the red stools on its chrome stalk as she eyed him with a smirk.

"You got that look, that *glow,* like you gettin' laid, Jack."

"You're observant."

"Seeing stuff's a survival skill these days. Hope she's worth it."

"Me, too. She's pretty scary."

Josette laughed. "Man, don't be disturbing his figurin' for long. I told him, spend it all before you got to pay up, but he don't listen. He gonna get his butt kicked by the state equalization.''

The security door opposite the employee rest room was ajar an inch and he knocked once and pushed it open. Ivan Monk sat at a flimsy table, where he was jabbing at an old PC with two fingers.

''What's up, Jack?''

''Hopes.''

''Same old same old.''

The doughnut shop was only the butter on Ivan Monk's bread. He made the bread tracing bail skips and doing all the other odd dirty jobs people left for detectives. He was good at it and Jack Liffey had passed a number of runaways his way, particularly when the kids ran south of Jefferson or east of La Cienega.

''Hey, you ever work a spreadsheet?'' Ivan Monk asked. He pushed away from the keyboard that looked ridiculously tiny and frail under his big hands. He was a nice guy, but he always looked like he was about to break your arm.

''Man, when the Arabs invented the zero, they came up with everything I needed to monitor my finances.''

Ivan met his eyes skeptically. ''You need to get yourself a doughnut shop for fallback money.''

''Always wondered where you came up with the capital.''

Ivan Monk took a sip of what was probably good Scotch from a tumbler. He knew better than to offer. ''That's none of your business, so I'll tell you. It was my savings from the merchant marine. Where's your savings from making all those fighter planes that they went killing babies with?''

''My own babies ate it up.''

''Man, I happen to know you don't pay your child support.''

''Ouch. You're right, but I think about it a lot.''

Ivan Monk snorted once. ''Maybe I'll track you down one day for Kathleen Liffey. What can I do you for?''

''Do you know a Jamaican named Terror Pennycooke?''

''You got business with him?''

"Maybe."

"I hope you're kidding me. Tyrone P is one crazy fuck. He used to be in one of those Jamaican posses that carried the good dope from L.A. to Kansas City and beyond. Latterly he's become a general-purpose dirty doer. He plays bold for anybody that pays. Likes a big gun, C-4 plastic explosive, and what he calls petrol bombs."

And ginger beer, Jack Liffey thought.

"Most Rastas are gentle souls, but he's not on that track *at all*. Stay away from him, Jack, if you got any kind of good sense."

"Thanks, Iv. One more thing. What does 'irie' mean?"

Ivan's brow wrinkled up. "Spell it."

He did, and Ivan Monk laughed. "Man, that's pronounced 'eye-rye.' It's a bit subtle to explain to a man like you, a peckerwood from Babylon, mon, wit no linguistic suss." He laughed, then lapsed into standard English. "Dread talk does a strange and philosophical thing with its pronouns. Somehow they got the idea that the pronoun 'me' was subservient and fit only for slaves. Maybe it is, you know? It's an object form, after all, and the doer is always the subject. Anyway, they use I a lot instead of me and my: give it to I, that's I car, I did it I-self. Even the plural, instead of we, it's I-and-I. You okay so far, Babylon?"

"I got lost back at C-4 plastic explosives."

Nothing could slow Ivan down. "Now it gets really subtle. 'I' took on a kind of holiness to the Rastas and they started substituting I for initial syllables of a lot of common words. I believe in I-quality. You're my heart's I-sire. I'm gonna I-ceive a letter. And so on. It's half a verbal game, of course, but the other half's an I-claration of independence from the language forms of the slave masters. After you know that, eye-rye is simple. Rye is standard Jamaican English for right. So 'irie' is a form of all-*right*. Meaning something like right-*on*."

"Copacetic there, old buddy. Thanks for the seminar. Someday I'll teach you redneck."

Monk shook his head. "We already know it. That's the nature of being a minority, Jack, you gots to pay attention."

On the main drag they sold mufflers, window glass, bowling supplies, and karate lessons. A half-dozen townlets that spread across one end of Canyon Country had voted to merge in the mid-1980s to form the instant city of Santa Clarita, and Saugus was the poorest of the lot, caught in the middle, mainly just soil erosion bisected by a highway. What there was of a downtown had been hit hard by the last two earthquakes and left with a lot of skewed buildings and "For Lease" signs. Over the hill in upscale Valencia there was Cal-Arts, the snobby arts institute, and out to the east there were newer suburbs with postmodern ranches, but here in the core there were mostly Baptist churches and guys tinkering with Harleys.

On the drive up the freeway, he'd found that if he focused hard on the road, he could just about forget what a mess he'd made of his daughter's visit. As usual, there had been a whole lot of little steps that mostly made sense, and then all of a sudden you lay there tied naked to a bed with your daughter screaming in the hall.

Danny Firestack lived a few blocks off the main drag on a street without sidewalks where most of the little boxy houses had aluminum foil in the south-facing windows. A man at the corner had a compressor chugging away in his drive and he was spray-painting the dirt and weeds in his front yard bright green. The sky above the neighborhood was deep blue, as if that, too, had been improved.

He parked across from the address the DMV had given him for 2MDD576. Toward the back of the driveway, by a detached clapboard garage that was about to collapse, he saw a big antique Olds with the chrome rocket on the front fender. The house was easily the crummiest on the block, with plywood boarding up one front window and patchy shingles missing from the roof.

He watched the house for a while and then thought, The hell with it. He walked across the street and up the walk made of eroding pavers and knocked. It was the big guy all right, maybe twenty years old and the size of a linebacker, and he recognized Jack Liffey from the cemetery but tried clumsily not to show it. Maybe it was the black eye.

"Yes?"

"Wise up, Danny, you know I'm not the Avon lady. If I found my way here, all is lost." He pushed inside.

"Aw, Jeez . . ."

"I want to talk to Lee."

"Who?"

Jack Liffey took out Lori's cell phone and dialed at random. "Me or the Santa Clarita cops."

"Don't!"

Jack Liffey turned the phone off and looked around while the big guy tried to work himself up to it. The place didn't look like a residence at all. All around there were collapsed umbrellas that he recognized as light stands for film work, and cardboard boxes full of videotape cassettes, and a lot of electronic equipment.

"What sort of name is Firestack?"

"My granddad was born Festacci," he said glumly. "Dad changed it in the war." He had a hangdog manner, as if maybe his dad had been responsible for the war, too.

"Come on out, Lee."

And then, all of sudden, she was there. A girl with dark bobbed hair, older and taller than her picture, but terribly skinny and pigeon-toed. She wore a black T-shirt with the circled red *A* for anarchy and what used to be called hot pants.

"How did you know?" she asked plaintively. She wore big black-framed glasses like Buddy Holly's that made her face seem much too small. She didn't seem to be able to stand still and moved about restlessly, giving the impression she was all elbow and knee.

"You're the one who chopped me down at the ankles, aren't you?" he said.

She grinned. "Boy, did you take a tumble." She circled

him like a dollying camera, looking him over. "You're kind of a scruffy-looking guy, even without that shiner. Did I do that? Wow. I don't know, not counting that mouse on your cheek, maybe you're sort of kindly looking. You look like a man who'd stand around with a big net under the trees in the spring just in case the baby birds start falling out of the nests." She grinned. "A grown-up Holden Caulfield with his hands in his back pockets worrying about the duplicity of the world as he waits to catch the kids that might run off the edge, and in between erasing all the Fuck Yous painted on all the walls. No, I know, you look like the kind of guy who'd still be standing there holding the Alamo when all the rest of them have fled out the back door and left you to Santa Ana."

"Actually, I'm the kind of guy who lost his job in aerospace and finds missing kids." He turned to Danny Firestack, standing there with his eyes going watery and frightened. "You're peripheral in this, aren't you?"

"He's just a film student at Cal-Arts. I made him do it."

"Beat it. I won't hurt her."

A terrible relief spread over the boy's face and he made a cringing smile and went straight out the door.

"He's not much," she said, "but he's company, and the camera's heavy. I want you to know I'm doing exactly what I want to do and I'm not going back. I have declared my personal independence from that omnivorous woman who calls herself my mother, and anyway, I'm right in the middle of finishing up a real important documentary about the resurgence of fascism in California, and artists are permitted to do exceptional things if it's necessary to their art."

"Sounds like you've absorbed the essence of fascism, all right. Hush a moment and stop trying to impress me. I've never yet taken a runaway back to an abusive situation, but you've put me in a tricky position by committing a felony." He had no idea how he was going to handle it.

"Can I make you a little drinkie-poo, Mr. Detective, I mean, before din-din?" she said. "Isn't that what all your femme fatales say? As a big handsome shamus, you must get a lot of femmes fatale-ing at your feet, right?''

"Coffee would be nice." Maybe if he set her to a simple task, her mind would stop zigging around.

She wiggled her hips in an exaggerated way as she headed for the kitchen. "Walk this way. Now, you're supposed to say, 'If I could walk that way, I could make a fortune on Hollywood Boulevard.' ''

He followed her into a kitchen with a week's worth of plastic dishes dumped into the old cast-iron sink. She plopped a tin kettle on the stove, then, frowning with the concentration it took, measured three spoons of instant coffee into a cup.

"You don't drink coffee much, do you?" he said.

"More?"

"Less."

"Here, you do it, then." She shoved the cup away in a flash of anger at being criticized—and in that she reminded him a little of her mother. She rocked from one foot to another, and he wondered if it was drugs or just nervous energy. "You know, they gave me an IQ test when I was ten, but the testing lady really fucked it up. First thing, they wouldn't accept my definition of the word 'tolerate.' The stupid cow had never heard it used in a negative sense, I guess. I said it was like 'abide' as in, 'I would never abide that sort of behavior.' Or maybe she didn't know the word 'abide.' And then she showed me a series of numbers and asked me to complete the sequence. That one wasn't even her fault, it was the test makers. It was three numbers that made an obvious arithmetic series, but if you looked a little deeper it was a Fibonacci series, you know, with each number the sum of its two predecessors. I tried to explain it to her but when I said Fibonacci, she looked like I'd just fallen down from Mars and was going to infect her with some space disease. I try to be tolerant of idiots, but sometimes it's hard, especially when it matters. You know, she probably got my IQ wrong by twenty points."

He emptied half the coffee powder back into the jar and shook the teapot once just to make sure there was water in it. "The only three-number sequence that could be both arithmetic and Fibonacci is one, one, two, three, if you leave out the first one," he said. "That must have been pretty stupid of the test makers." Normally he let kids run, let them tell tall tales and impress him, and let them top his jokes, but he could see Lee Borowsky was going to require special measures. She wouldn't like being patronized, for one thing, but she sure didn't like being called out, either, and she glared at him.

"You needed the money to complete your documentary?" he said.

"Are you about all done?" she said fiercely.

He glanced at her, twitching there in the doorway, unable to find some way to hold her hands still.

"Trying to take me down," she explained.

"How would you like it? You must be a real special genius for such a cute little girl. Is that what you want?"

"Fuck you, and the horse you rode in on."

"You don't think you ought to offer a little deference to my advanced age?"

"Not your kind, I know old people like you." She trembled with indignation. "You just curdle up in your head and everything in there gels into idea aspic and you close your mind up tight and forget what it was like to get excited about something like poetry or semiotics. 'I grow old, I grow old . . . do I dare to eat a peach?' "

I shall wear white flannel trousers and walk upon the beach, he thought, but he let it go. "You don't always have to be the brightest light in the room," he said. "It can be enough to be someone others can depend on. Smart or not, curious or not, maybe not even passionate or quick, just dependable."

"Windup clocks are dependable."

No wonder she and her mother threw sparks.

"Truce," he said. "You're stuck with me now, Miss Borowsky, because I know your terrible secret. I'll let you forgive me for growing old, and I'll forgive you for being a pair of ragged claws scuttling across the floors of silent seas.''

She laughed, but it was a phony laugh, trying to be knowing and streetwise. "Okay, you read books, too. I'll accept the truce if I don't have to go home."

"While we're thinking about what to do with you, why don't we get something wholesome to eat. I'll bet you haven't eaten properly in days."

She turned sideways and sucked in her stomach. "You must be referring to my svelte looks. I am not anorexic, I'll have you know. Did you know that anorexia is often linked to cats? Some of the girls act like cats, let their claws grow, lounge and move like cats, sometimes they can even trace it to witnessing one of those dreadful acts of feline infanticide when a mother cat eats her young. It's probably a kind of species adaptation to the pressures of overpopulation and underfeeding. Maybe anorexia is, too."

The water wasn't quite hot enough, but it wasn't going to make much difference with instant coffee, so he poured the cup full just to get it over with.

She kept moving, bobbing, peering at things and poking at herself as she talked.

"It's probably like homeostasis in the human body, you know, the self-regulating mechanism with hormones pouring into your bloodstream until you reach some state where the deactivating hormone starts to flow. In machines, the same thing was called cybernetics by Norbert Weiner back in 1948—the same year Orwell wrote *1984,* by the way—and in programming the exact same thing is called error-correction coding. Even in the nineteenth century they had governors on steam engines that released some of the steam pressure if the machine began turning too fast. It's all just a branch of information theory really, the use of feedback for control."

The coffee was too terrible even to pretend he could drink it. She poked at the dishes in the sink and cringed as a minor avalanche revealed further depths of the unwashed, but it didn't even slow her down.

"Wouldn't it be funny if cancer turned out to be feed-back, too, just a kind of homeostasis for the whole race, some kind of yearning leaking out of our DNA or some-thing to get back to a manageable population level. Actu-ally, I think I'd be pretty pissed if I found out that's true and my granddad died of a brain tumor because a hundred thousand Dexter Weenies overpopulated his area of the world and overused his allotment of resources. That would be cold."

"Do you carry one of those little cards in your wallet?" he asked. "You know, 'in case I die in a traffic accident, I donate my ego to science.'"

She looked sharply at him as if about to launch herself across the room with fangs bared, but then without warning she burst out laughing. It got more and more convulsive and she didn't seem to be able to stop it. Tears rolled down her cheeks, then her eyes went wide as she lost her footing on something on the floor and went down hard on her bot-tom. After a moment's stunned lull, the laughter came back redoubled. He'd never seen anyone actually roll on the floor laughing, and he wondered if it was a kind of epilepsy. A kind only geniuses got, of course.

He waited it out, holding his coffee cup at half-mast, trying not to see the evil foam on the surface of the brown liquid.

"What's your name?" she said finally, levering herself up to a sit.

"Jack Liffey."

"Pleased to meet you, Jack Liffey."

ON the way, she launched into an earnest discourse on how Coco's was *much* better than Spires which was better than Norm's which was better than Denny's, but the Hojos that were just moving into Southern California, they were un-speakable. It seemed to him a ridiculous subject to waste all those powers of distinction on, like a sensitive grading system for brands of kitty litter, but it mattered a lot to her, and it mattered that she always chose the very best of everything. He wondered where his 1979 AMC Concord would lie in her hierarchy of automobiles. Probably just above a Yugo. Hopefully.

There was a Coco's not far from Cal-Arts. It was a short run through an earth-tone postmodern suburb where every front window was topped by a pompous Spade & Archer fanlight. He smiled at himself. With a little effort he could become as pointlessly opinionated as this poor lonely girl.

Every once in a while the staccato of data and lore would shift down a gear and she'd launch a little trial emissary of a question in his direction.

"Did you grow up in L.A.?"

But it didn't really matter what he replied, her mind would be off somewhere else on its careening getaway from the ordinary. Then there was a lull in her hubbub, and he followed her gaze to a candy-green football field, and mesmerized, he pulled the car over at a hand-lettered sign that read, POP'S WARNERS' CHEAR TYROUTS.

In the distance, what looked like six-year-old boys in full football pads and helmets ran at each other with abandon, under the direction of men who looked like giants. Nearer, just beyond the chain-link fence, a line of perhaps twenty-five six-year-old girls danced and kicked in approximate unison in gold-and-blue uniforms, waving pom-poms half-heartedly. A woman in a big version of the same outfit walked along the chorus line pointing and blowing a whistle. Those she pointed to came forward and worked harder, shaking their gold puffs into fits of abandon. The little girls all spun around and flipped the tails of their miniskirts up to show gold panties. The chosen ones executed a rolling somersault forward, but about a quarter of them didn't make it and had to right themselves by main force. At one end, two girls were suddenly pulling each other's hair and then they locked together and went to the ground. As if on cue, two more fights broke out.

Through all this, Lee Borowsky sat with her jaw dropped open an inch.

"Man," she said finally, "I escaped some stuff. If somebody dropped down from Mars now, I don't think I could explain this.''

''Mars, hell. England.''

'' '*Tyr*-out,' '' she said scornfully.

''Look carefully. Every word on that sign is wrong.''

She snorted once, but she was quiet for another minute as he drove, and then the eye of the storm passed and she launched into a treatise on how it was only the teaching of structural linguistics in high school that could possibly save the American language from galloping illiteracy.

"I want two eggs over medium, so the yellows are still runny but the white isn't runny at all. They have to be taken off the grill at just the right moment. I hate runny egg white. I want four bacon rashers well done but not burned. I don't want any glistening transparent fat, I want it all white and translucent, but I definitely don't want that charred taste when it's overdone.''

The waitress was being remarkably tolerant, appearing to add codes to the order form that would record all this.

''I want hash browns cooked in butter, but make sure it's hot enough so they don't absorb a lot of the butter and get gummy and greasy. They should be separate little shreds of potato. And I want sourdough toast with the butter on the side and a decent jam like strawberry or orange marmalade not grape or that horrible stuff they call allfruit. A tiny glass of orange juice, but only if it's fresh-squeezed.''

''It is. For you, sir?''

''Coffee and wheat toast, but only if the bread is sliced north to south.''

The waitress tried hard not to laugh as she walked away.

''That wasn't necessary.''

''You sure you wouldn't like a little food with your cholesterol?''

Lee Borowsky started laughing again, but reined herself in before it went out of control. ''It's been a long time since somebody's teased me without being mean about it. I know

I can be a pain in the ass, but I think more people should insist on getting things right. Or getting things the way they *want* them, even if it isn't right. There's nothing worse than a bunch of Milquetoasts who never get what they want because they're afraid to make a tiny little peep of complaint.''

For a moment her voice had trembled with messianic energy.

"I can think of a few worse things, actually. But let's try another subject. Let's try you and your mother."

The fidgeting changed gears immediately. "Out come the testicles," she said.

"I'm paying, I choose the subject."

She made a lot of expressions with her mouth, one after another, then with her eyebrows, then she seemed to subside into a guarded neutrality that made him sad for some reason. "Mom's a subject, all right. They do master's theses on her, you know. Really—at least on her famous image—the whore from next door. And they do features in the press all the time: Where is the delicious Lori Bright now? Whole books on her career have been written in French, La Bright, la Grande Voluptueuse. In France, she's as famous as Jerry Lewis. They have festivals of her movies at the Cinematheque, they even throw in that early softcore movie where she bares her big tit to the vampire. She gets a kick out of all the fags making a cult out of her dress epics, but she denies it. You probably know that. Hell, you probably fucked her. Everyone else has. Did you fuck her?''

One way or another she was going to make him pay for choosing this subject. "Tell me about growing up with her."

She was so self-focused that she didn't even notice he had ducked the question. Her hands worked in her lap like live animals.

"What was your family life like?"

It took her a while to decide to go on. "Living with Mom was a daily depletion allowance. It was a steady drain on your headway in the world. She grabbed everything around her for herself—food, friends, light, *air*—she couldn't bear anyone else having anything. If I came in second in a spelling bee, she'd find fifty ways to remind me of the word I missed. She had to trash it if she couldn't have it. The big cheese in the cosmos, the only cheese.

"I once had a birthday party, I think I was eleven, and she flounced all around the house in that blue satin ball dress they'd all seen in *Time of Trial.* Nobody even remembered me at my own party, and even my best friend couldn't understand why I was getting so mad. And later I'd have a boy over and she'd come in with some shirt unbuttoned down to her belly button and bend over to give him a Coke. Dad couldn't take it and he was gone by the time I was four. He was no angel, but he didn't have to own the fillings out of your teeth. I can't even listen to her talk, you know? I can't listen to one goddamn word without hearing the subtext screaming at me, 'Look at me, Look at me, Look at me!'

"Yeah, she's insecure, sure, but I get tired of making excuses. Some insecure people are modest or quiet or generous. *I'd* like to be modest and generous, but she's made me what I am now. I had to scream and fight and grab for any space at all in the world. She would have crowded me right off the edge of the goddamn planet."

The food came and Lee Borowsky tore into it as if she'd been starving for days. The coffee was only tolerable, but even that gave him a little rush of pleasure.

"She didn't seem insecure to me," he said.

"She's an *actress,* you berk. What do you think? She's played Catherine the Great, she can't fool you about something like that? You don't really have a clue."

His mental image of Lori Bright hadn't shifted much, but it had grown fuzzier at the edge, as if preparing to move when more evidence was in. It was amazing what a second viewpoint could do to what you thought you knew of someone. He figured the daughter was overstating, caricaturing her mother because of a thousand resentments, but there was probably truth there, too.

"Actually, I was always surprised they didn't put the famous horse in that movie. Mom would have loved that."

"That's a folk myth," he said. "Catherine the Great didn't die trying to screw a horse. She died of a stroke."

Lee Borowsky wagged her fork in the air like a conductor's baton. "Some things *should* be true and that's that, man. It's just like this town. All those stories of old Hollywood that I've heard ad nauseam, blah-blah-blah. Gable and Lombard falling in love and Bogie and his first wife punching each other up on their yacht and Tracy and Hepburn not being able to marry, and Rosebud being the pet name for Marion Davies's clitoris, and the one-way mirrors on Errol Flynn's ceilings, and Steve McQueen doing his own motorcycle stunts in *The Great Escape*, which I know for a fact is bullshit, I've met his stuntman. Who knows what's true? It's a kind of epistemology of lies, and it's all about people whose careers are a kind of telling lies about who they are every day. I can't deal with any of it anymore."

"You don't look much like your mom, either."

She met his eyes fiercely, as if wondering why he'd said that. "I'm adopted, didn't she tell you?"

He hadn't known, but she seemed to find his nonresponse acceptable.

"Don't start making a big deal out of it. I don't like the great Lori Bright very much, I don't like who she is and what she did to me, and I reject her as a real mom, but she's still my mom, you know? I think at a certain age she got a whim that she was missing out on being a mother, or one of her publicists told her she ought to be a mom for the sake of the great unwashed in Dubuque, and I was the most painless way of doing it, without losing her figure, and then she just kind of lost interest in the whole thing and turned me over to nursemaids and au pairs. But she chose me and every once in a while she took an interest in me and I'm not about to try to hunt down some bitch who abandoned me.''

''That's pretty harsh on everyone concerned.''

She shrugged. ''I bend my eye on vacancy and with the incorporeal air do hold discourse.''

''*Lear*?''

''In a girls' school you get to do ridiculous things like that. I played a lot of male parts, but I wasn't much good.''

''It's not the gender. Nobody in high school has seen enough of life to do *Lear*.''

''Everything's accelerating, old man. Our first mortal sins are at six now, big betrayals at eight, dark night of the soul at ten, world-weary cynicism by twelve, and deathbed repentance at fourteen.''

He laughed. ''I think I can picture it. A couple of dry martinis and then storytime before bed.''

She laughed, too. ''Oh, I'll bet Mom's fallen for you. You're just too tasty, as she'd say.''

But she didn't follow it up. She regained her interest in the hash browns and began shoveling.

''We have to negotiate,'' he said finally. ''I won't drag you home right away if you call your mom and talk to her, and you've got to give the money back. If it's for the movie, ask her for it and I'll argue your case. Will you give me your word not to make a run for it?''

''Cross my heart and hope to die?''

''Something like that.''

She laughed and shook her head in disbelief. ''Men are amazing. What makes you think, if I'm willing to make up an extortion scheme and run away from home, you'll compel me to be honest by making me say a few magic words?''

''It's what my computer friends call waving a dead chicken at the problem. You know it won't really do any good, but you hope.''

''That's a good one,'' she said. ''The chicken.''

The waitress left the bill on its little brown tray and he put a twenty on it.

"Don't cha use plastic, old man?"

"All my money's tied up in cash," he said.

15

CAUGHT IN THE CROSS FIRE

As he headed south a big grasshopper crane swung a truss high on the hills above the Sepulveda Pass. The concrete slabs and granite of the Getty Center abuilding up there looked like a giant burst lunch box dropped from outer space. Textures and styles waged their edgy war above the 405 and he found all that fashionable disquiet suddenly edifying. It made him think of Lee Borowsky in a new way. Maybe she was the true postmodern child, the girl who was just too restless and energetic to adopt any one sensibility. Lee had been a fizz of attention, deadly earnest one moment, then refusing to be taken the least bit seriously, skating over the surfaces of modern thought and quoting all her ideas out of their proper scale like the boasts of little children. She insisted on her right to her own postures and her art, but she never let herself be questioned because she refused to plant herself in a place where she could be wrong. Nothing had a frame of reference and nothing evolved, nothing ever grew up gradually. He wondered if all the kids were that way now, if it was the only way to adapt to circumstances when the circumstances went out of control.

He was getting old, he decided. He was out of sorts with the time.

•　•　•

ABOUT Wilshire Boulevard, he noticed the pickup following him down the freeway. Two heads were silhouetted in the cab. He recognized the rope lashing down the hood and figured they must have picked him up at Lee's. The one with the zigzag tattoos had boasted he knew where Lee lived, but he didn't figure they had it in them to go this far out of the way for revenge. He changed lanes a few times, and they were too stupid not to do the same.

It was a wrinkle he didn't like very much and he stopped at a busy supermarket and ran in. They were waiting in the pickup, two rows over, when he came out with a small bag, but he knew how not to look. They followed him again as he drove up to Ridge Glen in the Windsor Hills and parked behind the green Explorer as if he belonged there.

Jack Liffey carried his bag up the lawn and noticed the screen door was shut but the door within was open. "Stay inside, Tyrone," he said softly. "You'll want to hear this."

He sat on the glide and kicked lightly to set it going. A little wind ruffled the peppertrees and filled the street with their sweet smell. The pickup parked on the street below and the two got out and stared. It was the tattooed duo, all right, still in strap undershirts to show off all the blue tracery.

They strode up the lawn but then seemed to lose confidence and waited facing the porch.

"Hello, gentlemen," he said.

They seemed disconcerted by his calm.

"Fuck you. We goin' to paradise, you and us." It was the one with the South Seas tracery. The zigzag one had always been quieter.

"Last time we met down in Orange County," Jack Liffey said, "you were starting to tell me about a young black woman you knew in high school, but we were interrupted."

His eyes puzzled over it for a moment. "Oh, yeah, Tamille Hudson. She was one stuck-up nigger, I tell you. We both remember her, huh?"

Zigzag nodded once. He probably remembered the auto-mag in his mouth, too, and he didn't seem to feel like chitchatting.

"That one thought she was as good as a white bitch. She got all A's and she talked like she had a plum in her mouth. If you heard her on the phone, you couldn't even tell she was colored. When she started dating that white boy, we had to teach her a lesson." He snickered. "We said we was his friends and we took her in the car up to the reservoir. We made her read poetry and she didn't mind that so much, but she objected when we gave her some white-power stuff we got and we had to force her to read it aloud and put some feeling into it." He chuckled a bit. "She had a real problem saying the word 'nigger' with enough abomination."

Jack Liffey heard a faint noise from inside the house, and he hoped Pennycooke held off a little.

"We figured she'd actually be pretty if she wasn't a nigger. Like you just take a pretty girl, all normal, and dip her in ink, she still looks pretty good, you know? But you just can't shine shit, huh? Still, she had all the apparatus, and we made her take her clothes off and do both of us and we said we'd get her and her boyfriend both if she told on us. She ain't been so nearly stuck-up since. Dropped her white boy, too, and went back to her own kind, the way it ought to be."

The screen door slapped open, and the boys' eyes went wide. "Whoa!"

Jack Liffey glanced at Tyrone Pennycooke out of the corner of his eye. He stood with his hands on his hips, looking as flamboyant as he'd ever seen him with black-and-white-striped bell-bottom pants, a yellow flowered shirt, and a bright green vest with a matching puffed-up billed cap. He made a sucking noise through his teeth, like a rattlesnake warming up.

"I want you to meet my friend Tyrone," Jack Liffey said.

"What I want ask you naow, bwoys, you tink you de true baldheads of Babylon?"

Almost like a reflex, the boys went into their martial-arts stance, bowlegged and elbows out, side by side. They shouted in unison and yanked on an imaginary bar over their heads. ''I'm a proud white Aryan warrior!''

Heads snapped left, their tongues came out, heads snapped to the front, arms flailed up and down.

''Protect our blood! Protect our culture! Protect our folk!''

They stamped one leg, then the other, snapped their heads up and down, and Pennycooke just waited, watching coolly, as the dance and chant carried on and on. Jack Liffey decided it was the oddest minute and half he'd ever lived through, and he didn't want it ever to end.

''Death to the mud people!''

Tyrone Pennycooke must have guessed they were winding down, because he reached into the waistband behind his back and came out with his big clumsy-looking Webley-Fosbury pistol.

''Dat's enough naow. I-an'-I penetrate de simple concep dat you two baldheads tink you is ugly bad, you is steppin' razors; and you got you a karate of de great white spirit. Well, I-an'-I got de karate of de people.'' He gestured with the pistol. ''Time for you two to forward up hyere.''

Jack Liffey took the six-pack of Vernor's ginger ale out of the paper bag and set it on the end of the glide. ''It's the best I could do.''

The Jamaican almost smiled when he saw it.

''I think you and I could probably make a separate peace,'' Jack Liffey said.

''Blessings, I don't tink so, but I going to be busy right now. You listen me, bwoys, you step up hyere or I shoot you where you stan.''

They were starting to look worried. Jack Liffey gave them a wave and headed for his car. As much as he wanted to stick around, he needed to get to Musso and Frank's by noon.

• • •

"It's for G. Dan," Jack Liffey said to the tall headwaiter in the red toreador jacket as he handed him the envelope with a folded-up chunk of the morning paper in it.

The only guy sitting alone over on the left looked like Humpty-Dumpty, with broad green suspenders over a white shirt to show he wasn't embarrassed about the paunch, but the guy might not have been Hunt.

Musso and Frank's was all dark wood and snug booths in red leather and overcooked English grill food. It had been around since 1919, which was ancient by L.A. standards, but in L.A., ancient only really meant before Technicolor. The place was fancy enough to be discreet with celebrities of all kinds and the headwaiter had second thoughts, but Jack Liffey had nodded in roughly the right direction, so he delivered the envelope.

Jack Liffey followed it over. "Don't bother. There's nothing inside but the stock reports." He sat as Hunt set his knife and fork delicately beside a chopped salad that had been neatly sliced and diced. He remembered reading that the French thought it a cardinal sin for metal to touch salad ingredients, but nothing French had ever been within miles of Musso's.

"You can probably guess I'm Jack Liffey."

"Probably."

The waiter came back and hovered. "Is everything all right, Mr. Hunt?"

"Yeah. Scram."

They watched each other for a while. Nearby, a TV sports reporter he vaguely recognized was entertaining two stunning blondes and a little boy.

"Want a ginger ale?" G. Dan Hunt asked with a shadow of a smirk.

"I just left your boy administering that very beverage to some other guys."

"No kidding?"

"Long ago I used to read about Dan Hunt and Jimmy Frattiano," Jack Liffey said, "but you're too young to have hung out with Mickey Cohen."

"That was my dad. Daniel, Dan the Man. Him and Hooky Rothman and Slick Snyder and Jimmy 'the Weasel' Frattiano and Happy Meltzer. That was another era, for sure. They hung out at the men's shop Mickey ran, Michael's Exclusive up on Sunset, that was a bookie in back. But mostly I remember the Carousel, the ice-cream store he had later over in Brentwood. The ice-cream guy pushed a button if you were a friend and you went through a door by the drinking fountain into the betting there, too. I was eight or nine and I thought all ice-cream parlors had a place in back where guys talked about nags a lot. My dad watched over the Mick some of the time."

"Must have had the night off when they blew up the front of his house."

"Where were you then?"

"About that time my dad was lugging crates off freighters down in San Pedro."

Humpty-Dumpty nodded thoughtfully. "Too bad about this coast. Now, in New York you could always buy crates of stuff cheap that 'fell off the pallets.' You could never touch stuff out here. Too many fuckin' commies in the union."

He went back to eating. "It's your dime, Liffey."

"I find missing kids. That's all I do. I came in the front door of this thing looking for the fifteen-year-old daughter of Lori Bright, who I think you've heard of. That's all I'm here for. The cops keep dropping broad hints that there's a shooting war going on between a little company called PropellorHeads and your friends at Mitsuko-Monogram. You may find it hard to believe, but I just got caught in the cross fire."

He nodded thoughtfully. "You were smoking a little cigar, wore a Mexican blanket, rode your mule into the pueblito, and people started shooting from all the windows."

"Something like that."

"So?"

"I was hoping we could declare peace. You could call off the reggae band and we could all walk away clean."

"What's in it for my client?"

"My goodwill."

Hunt snorted. "That ought to get them laying on extra shifts in Nagoya."

"I know it's a little like a flea saying he can bring down an elephant, but I can cause a lot of trouble. For Mitsuko and for you personally."

The utensils stopped moving. "You don't want to start with the threats, believe me."

"I just want to be left alone."

The eyes came up and rested. There was something a little crazy in them, bright specks in the brown. "First, guy, I'd have to believe you're pure as the driven snow. Second, I'd have to care whether you get squashed in the fuss or not. I don't give big odds at the dog track on neither one. Now, if you ain't gone from here before the fish course, I get Mr. Winston over there and his pals to toss you into the alley."

The headwaiter was watching the table like a hawk.

Jack Liffey rose. "I'll tell Mitsuko you had a chance to head off all their trouble."

"You do that."

HE went straight to a pay phone down the street on Hollywood Boulevard. As he dug out change a couple of loungers came forward from the shadows of a shop that sold T-shirts and trinkets.

"Dime bag?"

"Want a date?"

He just shook his head.

"Hey, that you, Admiral? That business we were talking about earlier? You go right ahead. Rock-and-roll."

He hung up and turned to the redhead with the buckteeth who was still watching him.

"Sorry. You can have your office back."

16

A DAMAGED REALITY

ON THE WAY TO PROPELLORHEADS THE NEXT DAY, HIS EYE WAS caught by a shop on Little Santa Monica called Dirty Lingerie. A long line of women snaked away down the block under a banner: YOUR FAVORITE SOAP HUNK SIGNS YOUR BRA. A woman at the head of the line fled, squealing happily, and a fortyish matron stepped forward to a card table on the sidewalk and tugged a sweater up to reveal a thick white bra. A young man in a muscle shirt leaned forward with a Magic Marker to ask something and then write on her breast. Two other young men stood beside him, all with the dark chiseled sort of looks you saw in *Esquire* ads, signing away as women unbuttoned their blouses and bent forward with no apparent reticence. We're back to the postmodern, he thought.

"MUMBLE!"

"Mumble frotz!"

The two programmers exchanged something like a high-five, though Admiral Wicks couldn't reach very high out of his lightweight wheelchair.

"Gloat on. Hey! Hey! Hey! Hey! Gloat off," Michael Chen exulted. "We did it, Liffey-san. Well, we did segment *one*."

"Smile, man. You are looking very thirty years ago. Especially with that big goose egg on your cheek."

"I'd like to know what I'm smiling about," Jack Liffey said. The Australian came in carrying fresh bottles of Yoo-Hoo, looking like he'd watched the cat eat the canary he'd always hated. They opened the Yoo-Hoos and spiked them with vodka to celebrate. The vodka bottle was already half-way down. Admiral Wicks was peeling the plastic off slices of Velveeta and gorging himself.

"The lads turned the trick," Bruce Parfit said. "And it's so untraceable they may never get to claim their victory. In the wee hours of the A.M., the domestic wing of Mitsuko Enterprises donated their entire cash reserve in this country to charity, and the Japanese, being conservative business-men, had a gi-fucking-normous cash reserve over here, twelve million dollars. What's that in yen?"

"Some dumb-ass number," Michael Chen said. "Over a billion, I think."

"Not just one charity, or a few of them. We spammed their reserve everywhere. We sent a few hundred dollars to every nonprofit in the United States, even the ones devoted to maintaining the purity of the white race against the yellow peril. Some of the surprised administrators are already E-mailing their thank-yous back to Mitsuko. Imagine the consternation at Mitsuko Corporate over in Century City when the news penetrates. Of course they'll go after their cash, but my lads pipelined it so fantastically deviously that it'll cost them almost as much to find it all and get it back. It was wonderful, like stealing the Rockefeller millions in dollar bills and throwing it out of a helicopter over the Rose Parade. Here's to the unacknowledged genius of Michael Chen and Admiral Wicks."

He put an arm on each of them.

"Touch me if you love me." Admiral Wicks bridled.

Michael Chen did a little dance. "We're not done yet. Segment *two* is being coded."

"Do not fire until you see the yellow of their eyes," Admiral Wicks called out.

"Careful there, dark man."

"Just a thinko, my friend. I'm a little drunk and racism

surfaces in all drunks. You know I love my yellow brothers.''

''And I, my *frères noires*, unless they're weenies or spods,'' Michael Chen said.

They made it up with a Yoo-Hoo toast and a low five.

''Sounds good. What's segment two?'' Jack Liffey asked.

''We have yet to fire upon the home office in Tokyo,'' Admiral Wicks said. ''We have something different in mind for them, something classic and clean and honorable.''

''And utterly devastating!'' Michael Chen seconded. They touched bottles.

''Killer!''

''They'll be coining new words for us!''

''In time to come, when our grandchildren tell the net police what we did, every great revenge scheme will be known as a Wicks-Chen!''

''A Chen-Wicks!''

''Leave us not argue! A Wen-chicks-wen!''

''I object! That uses your initial letter twice.''

''But it rhymes with you twice!''

''Gentlemen, could I have your undivided attention,'' Jack Liffey beseeched. ''Do I get to know what's going to happen?'' He noticed Admiral Wicks's long, thin, delicate fingers, which he was working now against the tough bubblewrap on a packet of bologna.

''Nil.'' Admiral Wicks seemed to climb back down a steepness from somewhere far away, and the instant his eyes met Jack Liffey's, the package ripped open and slices of bologna sprayed out onto his lap, where he looked down again. ''Try us tomorrow, monsieur, and we'll tell you how it went down. All is illusion, but combat is the worthiest illusion.''

''For the digital samurai,'' Michael Chen added. ''And I'm not even Japanese.''

• • •

HE drove up Argyle through the lower hills where the big expensive houses all hid modestly from the road, crouching behind hedges or turning their backs, allowing only sly glimpses of Tudor framing or scrolled witches' roofs. He was apprehensive about seeing Lori Bright again. He knew how much he wanted her and how tenuous her own feelings for him probably were, and he had no idea what he would tell her about Lee. He thought he had a new handle on his integrity, but he was already getting chills thinking of her voice. It was the shifting from one world to another that was so hard, he thought.

At Avenida Bluebird a big workman's truck was parked in the front drive, lettered WE-BOLT-U-DOWN: EARTHQUAKE RETROFITTING, RADON AND AUTO SHUTOFFS.

Anita was nicer to him now, actually smiling as she showed him into the trophy room. He heard a banging down in the basement and then the whiz of a big power drill.

"Hope you feeling better, sir."

"Better than what?"

But she was already moving on. The photographs of movie stars had come down from the interior wall and the plaster had recently been drilled through in several spots, explorations that had left little tailing piles of silt on the floor. He had a sudden absurd sensation of kinship with the old house, of age and a dogged chivalry, working overtime to hold together things that should really have fallen apart. He wondered if the walls felt a sense of relief that help was coming.

Then she was there and he felt the burn spread up his chest. Her hair was wrapped in a towel—she always seemed to be just coming from a bath—and she wore a short terrycloth robe like something that might have come from Kmart. Her lower legs were absolutely astonishing, sculpted to just that perfect museum-quality Greco-Roman shape. Only above the shortie robe did he know that her thighs spread a bit more than she would probably like.

"Jack Jack." She kissed him and patted the tender lump

beside his eye. "My sweet warrior, my champion, my love."

She smelled of musk and something sweet and the voice was like swimming in warm custard, and he swam. Already her emotions were intense, excessive.

"How is the delightful Maeve?"

"Fine. She's home."

"I hope I didn't cause trouble with her mother."

Go for the sore spots. "Not yet."

He had to tell her now. "I found Lee," he said dryly.

She froze up and a hand went to her mouth, a gesture of caution or modesty or anxiety, and he wondered if she remembered it from some film. He couldn't trust anything about her anymore. After all, she'd played Catherine the Great.

"She's okay. She's fine. She'll be phoning you in twenty minutes. That was part of the deal for not dragging her straight back." He took out the fat envelope.

"She's giving back the money, all but a few hundred that was spent. That was the other part of the deal."

This time she looked genuinely shocked and her hand pressed her mouth hard. The other hand went to her chest as if the robe were threatening to burst open. He no longer knew quite what to make of any gesture she made.

"You must have guessed," he said. "You and your husband both warned me it was fishy." He put the envelope in her hand and she looked down at it as if not knowing quite what it was.

"Eeep." It was a little noise from her throat, probably quite genuine. At least he hoped so, the kind of actorish calculation that could invoke that noise did not bear thinking about. She put a hand on his shoulder to steady herself. He wanted desperately to carry her to bed and untie the sash and peel off the robe.

"You must have guessed," he repeated.

"Oh, Jack, it's so easy to know and not know. Where is she?"

"She's in L.A. She's safe."

"Where is she?"

"Ask her when she calls. I promise you she's all right."

"Jack." She tossed the envelope aside. Money meant nothing to Catherine the Great. "Where is my daughter?"

"I promised not to tell."

"You made a promise like that to a fifteen-year-old runaway?"

"I gave my word."

"Your word?"

"It applies equally to children. If I dragged her back now, she'd just run off again and she'd burrow deeper somewhere. Why don't we deal with what she thinks is bothering her? Then she'll come back on her own steam."

Her eyes were going wild and something he saw in there worried him a lot. It reminded him of the way she made love, like pure madness, and the fear of whatever it was settled over him like frost.

"I need you, Jack. Does that penetrate that thick skin of yours? I hired you because I need you and I've come to need you more than I thought. You can't let me down like this."

That was a new tack, he thought. He didn't know what to make of it. "Fifteen minutes now. Talk to her. We'll get her home."

Anita stuck her head in. "Madam—"

"Go away! So youth must be served," she spat at the closing door. Her eyes swept around like lasers toward him, then she caught herself, and he could actually see her shifting gears. "So she tells you I'm a bad mother and she gets to follow her hormones and her teenage rebellion and the hell with me."

"What did you do to her?" he said. "You tell me."

"We're all hostages to fortune. I couldn't always be there for her. Is it so terrible?" She opened her arms to an audience, any audience, and a lot of the robe pulled open, so he could see the curve of a breast, one blue vein like a lightning strike on the inner swell.

Things are tough all over, he thought, dredging the

thought out of some surprising reserve of irony, but he hoped it didn't show on his face because she seemed to be metamorphosing again. "Jack, darling." She loosened the tie on the robe, gently pulling back one lapel to show the full swell of her breast, then an edge of the cowrie-brown nipple, then the whole breast. "Millions and millions of men have wanted to see this. Don't you feel privileged? I'll do anything you want, darling. We'll do anything together you've ever let yourself dream about. Shall I suggest what I'll do for you? You're my champion."

She took his hand and placed it on her breast. She nuzzled against him and he felt like he couldn't get enough air.

"Ten minutes," he said. "Just talk to her."

Now she seemed to be crying, burrowing her head in his chest and pressing against him. The show of frailty inflamed everything in him that was not already inflamed and stiffened his penis, which up to then had been only half-decided. Yet he still didn't believe it. Maybe she was actually scared deep inside, but she would never let him see it, not the real fear. What he saw was a mask over a mask. The big Spanish-Norman house, her entourage of servants, her whole life—they all existed in a damaged reality.

"Oh, Jack, I don't know how to say this. That girl has me over a barrel. She's so fierce and so self-righteous. I can't face her on the phone. Not without an edge. I need to know something, where she is, something. She's too much for me."

He wanted to help her, to say the words that would ease the intolerable confusion and brighten her face again. His whole being was inflamed with wanting to please her. It was what she counted on, and he knew it. He did not know what his face looked like, watching her, but he guessed it looked hungry and sad, like a starving man too proud to steal the loaf.

"Jack." Never had he heard his name spoken so often. He wondered if it was something that had come out of bad screenplays. She walked suddenly to a photo album that lay on the sideboard. She fanned it open to show dozens of picture postcards tucked anyhow between the pages. "Look. This is me, Jack. All my life I've only written postcards. I can't sustain. After the horrible buzz of so much that's banal, I don't know what to say anymore. That girl is so *earnest* and she demands so much of me."

She rocked a little as if pulled between giant magnets. "All my life I've had this recurring dream. There's a castle wall made of rough stones and I'm inside the castle and there's narrow windows open to the city outside, maybe a dozen of them, and there's a monkey chained in each one, sitting there on the sill. Most of them are looking out at the city. Some are—you know, see no evil, speak no evil, with their little hairy elbows up in the air. I think some of the dream comes from this trite little monkey sculpture my folks had on their mantel, but that's the painless part. A few of the monkeys are chained looking *in,* and they're looking into the corners of the room where it's too dark for me to see what's there, and I get a real chill wondering what it is they're watching. But one little monkey is more animated than the others and lately I can see this one's got Lee's face, and these soulful brown eyes are watching *me.* The eyes follow me. And every time I'm about to do something, every time I'm about to think a stupid thought or do something petty, that little monkey rattles her chain a little. Damn it, that's all, just rattles that damn tinkly chain like a reminder she's watching. Jack, I wake up sweating."

"I don't know anything about dreams."

She looked at her watch. "When?"

"Soon."

"Help me, Jack. I'll be good to you forever."

"Try telling her you love her."

Her eyes rested on him, angry suddenly, and he saw it was the wrong thing to have said. "Don't judge me so easily. Have you ever worked without a net? They used to say it would kill me, but I had no choice. It was the only way I knew how to work. But then you have a baby girl and she insists on dragging the real world into the room with you. I try to talk to her and I get some sort of messages from her and I know they're sincere and I know the meaning of every word, but I just don't know the code. She terrifies me.''

He had no idea whether Catherine the Great had ever said anything like that. He wanted to take her to someplace simple for a few weeks and see if she could straighten out. He wanted to lie on a stiff bed in a warm climate and make love for a few days straight and then eat simple meals and swim with her and talk about movies that she hadn't been in. He wanted to brush sand off her feet and discard all the rings and studs so there was just the two of them and their unenhanced skins.

Then the phone rang, and she squealed. ''Go, *go,* get out of here, go now, *go.*''

He went out and shut the heavy, carved oak door and then went through French doors to the back lawn. Stepping outside in a kind of primitive belief that the natural world would restore something that was spoiling in him, something that he'd left in the back of the fridge. If he'd been a better man, a voice deep inside suggested, he wouldn't have forgotten it back behind the mayo and pickles.

I require something holy, he thought. He needed something to wash him clean. The grass was too green and smooth, the way fifty years of expensive gardening would keep it, and across the steep canyon there were the usual houses on spindly iron stilts, so strange looking that only a generation of familiarity and repeated viewing, TV revisits after each earthquake, had normalized them.

As a boy he had played in a canyon on the east flank of the San Pedro hills much like the one down below. He'd called it Mystery Canyon. Mystery because it held a dark culvert pipe, a melted green glass insulator from a power pole and a handful of spent .45 shell casings. Dimestore mysteries, really. But he remembered the thrill the sense of mystery had given him, the feeling of passing into another world where you could make up stories, and he marveled now at how manageable mystery had been before he had come to understand just how villainous people could be.

Lori Bright's garden, by contrast, had conquered mystery through the use of the picturesque, a gazebo, a pond with a Japanese bridge, the smells of wet rocks and jasmine. He tried to imagine Lee playing there as a toddler, running unsteadily in her knock-kneed way toward the edge and being swept up before she reached it by a convenient servant. Or playing with a china tea set in the quiet of the small gazebo by the rose garden. He did his best, but it was Maeve he kept seeing, and she was on the topply swings in his old yard in Torrance instead. Lee and Lori were too extreme for him to picture, like golden czarinas playing cookstove with Fabergé eggs, like the millionaire boys in the silents who always wore the little sailor suits with the big collars.

The rent-a-cop her husband had hired to watch over the house was at the far side of the garden. He sat on the stump of what had once been a huge eucalyptus staring off into space. The man was tearing memo slips off a pad, folding them into little yellow airplanes, and sailing them out into the canyon. He supposed it was a pretty boring job guarding a back lawn.

Jack Liffey strolled in the opposite direction. Some bird cried out twice like a tormented soul in the still air. The sky was a gunmetal gray and featureless, like a phony stage drop for some dreadful didactic morality play. He had hoped to run into the old Latino gardener or anyone he could exchange a few pointless ordinary words with. Then he heard a crash of glass from the house. He ignored it as long as he could, but it wasn't very long. He had made it halfway around the house, to the alcove with the lion fountain where he'd met Lori—when had it been?—only a few days earlier. He had a sense that when he went back inside, he would be engulfed by a world that was profoundly different, and he wasn't sure he was ready to give up the old one.

Anita was down the dim hall, framed by a plaster arch, motionless, as if she'd been set on pause. She offered him an expression that eluded him, but he thought for some reason that he sensed sympathy plus something else in her liquid brown eyes, something dark and ominous—a warning? In the trophy room, Lori Bright stood in front of a shattered display case with the telephone fallen through to lie among plaques and *Life* magazine covers. Her eyes were red, focused on the envelope of money that she was clutching for some reason, perhaps just a talisman of her daughter, and the robe was clasped tight and knotted shut.

"Can't you help me?" Her voice was coming from a long ways away.

"I won't ask how the call went," he said lightly, but he could sense he wasn't going to get away with it.

She had never looked more beautiful to him, smoothed over with a kind of fury or madness, and never more unapproachable.

"I require Lee's whereabouts."

"I'll get her back."

"Jack, it's not a game anymore. I have to know exactly where she is."

"No."

She held up the envelope and met his eyes for the first time. Hers were depthless, as if shutting him out. "Your fingerprints are all over the money. I'll tell the police you're part of the conspiracy. Hell, you *are* part of it if you won't help."

This was a turn he hadn't expected, and he wondered if it was a bluff. He couldn't grasp the magnitude of the betrayal at first.

"I'll have her back soon."

"No, Jack, I mean it."

"Yes, Lori, I know you mean it. People like you always mean it, while I never mean it much, myself, not being a big star or rich or connected." Now he could see his whole concept of things unraveling. It was absurd, but what he regretted most just then was the sense that he would not get to make love to this troubled woman that night.

She glared dully, as if passing his words one by one over a scanner until the whole made sense.

"I gave my word to Lee," he said as he walked out.

"Jack!"

He looked back.

"You don't owe anything to a fifteen-year-old runaway who tried to extort money from her mother."

He shrugged. "Maybe not. But I owe something to the way I've always tried to live my life."

HE didn't even get down the hill before the white Caprice flashed its red light at him. Flor was driving and he seemed really happy about something. Malamud got out first and made the rolling gesture to get him to crank down the window.

"Kidnapping is an A felony, so we got no choice in this."

"If your role in life is playing gods and keeping things even, how come you're always stepping on the little guy?"

"We do things correctly, Liffey. It's our protection."

17

IT WAS THE FIRST TIME HE'D ACTUALLY SPENT A NIGHT IN A cell and by late in the evening he'd learned one thing new, that guys in jail had more imagination than the flat average, not a lot more, but more. He listened to stories about ways guys had committed suicide with smuggled drugs or wet sheets that didn't tear or splinters of wood pulled off benches. He heard about mysterious sicknesses that swept over guys in the middle of the night and ate the flesh off their arms until you could see through to the bones, and about feuds that ended with guys getting their faces blow-torched off while other guys held them down. The stories were all bigger than life because jail time was more intense than real time. On the way to all this entertainment value, though, he hit a bit of a bad patch.

He'd been booked in front of a window that was dark on the other side so it became a mirror. In the mirror he thought he saw a guy who was up to things, and he told himself it would be okay, but it didn't quite work out that way. After the booking, he had been pushed here and there by bored guards, as if waiting for just the right room to open up, until he'd complained about it and then he'd been frog-marched into a dim cell at random.

"Happy now, wiseguy?"

"Have my luggage sent on."

Two bunk beds filled a space meant for one and there

was only room for one man to stand up at a time, or two if they wanted to be very friendly. Less than a mile away, he knew there was a brand-new twin-tower high-rise county jail that had stood empty for years, its echoing pristine hallways guarded by a handful of deputies to prevent anybody breaking in and spraying graffiti around. In the wisdom of postmodern politics, there had been plenty of bond money to build it, but none to staff it.

He lay on the bottom bunk where a sullen white guy on the top had jerked his thumb. Another big stone-faced white guy with a ponytail and tattoos and missing teeth who said his name was something like Jolly-o was on the lower bunk opposite, and after a half hour of desultory monosyllables, the fourth man was brought back from somewhere, a middle-aged black named Fitz who was technically on the top bunk across the nine-inch aisle, but he took up a standing position with his back in the corner as if he expected something.

"Fucking county," Jolly-o said after a while. "They used to have this pogie sorted out. Now they so fuckin' crowded they puttin' niggers in with real people."

Jolly-o looked over for confirmation, but Jack Liffey kept his mouth shut. He didn't like the way things were turning.

"There it is," the guy on top said.

Jack Liffey met the black guy's guarded eyes. No wonder he was in the corner.

You never got to make the kind of principled stands they wrote books about, he thought. Here it was—he'd say something angry and ineffectual about brotherhood, and Jolly-o would knife him with a sharpened toothbrush and the old black guy would stay out of it and it would all go down as pointless jailbird violence. But he had a code that said something about standing up straight, and this was one of the situations where it seemed to apply.

"What do you say, new guy?"

"About what?"

"Puttin' niggers in with Americans."

"Shit," Jack Liffey said sleepily, "if we got to choose

up sides, I hope the black team takes me this time. They got a lot better jump shot from the foul line. And they got a better idea of who their enemies are.''

Fitz almost smiled. Jack Liffey brought his eyes around and fixed them on Jolly-o, who outweighed him by fifty pounds. Now or never, asshole, Jack Liffey thought, knowing every word could be read across their locked eyes.

''Don't you mad-dog me, *fool*.''

''We're all friends in here, aren't we?'' Jack Liffey said, giving him a chance.

''You want me to fuck you, is that it? You want a boyfriend?'' He sat up in the bunk, ducking his head to clear the upper berth.

''If you even try it, one of us ends up dead. I don't care which.'' Jack Liffey used a flat tone. It didn't give the man a lot of room to back down, but it left an inch. He kept a weather eye out as the man shifted his weight back and forth, only a foot away.

''Gentlemen, puh-leaze,'' Fitz said. He had a wonderful baritone. ''Flattered as I am to have men fighting over my honor, they's only two more days on my time and I wouldn't be seeing kindly to have my sentence extended by no *business* in here.''

He launched straight into the tale of how he'd ended up in jail, grasping their attention by sheer relentless oratory. He said he'd made a living for years going around the bars betting he could multiply two four-digit numbers in his head, a skill he'd had since he was a boy, and he'd made plenty of bar money on it, a few bucks at a time, until he ran into a guy who thought of himself as a big operator who'd bet him five grand on one pop. The guy worked out his figures on paper but his math was so bad he always got it wrong, and when Fitz asked for the money due him the guy had his friends drop a dime on him for being a sneak thief and pickpocket. Fitz demonstrated his prowess with numbers for a while and had them all laughing and awed, and the fight blew over, so at last even Jack Liffey and Jolly-o became warily civil.

He slept badly, his dreams full of breathing and cries and bad smells, and after a dreadful breakfast, they told him somebody was bailing him out. Just before he left the cell, wondering who in the hell it was with the money and hoping it wasn't his wife, Fitz held out a fist and they popped fists together. "I don't forget, Jack Liffey, it's my stock-in-trade."

"Come see me. I'm in the book. I'll give you some digits to rub together."

Fitz smiled. "I don't know about that. Here's my gift to you now in case I don't make it over to your side of town. It's a fact that love and death are the only two facts." There was a remarkable sense of peace emanating from the man, and Jack Liffey was afraid he was in for some religious two-step, but he wasn't. "Love and death, they's the two things, they one thing, they make each other significate."

He waited, but that was it. "I'll think about that when I get a chance."

"Come on, Charlie," the guard said. "I ain't got all day."

THE little, balding lawyer led him out of the building, and she was waiting for him by a jet-black Grand Cherokee. She was already crying, standing there in Mexican peasant skirt and blouse with tears streaming down red cheeks.

"Jack, Jack, I'm *so* sorry. I have such a temper when I'm crossed and Lee got under my skin on the phone so bad and then you wouldn't help and I blew like a five-cent fuse. It's what you've done to me." She turned abruptly to the lawyer. "Go away, Mo."

He did, nodding his parting and then scurrying across Bauchet ahead of a big gray bus with wired windows that beeped him on faster.

"You've reduced me to this state with your strength, Jack. I was your concubine and slave woman, and you didn't even know it. In my inner life I'd found someone who would envelop me and protect me and who wasn't after the movie star or the idol or the magic image or the sex goddess but *me,* and it was someone who could help hold me up. Look at my eyes. Look. Whose eyes are they?''

He shrugged.

She reached out and pressed a hand gently against his cheek and his face burned where she touched him.

''I needed you and you turned away. Oh, Jack, before all the laws invented by men''—she put her second palm up to sandwich his face—''what was natural was the strength of the lion and the need of creatures like me who suffered from hunger or cold. I'm the weak creature, I'm the need. I know it's going to be hard for you, but you've got to forgive me my moment of weakness.''

Actually, he thought, he didn't have to do any such goddamn thing, but she did have him in a bit of turmoil, and for all the baroque sentiment that she must have memorized off some old movie script, she had him starting to want her again. The touch of her hands suggested such sexual power that he could barely see through the pink fog.

''Look in my eyes. What do you see?''

''Tiny blood vessels.''

''Don't do that,'' as sharp as Catherine the Great. ''Don't make a joke, *please.* Look at me. These are your eyes, I've become you. I mirror you. I spent the night in jail with you. I'm lost in my need for you.'' She looked down demurely. ''Get in, please.''

He got into her Jeep Cherokee, which he'd never seen before, and immediately he thought of it as her contrition car. The Mercedes would have been too decided, too confident for this strange scene. But he was along for the ride, he guessed that much. In fact he had a feeling he would ride this vehicle until the wheels fell off, though he would probably never trust her very far again.

''I owe you getting your daughter home. That's my job. Nothing changes that.''

''Oh, there's so much more than that. Don't you hear my chaos? I need you, Jack.''

The strange thing was she was bringing it off. Even with

the phony actorish repetitions of his name and all the rest, she seemed to be offering up all the sincerity in the world. He wondered if she believed it, if she could even tell the difference between what she believed *tactically,* for the moment, and what she truly believed. Or if there *was* any difference. It worked for her and that was what seemed to matter.

Somewhere under his caution he found he actually did care for her. So much confusion created a loyalty of some kind. But he was still angry, too.

"Right now I want a shower in really hot water."

"I'll scrub you with my own hands."

"I've already had one group shower today, thank you."

She tried to put the key in the ignition but dropped the ring on the floor and then gasped. She turned her palms upward as if checking their color and he could see her hands were trembling.

"Maybe I'd better drive."

"This hasn't happened to me for years."

"What is it?"

"You big Dudley Do-Right jerk." She turned her face to him and he saw tears that looked real enough. "I'm *in love.* And I probably threw away my chance with you, the only decent thing that's happened to me in years."

The Cherokee rocked with the rush of a bus going by too close.

"Don't give up just yet," he heard himself say softly after a moment. And his insides were getting pretty worked up, too. Once again his vanity had him picturing camera flashes and gawking crowds at the entrance to a nightclub. His anger grew transparent, faint, flickering to a wisp. Looking past it, he sensed entrée to a world that lived somewhere deep in the heart of dreams and, yes, it offered the promise of insulation from all disappointment.

AFTER all, she seemed to be able to drive well enough, and he decided not to worry what it meant about her self-control or her acting skills. Halfway up the steep stretch that was

just before Avenida Bluebird, though, she put her full
weight on the brake and brought the car to a stop three feet
from the curb, where the engine stalled. It took him a moment to see what she saw. Just ahead of the car a big tarantula ambled across the asphalt, delicately lifting and then
replanting pairs of hairy legs like some slow modern dance.
He knew tarantulas were ordinarily nocturnal, and he wondered what had chased it out of its lair.

He took her hand and she squeezed back, still trembling.
"Kind of you to stop," he said.

She smiled ruefully. "I know they're great jumpers. To
be honest, I was afraid it would jump on the car and then
come in a window."

The spider seemed to slow ominously and glance at
them, as if considering her version of things.

"Beat it," Jack Liffey snapped at the creature.

The instant he said it, the tarantula leaped, just vanished
into another reality. Lori Bright screamed and grabbed for
him and the car began to roll. She was too disoriented to
do anything, and he dived headfirst under the wheel to cram
his hand on the brake pedal. With the engine off, he
couldn't put enough pressure on the pedal to do much and
the car kept moving nightmare fashion as he pumped and
grunted and fought with his other arm for leverage. Finally
the car stopped with a thump that didn't sound too dangerous, just wheel against curb. He heard the ratcheting of
the parking brake.

When he came up she clutched at him, sobbing convulsively. "Oh, Jack, *save* me from everything. I've always
had to be strong. I don't *want* to be strong."

HE'D never noticed the carriage house on the far side of her
estate where the gravel drive fanned out. There were doors
for six vehicles, hacked out of the bougainvillea that looked
like it had been taking over for a generation. Once inside,
he saw the Mercedes, then a little yellow sports car back
in the dimness, and, improbably, a snowmobile or something similar under a tarp. It smelled of oil and cool damp.

They both sat unstirring for a while after she switched the car off, as if afraid to turn the page and go on reading.

"What did you and Lee say to one another?" he asked.

"What do cats say to dogs? We called each other names, it almost doesn't matter what names. It's an ancient feud, as old as daughters trying to separate from mothers."

"It might help if I knew."

She put a hand on his chest to stop him speaking and shook her head. "It would only make me look bad and I don't want to look bad in front of you."

"What if I mediate? You two need something like that."

"Can you be neutral?"

He thought about it, or let her see him thinking about it. He was pretty sure he could, but he realized she would probably see neutrality as a betrayal.

"I've wrecked enough things in my life," he said. "I'd like to try to fix one."

Without preface she tugged the loose skirt up and straddled him gently to sit on his lap. She looked down into his eyes. "If I made love more demurely, would you love me more?"

She tugged down the elastic neckline of the peasant blouse, slowly baring her shoulders and then the thin, almost transparent silk bra, the shimmery pink of ectoplasm.

"If I were less abandoned, would you respect me in the morning?"

"Possibly, but could you start this whole new demure regime tomorrow?"

He thought he heard her chuckle once just before she drew his face down hard into the heady perfume she'd taken the trouble to dab between her breasts. But maybe it wasn't a chuckle, after all, because the last thing intelligible he heard her say for quite a while was, "You must mean something to me because you *hurt* so much."

THE banner along their hallway had changed again. Now it said, BOUNCY BALL IS THE SOURCE OF ALL GOODNESS AND LIGHT. A big inflated peach hung from the ceiling and someone had suspended a motor from it that was rotating a small Sputnik model so it orbited the peach slowly with an eccentric little hiccup each rotation. This time Bruce Parfit led him into the cluttered office Michael Chen shared with Admiral Wicks. They worked back-to-back at their complex workstations against opposite walls, stacks of beige boxes, big color monitors, and open circuit boards trailing cables, all pasted over with Post-it notes.

Admiral Wicks had a row of vitamin bottles glued upside down onto the chalk rail of a whiteboard where someone had written DYSLEXIA RULES K.O. Some sort of mechanism seemed to be able to dispense a pill from each bottle into a slanted raceway.

Opposite, Michael Chen was stashing away a box of Dove bars beneath a printed card that said, "THE SLACK THAT IS NOT DESIRABLE IS NOT THE TRUE SLACK."—BOB, CHURCH OF THE SUBGENIUS. There was also a framed photograph of Chairman Mao with the inscription *To Michael, a world-class coder and a real killer Marxist-Leninist. Your pal Mao*.

They both grinned when they saw Jack Liffey, and Admiral Wicks seemed to have got over his grudge, whatever it was. Together they made the one-arm pumping gesture that tennis stars make when they win a big set. Two wine bottles were half-empty, and the programmers seemed pretty happy.

"We did the deed, *dude*. Feetch feetch. They fell over hard."

"Crash and burn!"

"Fear and loathing!"

"Laurel and Hardy!"

Admiral Wicks held his hands flat and Michael Chen came around to the front of the wheelchair and gave him a two-hand slap, then he turned to Jack Liffey, who shrugged and followed suit.

"Has Mitsuko just made a big donation to UNESCO?" Jack Liffey asked.

Admiral Wicks smiled and shook his head. "We took a

very different cyber route this segment.'' He was holding it back for some reason, savoring the secret.

''No fair being mysterious,'' Michael Chen said. ''It is *I* who gets to be inscrutable. *You* get rhythm.''

''Did I say anything about your scrotum?''

''No puns! Puns are brain-dead humor.'' Michael Chen closed his eyes, as if in pain.

''Why do you close your eyes, O wise Buddha?'' Admiral Wicks asked in some ritualized singsong. These two had roomed together too long, Jack Liffey thought.

''So the room will be empty.''

''I am enlightened, master.''

''I'm not,'' Jack Liffey said.

Parfit dumped a can of some Australian beer into a tall glass so it foamed right up to the lip, but stopped as if by pure will. ''I'll tell you what it was, mate. Mitsuko's home office had a damn good firewall on their old mainframe and we couldn't get into their files. We couldn't get much of anything out of the heart of their computer system. But we could read between the lines to see the kind of equipment they were using. Trust the Japanese. Out in R-and-D land, their design and production tools are always cutting edge, but you can count on them being two generations behind where they do the accounting and billing. It was a real dinosaur pen.''

''IBM 360s, can you believe it?'' Michael Chen said. ''From the elder days. Card wallopers. And they had the old fourteen-inch magnetic drives. DataStars.''

''You've seen them in movies. They look like top-loading washing machines.''

They were all grinning, fidgety, as if they'd been doing some kind of speed under the wine. A pager on the table went off, buzzing and then hopping around like a wounded insect. It killed all conversation as they watched it with a kind of morbid fascination, and then Michael Chen laughed convulsively and the laugh seemed to shut the pager off.

''The drives've got big heavy sets of disks called media

packs,'' Admiral Wicks explained. "But DataStars have always had one flaw."

"Tell it!"

"One *little* flaw!"

There was another round of palm slapping.

"Ever seen an out-of-balance washing machine?"

"Ever seen an electric typewriter walking across a desk?"

"If you get just the right seek pattern . . . say, a nice slow access one way and then send it the other way on a fast seek across the whole width of the disk—"

"All the way to east hyperspace—"

"Stick-slip, stick-slip—"

"Angular mo-*men*-tum—"

"The whole washing machine gets up and walks! There is a legend that hackers in days of old used to write seek routines to race their DataStars across the room."

"Mitsuko had eight of them, mate. Most computer rooms run twelve-hour shifts, three-day weeks. We hit them just before shift change when the ops were all drowsy."

"We hosed them! Film at eleven!"

"Moby hack!"

"What lossage! Tramp-tramp-tramp, went the drives!"

Michael Chen did a little war dance around the wheelchair while Bruce Parfit picked up the story again. "We called up an hour after we sent our seek program into the drives and said we were tech support from DataStar and we'd heard there was trouble with the drives. The ops were hysterical. Two of the drives had walked up to the mainframe and wedged there, one had walked to the door in the computer room and jammed it shut, so the next shift had to come down a ladder from a crawl space, one broke the feed tray off their high-speed printer, one fell into a hole where they had the floor up for cabling, and one just kept hopping around in circles like an old dosser with a hotfoot. The others didn't get off the mark for some reason, but who cares?"

"Tell him the rest, tell him!"

The two younger men made hysterical pumping gestures, jabbing both arms in sync a few times and then alternating them, as Parfit just leaned against the whiteboard and beamed. For an instant Jack Liffey thought of the racists doing their Maori karate dance for the Jamaican.

"We told them our tech support had a simple software fix for their problem, and we gave them a bogus fix. *We can do it all again tomorrow!*"

Jack Liffey let them hoot and pump again for a while and then he tugged on Bruce Parfit's linen jacket. "A word."

He led Jack Liffey into his office. "You have that stilled look of a man getting ready to go to war," the Australian said.

"My war's just starting." He hesitated a moment, watching a bobbing bird toy on a cabinet dip forward to stab its red beak into a tumbler of water. "You're not my client, but I figure you owe me something for getting them off your back."

"What do I owe you?"

"I want an ounce of coke."

COMING out into the afternoon breeze, something up Little Santa Monica caught his eye. Two boys with Mickey Mouse ears were standing in the dirt between Little Santa Monica and Big Santa Monica where the Red Cars had once run. They were twenty yards apart and each had a fistful of those square metallic helium balloons. As he watched, the two of them shouted out a countdown and released a pair of balloons, with some gossamer thread between them. They wailed and hooted and tried to direct the balloons with their body English, like golfers on a long putt. Then he saw they were aiming for the high-tension power lines. He winced as the trailing balloons nearly caught on the wires, but wind took them too far east.

The boys trotted westward. Up the street he noticed the Dirty Lingerie shop. The crowds were gone but a big poster in the window said, MONDAY SCANTY PANTY SIGNING.

BASEBALL HEROES. His imagination wasn't up to it.

He heard a boy's screech of delight and looked up in time to see a torrent of sparks dropping out of the sky like slag in a steel mill. All the balloons took off at once and the boys fled. He decided it was time to get out of there.

IT was going dusk as he got back to his condo. The table lamp on its timer was on through the curtain, as it should have been, but there was a brown envelope by his door that shouldn't have been there. He picked it up and felt it for a moment, the rectangular shape within, wondering about explosive devices, but then ripped it open to find a tape cassette. It was a Bob Marley tape called *Burnin'* and the meaning was pretty obvious.

Then he found the dead bolt wasn't set and a chill went all the way up his arm. He froze with his hand on the key and listened, but heard nothing. He always set the dead bolt, a habit as rigid as logic.

He pushed the door open and waited out of the line of fire, wondering how a flamboyant Jamaican could have got past the guarded gate into the Astaire. There was a small sound from within, just enough to cause the hackles on his neck to rise. Then Loco stuck his muzzle into the light and gnarred softly.

Jack Liffey sighed and stooped to pat him.

"Jack, is that you?" It was Marlena. "I'm just feeding Loco."

By the door he saw the white plastic trash bag out of his kitchen wastebasket, tied off and waiting to go out. She'd probably dusted, too, and washed out the sinks.

"Thanks, Mar."

Sure enough, she was wearing his kiss-the-cook apron and had a sponge in her hand. It was half-annoying and half-touching. She smiled and licked her lips in the uncertain way she had, and all of a sudden her sanity and ordinariness and even this mundane way of laying claims on him seemed very, very appealing.

The least he could do was offer her a drink. "The least I can do is offer you a drink."

"Thank you, I will have some wine. You have a hard day on the hunt?"

He laughed. After Lori Bright's mannered dialogue, it was metaphor back where it belonged: tamed and docile. "I shot two gazelles, but the lions got away."

He put on a teakettle for himself and then hunted under the old supermarket bags in the tiny pantry and found the Cabernet he'd been saving for special guests.

She put her hand on his shoulder. "It's good to see you, *querido*." She drew close and then he heard her sniff Lori Bright on him and she stiffened.

"Oh."

"I'm sorry, Marlena. I'm caught up in something I can't help right now."

She nodded fast. "Uh-huh. I know."

"Remember when you had a thing for Quinn and you just had to do it? It's like a poker hand you got by some strange luck and you're not sure if it's good enough or if it's even the right thing at all, but you've got to play it to find out."

She didn't seem very interested in making analogies. "I don't know about poker. Are you in love?"

He thought about it a moment. He didn't know about love, but he knew he wasn't going to walk away from Lori Bright until something made him. Jack Liffey turned to look at her, at the pain and uncertainty in her big brown eyes, and he held her forearms. "Imagine a young Ramon Novarro walks in now and sweeps you off your feet."

She shook her head. She didn't want to play imagine games, either.

"What movie star made your knees weak?"

"Burt Lancaster."

"Okay, imagine it's Burt and he's fallen into your life, fallen bang into your bed like he just dropped in through a skylight, and he's being *very* charming and seductive and he says he wants you."

"Is she good to you?"

"I've got to see it out."

"You're better than that, Mr. Jack Liffey."

"No, I'm not."

There was a sudden bark and growl as if another dog had attacked Loco. They both looked around and Loco's pale haunches backed trembling into sight, then his fore-paws and then the powerful jaws, dragging the remains of one of Jack Liffey's only decent pairs of shoes, a black Rockport wing tip. The heel was chewed away and the solepad protruded like an orange tongue.

"Oh, damn."

She took only a glance at the dog and shoe and then dismissed them out of existence and looked back at him. He tried to enfold her in his arms, but she brought her elbows in stiffly between them to keep a distance.

"We're good friends," he said, feeling dull and stupid all of a sudden. "That won't change unless you want it to. I've just got to do this thing."

And he had to deal with Terror Pennycooke and G. Dan Hunt. He couldn't go on living with bombs in every en-velope.

18

A TUMBLEWEED WITH TEETH

HE WOKE UP TO A TREMOR SO FAINT HE DIDN'T KNOW WHETHER it was a little jiggly aftershock or just the woman upstairs trundling open the sliding-glass door to her deck. He held his breath, waiting, heard a tiny mewling sound, and saw Loco nose the bedroom door open and scamper almost noiselessly into the closet. One vote for earth movement, he thought, but there were no car alarms and he was not convinced of the mystical power of animals to herald seismic events, so he could still interpret his waking as the consequence of a half stumble in a dream or of a barely subperceptual local occurrence.

Definitely not an omen. There were no omens, that was an article of faith. There were just events one after another and a dog that was wound too tight.

The clock said five. The paper would be there, so he got up. For a long time getting up without a drug of some kind, without even a place to belong effortlessly and reassuringly, had been a real ordeal, but it was getting easier. Eventually everybody lived in some relation to detachment, and the differences were mainly in the ways you came to it. For a minute or two, drowned now in the familiarity of his surroundings, he didn't even think about Lori Bright.

"Loco, you eat any more shoes, I'll trade you in for a Chihuahua," he said mildly to the closet door. Marlena would like that, he thought. She fancied the little rat-dog breeds that were all vibration and drool.

"You hear me?"

There was no reply. He thought of playing Marley's *Burnin'*.

HE dropped by his office to get the .45 that he'd put back in the big hollowed-out *Oxford Companion to English Literature*. Marlena Cruz was on the landing outside his office watching her nephew Rogelio tape gold decal letters above a blue crayon line on the glass door. For a year Jack Liffey had only had a posterboard in the window with his name and livelihood stenciled across it. The decal letters seemed to be following the model of his poster, and the top row had already been glued to the glass:

LIFFEY INVESTIGATIONS

The second row, smaller, seemed to be going up temporarily for alignment:

WE FIND MISSI

Thank God they hadn't been able to find a big eyeball.

"Shouldn't it say Spade and Liffey?" he said.

"Huh?" the kid said.

He gave her a one-arm hug her for the gift. "Or do you prefer Liffey and Cruz?"

"That could be arranged," she said in a throaty voice.

He shouldn't have said it. "Hold up a sec, Rocky." Jack Liffey unlocked the door and slipped in ahead of the *N*. He left the light off and found the big book by feel, using his body to shield the operation from sight of the door until he got the pistol under his shirttail, where it cut uncomfortably into his leg. That couldn't be helped.

He wished she would make fewer claims on him, but there was nothing he could do about it and the devotion was poignant in its way and warmed him a little when it wasn't worrying him. He came back out.

"Now when Rocky goes missing," he said, "I guess I've got to track him down for free."

"I ain't going nowhere."

"Give me a kiss, Jack."

He held her and she took the opportunity to press hard against him and kiss longingly, and it was all he could do to torque around and keep her from feeling the pistol. He pulled back, but she still clung. Finally she let him go and talked a bit about some designs she could have done for his sign. Over the railing, he watched a homeless woman in a half-dozen overcoats make her way out of the bushes up the street. She clapped her hands as if trying to jump-start her circulation.

He wondered—if things went really bad and if he started free-falling, and if the last of the money went south, and nothing would break clean for him, he wondered if anything would arrest his fall before he hit the streets like that. He made a mental note to toss an old blanket and some money over the shrubs for her.

"Thanks for the sign, Marlena. It's kind of you."

"It's nothing at all."

"No, everything is something."

THE big bungalow on Ridge Glen was still for sale and the green Explorer was still in the drive. He thought of doing something cute but instead just stuck the .45 under his belt and rang the bell hard. It was almost nine.

The man swung it open, tugging up multicolored wrestler's pants with one hand.

"Hi, there, Tyrone." Jack Liffey lifted a shirttail to show him the pistol.

There wasn't any fear in the man's eyes, but definitely some consternation. "Bwai, tings dread naow."

"I hope you didn't kill the Nazi boys." He came in as Terror Pennycooke backed away.

"No, but dey step like hell back to dere own place."

Jack Liffey tossed the Marley tape on a little table by
the door. Pennycooke glanced at it without a sign he recognized it.

"I-an'-I no big man in dis ting, just a scuffle for my
bread. You no see it, Babylon?"

"Sit." He took out the .45 just to make sure there
weren't any disagreements. The man sat with his back
against a stack of identical cardboard boxes that said they
were Sony MD-1401 stereo receivers. The rest of the room
was jam-packed with appliances, TVs, computers, and mi-
crowaves, but these were all used.

"G. Dan tell you to keep after me?"

His eyes looked around, as if for a way out of his pre-
dicament, but he said nothing.

"If you escape this in one piece, it's only because I'm
a little sensitive about the image of a white man beating up
a black man in the home of Western imperialism. G. Dan
Hunt told you to shake me up, right?"

"You a-penetrait."

"The war's already over and your side lost. The only
thing left for me to decide is whether to send you home on
a plane or in a box."

Jack Liffey found a couple of old IBM Selectrics among
the inventory and scowled at them. He was careful to keep
the .45 on its target while he ferried the heavy Selectrics,
one at a time, across the room and set them on either side
of Tyrone Pennycooke. Then he took two pairs of Peerless
handcuffs from his back pocket and tossed them to the man.

Tyrone Pennycooke said something that sounded like,
"Raas klat licks."

"You know, Terror, I bet you can talk Standard English,
if you try hard."

"Fock you."

Jack Liffey laughed. "See how easy it is. Cuff your
wrists to the typewriters, right through the frame. Nothing
personal, it's just to slow you down a little. Conservation
of momentum, like that."

"You tink I a fockin' puppet?"

"I think you're fuckin' *dead,* friend. Don't push it."

They locked eyes and at last Tyrone Pennycooke decided to handcuff his wrists to the two Selectrics. "That'll put you in real good with your boss. We're going to go see him."

He called first, just to make sure the man was home, and Hunt was curiously subdued on the phone but agreed to meet.

THE big Jamaican and the two Selectrics were a tight fit in the passenger-side bucket seat of the Concord, but there weren't going to be any sudden moves.

"I-man nah end my life lockdown wit no typewriters."

"Just take it easy and you'll be fine."

A station wagon was parked at the corner, and a half-dozen scrubbed white boys with flattops and skinny ties were lined up at the tailgate where an old man with flyaway hair was breaking open cartons and apportioning what looked like big presentation Bibles, an armload to each. He wondered what peculiar turn of logic had a Bible company using cracker boys to sell King James rhetoric to middle-class blacks, if it was some curious appeal to reverse guilt. But he didn't think about it for long, and he drove past the station wagon and headed north.

"Dis a bitch naow."

"Just let it go."

It was twenty minutes to the blue glass mid-rise on an unfashionable stretch of Sunset—a legendary L.A. distance. You said anything close was twenty minutes, and anything far was forty-five. Farther than that was out of town. The building looked like an upended Kleenex box, wedged between a banner-draped lot called Muscle Machines that sold big candy-colored Detroit cars of the seventies—Dodge Hemis and Chevy 409s—and a strip mall with a Chinese takeout, a liquor store, and a ninety-nine-cent store. There was no guard in the empty lobby. He herded Terror Pennycooke ahead of him, the man's big fingers hooked onto the heavy typewriters, pushed him into the scuffed, piss-smelling elevator, and hit eleven.

The doors on eleven were all solid wood, so there was no chance of catching the silhouette of Sidney Greenstreet or Peter Lorre through frosted glass. The door at the end said G. DAN HUNT, PERSONAL SERVICES.

The Jamaican's eyes were puffy and angry, and he seemed to realize this was actually going to go down. "I-an'-I gwaan fock you up good."

"Sure you will."

There was no anteroom and they went straight into a cluttered single office. The big desk was sideways to the door, but what you saw right away on the far wall was a life-size photograph of a grinning John Wayne arm in arm with a fat man on a boat dock beside a big cabin cruiser. The fat man, twenty years on, was there in the flesh, too, behind the desk, the Humpty-Dumpty from Musso's.

In the center of the desk there was a large revolver with ostentatious notches on its wood grip. The Jamaican started to say something, but the man just shook his head and shushed him. Then he turned a little and put a foot up on a drawer.

"So this is what makes the goat trot," he said to Jack Liffey.

"You got your big gun and I got my big gun." Jack Liffey patted his hip without showing it off. "But none of us is going to go shooting the place up. That's just to establish the balance of power. Why don't you have a seat, too, Terror?"

The Jamaican looked like he was about to blow, but the typewriters were tiring him out and at last he subsided into a hard chair in the corner to set his burden down. He started to speak again as he sat.

"For you someday cyan come a dance widdout no gun inna you waist—"

"Shut up, Tyrone." G. Dan Hunt didn't even look at the man as he spoke.

"I assume you've heard from Japan by now," Jack Liffey said. "They've probably had a couple bad days."

He didn't admit to any calls. Jack Liffey glanced over at Tyrone Pennycooke, who looked like he was going to be sick. The man's eyes shifted from one typewriter to the other, then back to the first, as if he was having trouble counting to two.

"What's the plan?"

"Let's talk about him first. We skip the arson, the assault, the kidnapping, the extortion, we just forget about it. You give him a one-way ticket back to the Big J. I figure that's probably negotiable."

"You got the whole secret of life right there, guy. Knowing what's negotiable and what ain't."

Pennycooke rustled a bit, but the big man hissed at him.

"The only other thing I want, I want to know what this shit is *really* all about. I'm tired of being the only guy in town who's in the dark."

G. Dan Hunt shrugged. "You ever hear of Tim-Tam?"

Jack Liffey just stared at him.

"You've seen him, you just don't know it. He's the little grinning round-face Jap kid with the baseball hat. You see him on burger wrappers and in the window at the 7-Eleven. Tim-Tam is the biggest fucking video game on the Omega Game system that Mitsuko owns. I might add that video games now pull in more money, gross, than the entire fucking Hollywood film industry. And Tim-Tam is like Mario or that hedgehog thing, he's a whole franchise all by himself. I believe Tim-Tam goes to rescue his sister, who's held by a bunch of bad guys in a dangerous world full of things you got to stomp along the way. Sort of like Terror, here. I think you got the picture."

Jack Liffey nodded.

"Was a lawsuit between Monogram, that Mitsuko owns, and this Australian character that runs PropellorHeads. It was a nasty business about some breach of contract, that doesn't concern us. Mitsuko decides to settle quick and in the settlement they give the Ozzie rights to use Tim-Tam and his pals in a CD-ROM game. Mitsuko doesn't make

CD-ROMs anyway and they figure he'll never get to first base with it, most of these games die in a week, and at worst, if he brings it off, the deal is publicity for the crown jewel of their game system. Any kids that want more Tim-Tam then got to whine to Dad to buy an Omega system.''

Jack Liffey remembered the display in the Propellor-Heads lobby, with a little kid on several screens zipping along in some imaginary universe. For a moment the whole world seemed to lose its reality, like a noun you repeated until it was only a sound. It didn't make any sense to him that that ridiculous little cartoon image could have touched off a whole business war that spilled out into a shooting war. Then he looked at Hunt's pistol on the desk and it came back into focus and seemed real enough.

''Well, the Ozzie is pretty good. He makes a game the kids love, and they build up one of Tim-Tam's minor enemies into a big deal in the game. It's this thing called a Zomboid, like a tumbleweed with a big mouth and big teeth that's always tryin'a roll up and bite your ass. Turns out the kids like what he's done with the Zomboid. They love fighting it off, and they make running away from Zomboids a kind of cult. So far, we're okay. But the Ozzie figures he's developed this thing enough that he owns it now and he makes three more games starring the Zomboid. Calls it something new, Mr. Zoom, or something. Word filters across the Pacific and the guys over in Japan have a shit fit. He licensed *one* game and he's building an empire on it, and to make things worse, *their* Zomboid isn't called Mr. Zoom, so the spin-off value isn't standing up and saluting for their flag.''

G. Dan Hunt swiveled and put his feet square on the floor.

''These guys in Japan don't even think in money, you know. They think in *face*. Maybe it's living on an island like the fucking Sicilians breeds all this permanently touchy dignity and shit. Anyway, these Nips need some way to get their face back. This is where they call in Monogram, which they own over here, and tell them, do something about it, and Monogram calls me because my dad and I been fixin' things for them since Lana Turner started footsying with mobsters, and they tell me, do something about it and they tell me not to be too gentle, neither. And I call Tyrone here. The *real* Mr. Zomboid. You don't got to tell Tyrone, don't be too gentle.''

He put his pistol into the drawer where his feet had been and shut it. Jack Liffey turned and glared at Tyrone Pennycooke. ''This whole thing was over a cartoon tumbleweed with teeth.''

''You, I wouldn't mind working with,'' G. Dan Hunt said. ''There's something of the old days about you. Maybe that's how we negotiate our way out of this, set up some kind of contract work.''

''That's already taken care of,'' Jack Liffey said. ''All I want is him on his way back to Trenchtown, then I lay off you and Monogram and Mitsuko and we're even. It's not a lot to ask for you guys having done me some real damage.''

Jack Liffey took out the plastic film tube with G. Dan Hunt watching him like a hawk. He pried off the plastic lid and displayed the white powder that filled the little canister the size of a thirty-five-millimeter film can. He dipped his finger and leaned over to wipe it on the Jamaican's nostrils. Tyrone Pennycooke's eyes went wide and his head snapped back.

''He'll report the quality.''

''Wooo, mon,'' the Jamaican said.

The top few millimeters of the can held about two hundred dollars' worth of Bruce Parfit's cocaine, and under that was about nine cents' worth of talcum powder, but if he was careful they'd never know that. Jack Liffey went straight to the filing cabinet, yanked it open, and whisked some powder across the files inside. He blew on it to spread it around. Then he hit the next drawer. G. Dan Hunt watched as he dumped a little more on the big easy chair and then sprayed what was left across the carpet.

''Vacuum all you want. If I ever see you or him again,

there's gonna be drug-sniffing dogs alerting on all the shit you own. Have we got a deal?''

G. Dan Hunt watched him for a few moments neutrally, then his big round head tilted back and back until it looked like he had only one chin, and he laughed, jiggling and rippling. ''We had a deal this morning when somebody in Monogram called me up, crying and whining, to get out from under. Get the fuck out of here. I couldn't work with you, Liffey, you're a comic.''

19

A BIG ONE

THE MAN WAS DYED PURPLE FROM HEAD TO TOE. HE WORE
only a loincloth and that was purple, too, and he stood at
the corner, pinioned between two policemen who seemed
to enjoy snapping him back and forth a bit as if they were
toying with the idea of whipsawing him into traffic. Jack
Liffey came to a stop at the stop sign only a foot from the
purple man, and the man's eyes sought him out through the
glary windshield, startling white flashes against the violet,
eyes that were appealing to him for something. Jack Liffey
wondered if the cops were more offended by the aesthetics
or the morals of the situation.

The man lunged forward a foot, or was propelled, and
his belly brushed the Concord to leave a purple smudge on
the fender before the policemen yanked him back. Jack Liffey had no idea what a purple man would want from him.
One policeman pointed straight though the windshield and
gestured him on peremptorily and he decided to go. L.A.
was like that, but how long could you go on using that
excuse?

Within a block he had to brake hard to avoid three large
dogs that sprinted out of nowhere onto Sunset. The largest
trailed a leash and the others seemed to be snapping at his
heels like dog bounty hunters. Jack Liffey waited a moment, expecting a breathless owner to appear, but no one
did.

His hand shook a little. It wasn't the dogs or the purple man. It was Lori Bright. He'd phoned to tell her he was on his way to get her daughter, and her voice had immediately taken him right up over the high side. He still had no real handle on what it was she did to him, but he could tell her celebrity ruffled something down deep in him. Whenever his mind came to rest on thoughts of her, he experienced one of those vague dream feelings that you couldn't quite put your finger on, amalgams of desire and guilt and who-knew-what-else. In fact, he'd had a literal dream about her, just an image really. She was looking past him at something over his shoulder and he was waving both arms, trying to get her attention.

All in all, it was mostly the sex that was real, he thought, that was where they made contact, but even that was spoiled by all her games and extravagance.

A car honked angrily behind him and he realized he was stopped in the middle of Sunset. "Get off the dime, bud," he heard faintly. He threw up his hands to apologize and drove over to the Hollywood Freeway to head north for Saugus.

The traffic was light and fast over the Cahuenga Pass and he brought himself back to the present. Driving was always the best tranquilizer. He knew he should have been happy. He'd outwitted a big Japanese *zaibatsu*, and beaten their American surrogates, and all he had left to do was what he'd been paid for in the first place, talking a confused teenager into coming home. He might even get enough of a bonus to make up some of his delinquent child support. It all seemed solid. Everything seemed exact and finite, which in his experience was just about when you were going to drop into the shit, but he couldn't find the hole in it.

SHE'D cleared out a big area of the living room and thrown down a plastic tarp. In the middle of the tarp was an easel with a large canvas clamped fast and she painted on it impetuously with a stubby brush and a lot of browns. Some spooky music was going very loud on a boom box that was out of reach of the spatters.

"Where's Godzilla?"

She rocked a bit on her feet as she slashed more brown across the canvas. "You mean Big Danny? He's over at Cal-Arts in one of their edit bays. You ever seen nonlinear editing? It's really fierce. You digitize all your footage and store it on these huge hard disks and then you can work through your movie deciding how to cut things together and you never even really make any cuts. The machine just remembers where you want to do a cut or a dissolve or something else, and you can go back and watch it over anytime and change it. Even a little smidge of a change or you can move the sound or put in another shot. You know, maybe someday everybody can take home some digital multiversion of a movie and make their own choices at home. You can let King Kong live if you want to or let Rhett stay with Scarlett."

"Some of us like to let the artist do that!" He had to holler to be heard and it felt absurd.

"Hey, give the viewer a choice and that makes them an artist, too. It's called deconstruction."

"It's called noise!"

She waved her hand with a little snap and somehow the music muted. In the dead echoing silence, she whispered dramatically, "You mean that noise?"

"No. As in physics."

"Oh, you mean random data. That's a cruel judgment on democracy."

She waved again and the other noise swelled into a kind of primitive chant. She worked in time to the chant, lurching into the canvas and recoiling.

"Come talk to your mom, Lee. It's time."

"I've decided not to go. You just head-tripped me into it, man. The worst thing in the world, the absolute worst, is getting yourself bored. I've got nothing to learn from that woman, and as far as I'm concerned, that's all she

wrote and the fat lady sang, if you like mangled metaphors.''

"I love them. We made promises to each other."

"I can't do it. She pushes all my buttons."

It was ironic considering how much he'd risked to keep
his end of the promise, but he didn't think simply insisting
would cut much ice with her.

He turned the boom box down a notch so he could hear
himself think, then noticed the oak barrel at the edge of the
tarp with a plank on it, the sort of impromptu table an
Impressionist might have set up to hold a pear, two apples,
and a red vase, but someone had set out three toy cars and
a fifties-style cocktail shaker. The shaker gizmo caught his
eye because it was the one his own father had used during
a brief period in the Eisenhower era when the old man had
gone back to JC to try to complete his education and leave
longshoring behind. The martinis were an affectation he'd
picked up for a while from a philosophy professor, but in
the end he'd liked the martinis a lot more than the books.
"Can't do it anymore, Jack, and that's the truth," the old
man had said. "I just can't sit in a room full of nineteen-
year-olds and listen to some dried-up asshole pontificate."
Patience had never been the old man's long suit, any more
than his own.

He picked up the martini shaker and admired the fatter
waist and then the narrowing to its silver top, a bit like a
Lava lamp. Recipes for mixed drinks like daiquiris and
manhattans were printed in red on the glass, mixed in with
line drawings of happy homemakers, and he could feel the
raised ridges of the drawings under his fingers. It was hard
to resurrect the fifties without conjuring up a sensation of
some rank evil festering away in the dark, back in the closet
behind the poodle skirts and angora sweaters, a big maggot
of fear that lay in wait under all that conformity. He had a
physical chill.

"You're painting the music," he suggested.

"You got it. It just comes. Maybe it's a cheat, you know,
I don't do anything, I just listen."

"Show me," he said. He cut off her CD and swapped in a different disc out of the pile. "Just tell me what you see."

The music was Baroque harpsichord, he had no idea who. She posed, eyes closed and a hand ostentatiously stretched out, as if for Prince Charming to plant a kiss on it.

"Red rolling hills," she said quickly. "There's a brighter orange light coming from out of sight beyond the crests, and a kind of speckling that shifts and darts in the air like Brownian movement."

He stopped it and put in a new disc, a woman wailing unintelligibly against a slow beat. Really weird stuff, he thought, and wondered if this was what they were listening to these days.

"Blue and green bars that pulse against one another as if one set is breathing in while the other is breathing out. They taper a bit as they go up."

He swapped discs again. A faster beat, with a strong backbeat, and then he got a momentary chill from a Jamaican voice.

"Big patches of color. It's too irregular to describe very well. The biggest is silver and then orange and yellow. The edges are ragged and there's a black rectangle to one side."

He went on for a while, working through the haphazard stack of CDs and sampling tracks. She seemed to enjoy it. She put down her brush and sat on a metal stool, then rested her forehead on a palm, like a clairvoyant concentrating.

"Fringes and tassels of a lot of bright colors, and they're rippling like in a breeze. That's really awesome."

"Yeah, I bet," he said. "Last time I played that piece, though, it was a big blue balloon with purple behind it."

He saw her stiffen.

"Let's try one more," he said, with terrible friendliness.

"I'm tired of this."

He fired up the CD and she sat in silence as the female crooner begged for relief from heartache.

"Cat got your tongue?"

She turned away from him.

"Let's see, was this the yellow turnip or the boogie-woogie blue?"

"Eat shit and die."

"You're not synesthetic, are you? It was just something to make yourself feel interesting, like seeing flying saucers."

"I *used to* see color. It went away."

"I used to have a good job, so we're even. We both feel abandoned by our destiny."

She stood up and rocked a little on her pigeon toes, glaring at him. "Are you making fun of me?"

"A little."

"Is all this easy for you? Manipulating people, humiliating little girls, lusting after movie stars?"

"Which of those questions would you like me to answer?"

"The lust would do."

"The lust is none of your business."

She grinned a surprisingly feral grin. "A*ha*! Mom's got you, too. The bitch goddess never fails."

"Let's go have a talk with her."

"I guess I have to, don't I?"

"Yup."

She studied the mess of browns on the canvas unhappily. "I may as well. I'm not much of a painter and Danny's got the movie under control." She considered, as if one more good reason might just push her over the edge. "And I'm not very happy here. I need to be someplace where I can be happier."

She sealed up the paint cans and tubes carefully, then smiled apologetically. "You never know, I might be back."

JUST as they came outside a big goat kicked out a couple of pickets in the fence next door and squeezed through into the weeds where a sidewalk should have been. It offered a terrified and bewildered bleat at its freedom and bucked once, like a basketball player setting up to change direction in midair. When it came down, it headed up the ratty street as fast as it could go, trotting a bit, then working its hind legs together like a kangaroo, then trotting again, as if it was trying to relearn all the gaits at once.

"Nature is out of joint," he said.

"Or something is rotten in the state of California."

He watched the goat diminishing up the street and thought about how seeing the animal burst its bonds like that made him feel the way he hadn't felt in a long time, that maybe it wasn't a good idea to try to control everything. It probably wasn't a bad lesson, but on the whole it wasn't his nature to let things develop at their own pace. It meant the really bad stuff would probably catch you with your pants down.

He took San Fernando Road out of the scrubby town, past a sign that told him William S. Hart had once lived up a hilltop, and then he caught 14 and took it down into the spaghetti of high overpasses where it joined I-5 south, the Clarence Wayne Dean Interchange, named for the poor motorcycle cop who'd ridden off into blackness when the old overpass had come down in the 1994 Northridge quake. Lee Borowsky had gone quiet for a while, brooding over something or other.

"Cat got your tongue?"

"I was thinking I'm too close to Mom to see who she is. It's like trying to study an elephant from an inch away. All you know is it's gray and rough and it's got coarse hair and it smells pretty bad, and you don't think it could be any other way because it's all you know. It's a dumb comparison. What's my mom like to you?"

"You can't get past being her daughter. I can't get past the fact she's a movie star."

"So what?"

"Maybe in your world that's a so-what. But I was just a poor kid from the harbor. Where I grew up, most of the men worked with their hands and kids could play in the street after dark and divorce was pretty much unthinkable and everything that mattered, all the people that *Life* wrote about, belonged to some other world far away. When I saw her, her face was twenty feet high on the screen at the Warners.''

''But you've seen her now as a person.''

''And every time it carries all that baggage.''

All of a sudden he had a revelation and it all seemed so simple—all that weird guilt he felt toward her. Back in his youth, Miss Lori Bright had lived in the magic faraway world of the powerful and carefree, courted by princes and kings. Now he was stepping across the magic line to touch her, and what he saw was a sad and anxious, slightly over-weight woman who clung fiercely to the few quirks that still made her seem extraordinary to herself. It was his own effrontery crossing over that line that annihilated her magic. The relation between what he saw and what he remembered refused to settle, and in that tension was his heartache.

''Are you in love with her?''

''God only knows.''

''Be careful of her, Jack.''

He didn't think he'd ever invited Lee to use his first name. He didn't really mind, but it seemed a pretty big leap for a fifteen-year-old.

As they descended into the San Fernando Valley she grew less intense. She started jabbering again, pointing out the sights, telling the names of the malls and the larger shops, and recounting adventures she had had hither and beyond. At the Ventura, he headed east, and he was just onto the Valley end of the Hollywood Freeway when it happened. They say being in a moving vehicle is one of the best places to ride it out.

''Jack!''

He was cursing the Concord, thinking the engine was acting up outlandishly, when he saw a Thunderbird slew across his path and come to a stop on the shoulder. He braked in time, but a minivan wasn't so lucky and plowed into the rear of an old Camaro. All of a sudden cars were slantwise all over the road and the road itself was bucking and rolling in a way that made no rational sense.

He heard a noise like the whistle of a teapot and thought he saw a flash of light and all he could think of was a junior-high teacher bellowing ''Drop!'' and a mushroom cloud rising in the distance. Then the car, which he'd thought he'd got safely stopped, jolted up and down, bottoming hard like an elevator that had hesitated a floor too soon before free-falling the last few feet. Something roared in his ears. Lee Borowsky threw herself onto his side of the car and clung to him, and he stuck an arm through the steering wheel for grip as if they might be bucked right out the open window. As his head jerked involuntarily on his neck he regained enough sense to realize what it was and that if they were still okay now, they'd probably live through it.

There was a starburst of sparks up ahead where a power cable tore out of a pylon above the freeway and he thought he saw a palm tree hurled straight up in the air, though it seemed pretty unlikely. When he got his neck stabilized and looked the other way, a jet of fire was cutting right through a house down the freeway embankment. The violent shaking had ebbed to a side-to-side roll like a slow ferry in a swell. A quarter mile ahead, the power pylon leaned at a precarious angle and he watched with awe as one more joggle of the earth sent it over in slow motion. Girders snapped like toothpicks as the big frame broke up across the entire width of the road, trailing cables and gobs of sparkler flare. To the south, the Hollywood Hills had disappeared into a haze of dust. He guessed the hills were probably still there under all the dust that had huffed into the air.

Lee Borowsky's hands worked hard on his biceps and she pressed against him with her eyes shut.

''It's okay, little one. It was just what it was.''

Just when he thought it was truly over, there was another quick tremor, and another, and he realized the aftershocks would go on for months, diminishing little by little but now and again offering up a nastier shiver as a tease and reminder. Months later, aftershocks would still start nightmares throughout the city and spook those pets that weren't already out of their minds. He thought of Loco and then put the dog right out of mind. There were more important worries.

He looked at his watch: 2:40. Maeve and Kathy were both still in their schools, and after a generation of study commissions and rebuilding they were the safest buildings in the city. Marlena would have been down in her mailbox shop. Nothing he could do could help her. The phones would be down for hours and clogged for days after that and the major roads would probably be impassable.

He felt a strange nausea of dislocation. Things wouldn't be the same now, and he didn't know how he felt about that. His heart thumped away in his chest like a trapped animal. People were getting out of their cars to look around, unsteady on their feet. An old couple had made it up to the chain-link along the edge of the freeway and had their arms around one another, sobbing. A man in a leather jacket stood in the bed of a pickup waving a single finger up at the sky and shouting something that was lost in the din of car alarms and horns. Children bursting out of a yellow school bus were applauding and frolicking. Just past the off-ramp an old VW bus had slid into a Texaco truck that was beginning to brew up and he decided he'd better get off the freeway while he could.

Jack Liffey extricated his arm from the small, tight hands and started the stalled car.

"That was a big one okay, but not *the* big one." As if words would normalize it. Though he noticed his mind shied away from one word. Earthquake.

She put her head down and covered it with her arms, as if to make it all go away. He backed and inched the car around the Thunderbird. The surface of the freeway was cracked up like a dried mudflat, but none of the gaps seemed more than an inch or two wide. Far away there were plumes of black smoke and he heard a steady pop-popping from somewhere, like popcorn in a skillet. A policeman was working at righting his toppled motorcycle, leaning against it with all his weight. Not far off the road he could see a ten-story glass building leaning to one side, its grid of rectangles squashed out of true and a lot of the glass broken out.

Jack Liffey steered the car slowly down the Laurel Canyon off-ramp, and as he descended he lost his perspective on the city. Damage became local, personal. A chimney had fallen tidily across a front lawn, a family crouched in the street, craning their necks in every direction. A four-story apartment house was only three stories high, having collapsed neatly on its dozen parked cars. He was the only vehicle moving, and then he remembered the radio and switched it on. It crackled anxiously. Long ago the tuner had frozen up on an all-news AM station, but it seemed to be off the air. He turned the volume way down but left it on.

A big frame house was wrenched off its foundation, as if rotated a few degrees from true, and he felt a chill thinking of similar houses.

"Lee, honey. We're okay. You can sit up."

She sat back and uncovered her eyes, but there was something crazy inside, unfocused. It reminded him of the look he'd seen on Loco.

"The last time I was at your mom's house," he started, trying to keep his voice as calm as he could, "there was an earthquaking contractor's truck out front. Do you know what he was doing?"

She swiveled mechanically toward him and he braked as a little silver sports car went past very fast, honking its horn maniacally. He felt a tiny spurt of rage at the recklessness, but pushed it away. A thousand emotions spiraled through him—dominated by a deep unease that had been kicked up off the floors of an ancient sea. What was certain was not certain any longer. She started crying, her head jerking in spasms.

"Lee?"

"Dad was after her for years to get the house bolted to the foundation. He said . . . ''

Everyone in L.A. knew what the Whittier Narrows thrust-quake in 1987 had done to the old Cal-bungalows that had only sat on their foundations by weight.

"Do you think they had time to bolt it down?"

"How would I know?"

Up the higher slopes of the hills he began to see houses and trees appearing through the dust. They looked curiously untouched above the haze, part of a safer universe. He stopped at a dead traffic light. Ventura Boulevard had cars stopped every which way and people out of them to sit on the curbs or hold one another. Power wires looped slack from pole to pole, a few fallen to earth. A big sycamore was snapped in two right in the middle, the crown of the tree resting across a navy-blue four-wheeler.

"The freeways are going to be out of the question. We just might make it there over the hills, if they're not blocked by rubble. There's a Thomas Bros. in the glove box."

"I don't need a map. I grew up here. If you can get past that truck, turn at the doughnut shop."

He got past by jumping the curb and running half a block on a sidewalk littered with glass. The old Concord had a nice high clearance and his steel radials seemed to sneer at the glass.

20

JUST DOING YOUR DUTY

HE BOUNCED HARD OUT OF THE ALLEY AND HEADED UP ROBIN
Terrace, then had to swerve immediately to keep from running over a tiny dachshund wearing a plaid tweed suit. For
a moment he thought it was a hallucination and then he
glanced back and clearly saw the determined blur of the
little legs going downhill. Loco would have had the dog
for lunch, he thought, but would have spit out the suit.

"Do you think Mom's okay?"

"They do statistics at that rich-kid school?" He hoped
a bit of gruffness would help keep her from spinning out
of control. "The last two of these things killed less than a
hundred each, and the basin holds eight million people. Do
the math."

He could see by the glaze in her eyes that she wasn't
really listening.

"We can always hope she was out pruning the roses,"
he said.

Just before rounding the first big curve on the hillside,
he stopped for a moment and looked back at the Valley,
thinking of Lot's wife. Several pyres of dark smoke rose
into the unearthly blue afternoon sky and one really im-
pressive billow of flame far away shot up a couple hundred
feet where a big gas main had ruptured. There was little
major damage visible, though. The high-rises had been
strengthened and strengthened again after previous quakes

and quake commissions. Cracking the window, he heard a symphony of car alarms and sirens over the faint boiling hiss of his own dead radio. All this played out against a rumble that was like some machine turning over deep in the earth and was probably only his imagination. The traffic lights he could see were all out. It would be a dark night ahead.

As he drove on he saw there were people standing out on all the terraces and patios, looking out over the city below with binoculars and telescopes. He remembered reading about the rubbernecks who'd driven their horse carriages out of Washington, D.C., to gawk at the Battle of Bull Run. He noticed that these particular rubbernecks were not standing too near the edges of their suspended decks.

"Jack."

"That's me."

"I'm so scared."

She was shaking with some inner horror.

"I've got away with so much," she explained.

Looking over at her, he noticed the vulnerability of her thin limbs. Someone could have snapped her wrist like a carrot.

"I've been privileged. I had the best education money could buy in this town. I had all these famous and important people to dinner in the house. I had a big movie star get drunk and feel me up in my own bedroom. I sat in my living room and had a long conversation with Joseph Heller about how he wrote *Catch-22*. I never went hungry for an hour and all I'd ever give beggars was a quarter. I have this feeling that the time has come to make me pay for all that."

"You mean all *this* was so the gods could punish *you* for being ungrateful?"

She looked blankly at him, too frantically focused on her own feelings to see the absurdity.

"It doesn't work that way, kid."

He braked hard. A section of road was tented up like a giant dropped book and water gushed out of the opened pages. He steered close to the barrier at the edge of the road, closer, and felt his fender scrape gently along the metal. A little less paint on the fender, he thought, and so what? He was past.

"Why not?"

"From the first time some saber-toothed tiger killed somebody's beloved child, we've all had that urge to find the *reasons*. It's just human to want order, but you can't have it. There are no reasons for things, and it'll make you mad to look for them."

"I *feel* I did something wrong."

"Of course you do. Have you ever been punched out?" She shook her head.

"I was blindsided in a bar once. The guy was going for somebody else. The first time it always makes you feel *guilty*. That's that damn mechanism we have that demands reasons. If we get hit, we must deserve it. But we damn well *don't*."

She stared dully.

"And if that's not enough for you, Lee, there's not a god anywhere who could work it out so that colossal mess out there only punished those who deserve it."

"What if we all deserve it?"

"Then I tell you He's being damn lenient to let *me* off."

She smiled finally, but it was fleeting. "I'm scared, Jack. I don't really care why."

"So am I, honey. That's why we're going to find your mom."

THEY got through a number of minor roadblocks, scabs of earth and ice plant that had come down from the hillside, until they came around a curve on a steep patch just past Sunshine Terrace. A sparkling red Mercedes 450 was about two-thirds of its original length, nose down on the road. When he drifted up close, he saw the remains of an expensive Swedish table saw peeking out from under the car to block the last few feet of the road. There would be no eking past this mess. Up the hillside, resting on tall stilts, he could

see the garage where the Mercedes had come from, its back
wall blasted out and a fancy Swedish wood lathe still hanging precariously by a 220-volt electrical cable.

"Go back to Sunshine," she said. "I know how to get
through."

Getting-Lee-Home had become their whole life, the trials
involved substituting for any real thought process, and that
was just the way he wanted it. He backed down to Sunshine, where they could look out over the Valley again.
The monstrous gas flame had grown noticeably, and he
wondered if it was one of the big conduit pipes that brought
the gas in from Texas. There were a half-dozen other fires,
but he knew the Valley was much too spread out to be
gobbled up by fire the way San Francisco and Tokyo had
been. The eight-lane roads made great firebreaks.

Around a bend he saw the first sign of fire in the hills,
a small eucalyptus going up like a torch, and then a little
farther a hillside house was fully engulfed with no sign of
firemen. The flames were so bright they hurt his eyes, and
a neighbor in a bathing suit was up on his own roof with
a hose. Jack Liffey was surprised there was still water pressure.

"Jack!"

A motorcycle had come around the bend abruptly, idling
and popping on the wrong side of the road, an erect young
man glancing around himself in a daze. He corrected his
course and waved like a racer taking an exhausted victory
lap and then he was gone. Sunshine Street dead-ended on
Halcyon, and Lee pointed right, upward on Halcyon. It was
narrower than any road they'd been on, too narrow really,
one of those hilly lanes where you cringed at each oncom-
ing car, but nobody seemed to be coming down. And then
they found out why. About half of a stilt house that had
once inhabited the cliffside above Halcyon was in a heap
across the road, as if somebody with a bulldozer had simply
driven up and pushed it over the hill. A green sectional
sofa looked as if it had ridden the rubble down and now
sat proudly atop the pile of stucco and plaster, a dozen tones

of lilac and chartreuse and prickly with broken two-by-fours. A purple designer toilet stood on the pavement a few yards away as if guarding the approach.

"Aw!" she moaned. "Chrissake!"

She was out her door, staring up at the ragged edge of what remained of the house, and he stepped out, too. It was a day for dogs, all right. Whoever lived there had kept a rottweiler. The big dog had been leashed and the hand end of the leash had been tied off on a stair rail, and when the floor had gone the dog had fallen into space and now the motionless body swung in the breeze straight overhead. It turned as it swayed—*precessed* was the correct word, he thought. The legs were stiff, as if frozen in mid-stride.

"C'mon, Lee. We can clear enough of this to get through."

"It's an omen." Her head was thrown back, and her gaze was captivated. There were always details that stood for the whole and you had to keep them from meaning more than they should.

"There's no such thing."

"Mom loved rottweilers," she countered.

"I loved the Cambodians, but it didn't help them much, either. Come on."

They started by scrambling up the pile and hurling the sofa off to the cliff side. Under the sofa he saw piles and piles of plain brown books, some of which showed a fierce bearded face in silhouette. It was the collected works of Lenin, and mixed in were other works of politics and social history. If you really liked symbolism, he thought, you could probably find something in that. He kicked again and again, sending volumes of Lenin flying. Lee stooped to get hold of a reading lamp and she pried it out of the pile of muck and leaned it delicately against the bougainvillea on the hillside.

"Jack!"

This time the rumble was clearly discernible. Up the hill somewhere a man began to shriek. Metal clanged against metal like someone hammering away at sheet metal. The

pile they stood on shifted. Looking up, he saw the dog
bounce once like a bungee jumper hitting bottom. Lee Borowsky stumbled across the rubble and clung to him and
he tugged her away from the cliff face. Plaster dust sifted
down from above and a few more books swan-dived to join
their comrades.

Maybe a 4.5, he thought. She sobbed inconsolably
against his chest. He could feel the damp of her tears begin
to seep through his shirt.

"Let's find your mom."

He felt her nod. They'd lowered the rubble pile a bit and
he thought he could bull the car up and over.

"Wait here," he said. But her ninety pounds wouldn't
have made much difference inside the car.

He backed the Concord to the curve and then came on
fast with his foot down hard so the clunky old automatic
wouldn't upshift. The engine roared agreeably and the car
bucked a little, but it plowed straight through the edge of
the pile, blasting books and plasterboard in all directions.
There was one bad *clonk* on the underpan just before he
cleared the rubble, but the car didn't seem to mind. She got
in without a word, rubbing her eyes.

He looked back, but the angle of the hill hid the city,
and all he noted was the dead rottweiler swinging and twisting gently on the air.

"I'm so scared, Jack. I'm sick with it."

"Uh-huh."

"If only I'd stayed with Mom, if I'd been better . . ."

It wasn't rational, but he knew the feeling. If he'd only
beaten the drink sooner, he might have saved his marriage,
might have been there to protect Maeve and Kathy. . . . He
hadn't even been there for Marlena or Loco. Protect the
one you're with, he thought. That was all anyone could do.

A man who looked Indian or Pakistani knelt just off the
road with his palms pressed together in prayer. Jack Liffey
slowed and the man glanced up at the car, but made no
sign to ask for help.

"I know I could have made it up with Mom. She didn't

deserve the kind of contempt I poured on her. I feel so awful.''

"Maybe that's not such a bad way to feel," he said, noticing her past tense. "I want to tell you a story. Just sit back now and buckle in. In 1971 I was working in a big air-conditioned trailer out in the bush in Thailand, monitoring radar screens to watch B-52s head in to bomb the Ho Chi Minh Trail. It was two removes from the real fighting, the kind of war you tended to inherit if you'd been to college. We had a lot of free time off-shift. Not far away was a Catholic mission run by the White Fathers, and I got to know a French priest named Jules de Retz who ran a little bush hospital at the mission. We'd sit on his veranda and swap Pernod for Scotch and we became pretty good friends.''

He took the turns cautiously, navigating around the surprises that waited on the roadway, rocks the size of a proverbial breadbox, a flowering shrub with a perfect rootball attached, a redwood chaise standing on end.

"I corresponded with Jules after I came home. In 1975 the Khmer Rouge took Cambodia, which was only a few klicks away, and within a year Jules found himself running a big refugee camp that had gathered around the mission. One group of these Cambodian refugees were truly remarkable. They'd come en masse from a village called Suramarit not far over the border. It took months for Jules to eke the story out of them. For the first few months after the Khmer Rouge victory, they'd been marched around by the little gung-ho guerrillas that had been sent out to stamp out bourgeois influences. The villagers had to abandon their homes and sleep out in the bush, and they had to sing ridiculous songs and chant slogans as they cleared new fields where nothing would ever grow. They ate half rations and a few of the older people died, but it was nothing like what had happened to the city people. Then the word came down to arrest anyone who'd been a village leader. There were about a dozen of them. They figured there'd be some sort of reeducation. The KR kids lined them up and taunted the old men in front of the village and then shot them.

"The same thing was happening all over Cambodia. It's pretty hard for us to imagine. At this point nobody would be surprised if the whole village had got demoralized, but they didn't. Another order came down to cull out all the secondary-school graduates. That was another dozen, but a strange thing happened. The KRs had a list of the diplomates, but they didn't know the people very well, and when they lined up the villagers, the people of Suramarit all gave the same name. They picked out the name of some poor illiterate peasant and they all insisted they were him. No matter how the soldiers strutted and threatened, not one of them ratted out the graduates."

A crushed wardrobe made of stripped pine lay in the middle of the road, fallen from somewhere above, and it leaked what looked like silk dresses. He bulled it slowly out of the way with the car and went on. Lee Borowsky watched him with a fierce glare.

"It was one of those mass acts of bravery that happens from time to time, like the Huguenot village in France that refused to turn its Jews over to the Nazis and got away with it. In Suramarit it worked for a time, too, but they could see it wasn't going to last. One of the kid soldiers who'd gone soft on the villagers leaked the news that the next turn of the screw was going to be rounding up everyone who could read. Rather than wait around, the villagers jumped the soldiers in the middle of the night and disarmed them. Without their AKs they were just scared kids and they fled into the forest.

"The villagers knew better than to stick around. They packed what they could and fled into Thailand and just about doubled the size of the refugee camp Jules had set up. He got some more tents from the U.N. and never quite enough rice to go around and kept the place going. The villagers didn't sit around moaning, though. They planted a new crop of rice and set up a school system and a village council. They showed whatever-it-was quality that had helped them resist so long. It was all pretty good for a year.

"Jules must have told someone the story because the press heard about it, and the journalists starting coming and going. About then the Vietnamese, to their everlasting credit, got fed up with the genocide in Cambodia and sent their own army in to stop it. Maybe that was the trigger, or maybe the journalists . . . I know Jules blamed himself. Anyway, late one night a brigade of Khmer Rouge came across the border and shot every man, woman, and child in the refugee camp."

"Awww," she said, like something deflating. "That's sick."

"I was gone, but I got the horrible letter from Jules that summer. His English was great but a little stiff. He ended with the expression: 'Catastrophe like this is just too big for us to measure ourselves against it. I cannot accept this, Jack. Even courage such as that can be rendered meaningless.' "

"God," she said. "It makes you want to live simple and pure."

He must have frowned.

"You know, to even things up for all the privileges you had."

"That's the point I'm making," he insisted as he inched the car over the bricks of a fallen wall. "You *can't* even things up."

"Wasn't God supposed to spare the world from destruction if somebody found seven just men?"

"Terrific. So we're all gonna die if there's only six. Suramarit was a whole village of them."

"Then what's your rule?" she asked with real fervor. "What do you *do* in life?"

"You do your duty, you just don't kid yourself it'll save the world."

". . . Switchboards are jammed from Santa Barbara to San Diego." The radio blared out and they both jolted in surprise. "Please don't try to call. If you have a medical emergency, we've been told you should place a white bedsheet on your roof and rescue units will get there as soon as they can. Kelly?''

For the last few minutes he hadn't even noticed the crackle of the dead radio. Lee Borowsky leaned forward and stared ferociously at the volume knob as if to read some answer there.

''Bob, my uplink is still working. I'm out in Burbank and it looks like the IKEA store has completely collapsed. I . . . it's horrible. The whole three stories is just a pile of rubble, and the parking structure, too. I have no way of knowing how many people were inside and the police aren't letting anyone get close. They've blocked the road completely with their black-and-whites. Off to my left I can see a fire about two miles away toward the Burbank Airport . . . cracks in the pavement . . . Bonita . . . Glenoaks off that way. . . .'' The voice was breaking up.

''I'm sorry, ladies and gentlemen, I think we've lost touch with Kelly Stockman. As you know, at about two thirty-eight this afternoon the Burbank–North Hollywood area suffered a severe earthquake series that seems to have been centered somewhere near the edge of the hills. Our instruments in the studio gave a preliminary reading in the range of seven-point-five on the Richter scale, but we'll only know for sure when we reestablish contact with Frank Olmos over at Caltech. First reports said it was an unusual type of earthquake that we've never experienced before. There was one severe upthrust at two thirty-eight. That was the one you probably felt as a sharp up-and-down movement if you were close enough to the epicenter. The first quake seems to have set off a second tremor of a different type, a rolling shock about eight seconds later. The second quake may have been even bigger than the first one and it seems to have been centered a few miles farther south, directly under the hills. We'll know better soon when Frank— Frank, are you there?''

The reporter came on, working over a scientist at Caltech who insisted she didn't know anything more yet. The reporter badgered her for a while to reveal what she didn't know, and Jack Liffey lost interest. He knew what he needed to know: the second jolt, the one with the side thrust, had been right under the hills. He'd guessed as much, because the damage was getting worse and worse as they climbed the hillside. Probably the only thing saving the hill houses from even worse was the fact that they had resilient wood frames and were rooted in bedrock rather than floating on alluvium like the buildings down below. But some of the older ones from before the war, particularly on the south flank of the hills, might not have fared so well. Especially if they weren't bolted to their foundations.

"Oh, holy shit."

He braked and then stopped.

"Jack. What is that thing?"

He let the rear wheels drift back into the curb and then killed the engine. They both got out and stared in awe. The road simply ended in a crevasse up against a sheer granite cliff at least ten feet tall, as if the Great Wall of China had been built across their path. Up at the top of the cliff a few inches of asphalt projected into space where the road started up again. The new cliff ran as far as he could see in either direction and at its base there was the three-foot-wide crevasse. He stepped carefully up to the dark crack in the earth but could not see bottom. It might have been his imagination, but he thought he felt a cold wind blowing up out of the blackness, as if the break went all the way down to a chilly hell.

And straight in front of him, the Hollywood Hills were ten feet taller than they had been an hour earlier.

"Looks like we're on foot," he said.

21

GROWING UP IS NOT A SPEED EVENT

"How do we get up that?"

"Good question."

They followed the edge of the chasm over a broken-backed retaining wall, through a noisy bed of ivy, and across a deep green lawn that had probably once been as flat as a golf green but now tilted steeply toward what rubble remained of a house.

"Anyone there?" he called. He tried a few more times for his conscience, hoping they'd been away on vacation.

The earth here had been torn into big jigsaw-puzzle pieces and each piece tilted a different way. He took her hand and boosted her from one piece onto another. In a second torn-up backyard, they skirted a concrete swimming pool that had heaved up out of the earth like a spit melon seed. It had tipped onto its side and emptied through a half-timbered Tudor. Finally he found what he wanted along the new cliff.

"How far are we from your mom's?"

"Five or six blocks, I think. A couple blocks up to Mulholland and a couple down the other side. But things don't look quite the same."

A good-sized masonry house that had once lived above the cliff had collapsed into a ramp of broken concrete and rock and jagged two-by-four ends. Water washed down the gradient, trickling from ledge to ledge like a designer waterfall. It would be a rough climb, but it was doable. He took her hand and they climbed, planting each foot carefully in the wet debris. His mind drifted and he started musing about how life was an overlap of the processes of assembly and disassembly. It had probably taken six months to assemble this house and ten seconds to disassemble it. But not all processes were so one-sided, he thought. Within a few weeks a lot of the jumbled hillside would be scraped and leveled and the roads would be rejoined by the inexhaustible acts of men. We were like ants, he thought. Nature wanted its crazy picnic, but human persistence could swarm Nature under, at least for a while. He boosted Lee Borowsky up the last few feet by standing in the prow of an orange canoe that stuck out of the hillside.

At the top of the climb, a potbellied man in checked pants stood at the edge of a chunk of lawn swinging a fancy wood golf club to drive balls off into the city below. He had them set up a few inches apart and he stepped from one to the next, shimmied a moment, and then let fly with a distinct *swish-pok* in the stillness. It looked like a clean strong swing and with any luck he might make the freeway. Jack Liffey didn't like the look in the man's eye, and he shook his head at Lee and they skirted his driving green.

The houses they saw up here had mostly survived. All the chimneys were down and walls were cracked open here and there, but most of them stood. It gave him hope. As she walked, Lee seemed shut in with a kind of contrition, like a child expecting to be hit. Her face had sharp lines and contours and he wondered if she would be good-looking in another few years or if she'd make one of those gawky transitions to a hard-looking adult.

There didn't seem to be many people about. A helicopter wove noisily along the crestline but kept going toward the Pacific until he could no longer hear its *thwop-thwop*. What he could hear ceaselessly, without being able to identify it, was a deep systaltic throbbing beneath the city itself, as if a tunnel deep underfoot carried the earth's life force. It made his skin crawl.

They came on an ornate Victorian birdcage parked at the edge of the road with a jet-black mynah squawking again and again, like a mechanical timing device. He thought of releasing the bird, but the owner was probably in the process of moving the cage to safety.

"Hundred-dollar whore," the bird challenged, or he thought it did. The words had been fairly distinct, and Lee chuckled once.

"Did we hear right?"

"That's pretty cheap up here," she said.

"Maybe it's an old bird."

As they passed, the bird tried again: "Suck you off, mister."

Lee laughed out loud. There was a touch of hysteria in the laugh. "Don't be embarrassed. I'm not a little kid. I *do* know what a blow job is."

He thought involuntarily of his daughter. He imagined her in the back of some brutish frat boy's car, and shuddered. She would grow up to be whatever she would be and there was not a thing he could do to protect her.

"Growing up's not a speed event," he said.

"I could give you a blow job and show you."

"Knock it off, kid. You're not that tough yet and I'm not that corrupt."

A big Lincoln Continental sat abandoned in the middle of the road with all its doors open. He checked as they walked past, but the keys were gone. A plastic bag of tomatoes sat on the passenger seat.

"Mom made me this mess. You better face it. She even latched onto my boyfriends if she could. It's like a dark parable or something. She had this way of touching guys at the door or kissing them or holding their arms, you know, so you couldn't really object because maybe it was just one of those stupid greetings that all her Hollywood tribe use, those aging over-made-up women who are eternally kissing each other at doorways, and if you complained she'd just laugh at you like you were some naïf out of Kansas, but it was more than a big hello and the boys damn well knew it. They'd cop a little feel and she'd tingle a bit to show they had permission to do it next time and maybe do a bit more and, Jesus, the next time they'd show up for a date with me, they'd be all het up and nervous before they even got there.''

She seemed to need to jabber, but there was a brittle brightness that worried him. They passed two teenage boys who were slamming lengths of iron pipe into what was left of a stucco ranch house. They worked methodically, sweating and knocking off chunks of stucco as if they were paid on piecework. She didn't even notice them.

''There was a time I was away with my dad on location in New Orleans for a few weeks while he was making, I think it was *The Awakening,* and she hired two of my friends to paint the back bedroom. One was an ex and the other one of these Judases was still supposed to be seeing me. She got them working with rollers and edgers and things and then she joined them to help out, and *whoops,* she gets a little bitty spot of paint on her designer work shirt, *oh dear,* so she has to take it off to protect it and then they go on working until, *whoops,* here's some paint on her Calvin Klein jeans and they have to come off, too. And there she was painting away in her bra and panties in front of two of my boyfriends, nonchalant as hell, and she spatters a bit on one of the boys, and to be honest I don't know how far it goes after this because it's the damn ex who told me all this just to hurt me and I covered my ears and got away as fast as I could and the other one just turns beet red when I bring it up and won't talk about it. How can I forgive this woman for things like that? I mean, I'm serious, I think I actually *want* to forgive her. Even if she did buy me at a slave auction and then lose interest.''

''You ever do therapy?''

She scowled and took his arm as they walked.

''I feel there's this great big beautiful life waiting for me, waiting up ahead somewhere to bust into colors someday, but I got to get around Mom first. I don't mean avoid her. I've got to find a way to make all this anger turn into something good in me so I can love her, no matter what, like some kind of Gandhi.''

She gripped harder and harder and he sensed that forgiveness was indeed what she wanted, but she had no way to get there.

''Honey, you had a pretty exotic upbringing, all right, but you're not the only adopted kid who was treated bad. It may be a weird path you're on, but you're not Daniel Boone. Why don't you talk to some of the people who've left messages along the trail?''

''Who?''

''I don't know, but I'll find you somebody good if you want.''

''You've been sleeping with her, haven't you?''

This kid was a pretty tough nut, he thought.

''Is it just the sex?'' she said querulously. ''I don't get it. I mean, is it those big breasts or the things she does in bed or what? Do you really *like* her?''

He sighed. ''A minute ago you wanted to forgive her. She's a bright woman, you know. Way back when, when her contemporaries were off in college or out in the world learning how to relate to each other as people, she was too busy being a movie star. All she knows is her magnetism. It works for her, and she's relied on it all her life. That's *her* problem. Mine and yours—that's nothing so straightforward. Yeah, she's got a hook in me. Just like your boyfriends.''

She punched him in the arm. It wasn't playful at all. She hit him again, trying to hurt.

''Ow. Hey!''

''You lousy fucker!''

And then she was crying and holding him, and they had to come to a stop. ''I'm so scared. I think I've killed her with my hatred.''

THE top of their Everest wasn't far. Skyridge went up another steep block to Mulholland Drive, famous for following the crest of the whole range of hills. Unfortunately the big retaining wall that had held this bit of Mulholland up there at the top had given way and a whole lot of asphalt and fill had come down to where they stood, leaving a sheer thirty-foot cliff. All around he could smell the exhalations of damp earth and that mildewy root smell of ripped-up weeds. A good climber with ropes could do it, he thought, looking upward. Maybe a bad climber, but the ropes were still part of the bargain. Some contractor would get rich rebuilding that road.

"Jeez," she said simply.

"This is another fine mess you've gotten me into," Jack Liffey said softly. She gave his biceps a squeeze where she was hanging on.

She pointed and he could see she was right. A huge gnarled live oak that was probably 150 years old rose from a backyard where some homeowner in the fifties had gone to great trouble to build around it rather than leveling the expensive hillside pad. If they were crazy enough, they could climb the oak and shinny out the biggest limb and jump to the shoulder of a short stretch of the road that remained up the hill, jutting precariously, like a bridge to nowhere.

He didn't like heights, but he could probably handle it.

"Let's do it."

It was enclosed spaces that got him, the memento of a really bad afternoon spent treading water down a well where he had fallen when he was nine. Heights were a piece of cake by comparison. They picked their way through a rock and cactus garden to the big rough bole of the oak and he stood on a bench to boost her up to the lowest limb, self-conscious about placing his hand on her small, warm thigh. She reached down to give him a hand. She couldn't take much of his weight, but it was just enough to help him scrabble up the raspy black bark.

"We rise to fixed things," she said. "An ascent out of the circles of hell."

"Oh, be a kid for a while still."

They boosted one another up two more limbs. He was

getting queasy now, looking down at the redwood bench and cactus garden, and he kept a good grip on the jutting branches. It would not be a nice landing. Wind ruffled the deep green cupped leaves with their pointy edges, and his progress along the boughs stripped dried acorns that bonked off the bench below.

"Hey there!" It was a shrill but very calm voice.

He looked down to see, foreshortened, a teenager in a black homburg and curly locks. A young Hasidic Jew clung to a big black book and stared up at them hopefully, like a farmer looking for rain.

"Are you crazy?" the boy asked, as if it were a genuine question.

"Probably."

"I'm serious, sir."

"Well, if we weren't," Jack Liffey said, "it would be a very good time to start. We're trying to get over to Avenida Bluebird to find her mother."

The boy nodded earnestly. "Blessings on you." He spoke for a while in Hebrew, and then he undertook to translate. "I just memorized that, sir. It is from the end of the Yom Kippur service.

> "Lord though every power is yours,
> And all your deeds tremendous,
> Now, when heaven's gates are closing,
> Let your grace defend us."

"Thanks a lot," Jack Liffey said. "I hope the gates are open for a while yet, though."

"I think he's just peeking up my skirt," Lee said softly.

"Oy," Jack Liffey said.

"Good luck, sirs."

The boy waved and walked gravely away. They boosted onto the big high limb now, the one they needed. He sat with his legs on either side and she sat sidesaddle. He felt a wave of exhaustion, the kind you got after a long period of nervous tension and he knew he had to fight it, but for just a moment he closed his eyes and imagined a soft bed. Somewhere far away a carillon was tolling the hour and a donkey was braying. Both stopped at once.

"Jack," she said. "Wake up."

"Just a momentary ebb of energy," he said. "Let's do this one at a time. I don't like the size of the bough out there."

She nodded. "I go first so at least one of us gets through," she said melodramatically. It was academic because she was already ahead of him. She shinnied herself out and up. The branch slanted up at about the pitch of a roof and her weight didn't even disturb it. She gave a half-playful little "ooh" when she sidesaddled past a sharp place, and soon she was well above his head and the thinner bough was bouncing a little each time she boosted herself along. She nearly lost her balance once but tucked her legs up and stabilized.

"This is cool," she said, and he had no idea what she meant. She couldn't possibly have meant the danger.

Out near the end she hung by her hands and could almost touch the shoulder of the surviving bit of road with her toe. She swung back and forth, boosting higher each time, and let go at the right moment to catch easily on a stretch of guardrail. She sat on the rail and slapped dirt off her hands.

"Mickey Mouse," she boasted.

He wondered how stable that one stretch of roadway was, but there was a limit to what you could worry about. He blew out a breath and started inching out the limb. Balance wasn't much of a problem with his legs astride, but his progress was painfully slow. He noticed now that out toward the end he would be over a much more serious drop where the yard fell off to a ravine, perhaps another hundred feet down. He wondered why he hadn't noticed before.

"Cluck cluck cluck," she said, then: "Nyah-nyah, come get me." She stuck out her tongue. He wondered if she'd hit some drug when he wasn't looking.

The bough began to bounce and give. He went right into the sensation, the hanging in space, into the risk, until he convinced himself he was still lucky. It was all you could do. A little more than halfway out, where the taper had reduced the branch to about the size of his forearm, he heard a crack, like a pellet gun.

"Oh, jeez, Jack."

"I'm okay."

He hadn't felt any give at the sound. He shinned forward more gently, his hearing dancing anticipation of more cracking. The branch was starting to sag now and he was gaining less height than he wanted. It was clear he'd never make it the way she had, but there was nothing to do but go on. The yard was gone now and there were rocks far down, but he refused to look.

A *crick-crack* went through him like an electric shock and he felt the give this time.

She stood rigid on the cliff edge twenty feet away with both hands to her mouth.

He cursed himself for not losing those ten extra pounds. He thought of the rocks below, and then for some reason he thought of a tumbleweed with teeth. Celebrity will bite you in the ass, Mike Lewis had said. He could tell he was losing focus.

Crack. It came much louder this time, and he held his breath, expecting to fall.

Might as well get it over, he thought as he shinned forward straight into the fear. He'd never thought it would be heights. It was supposed to be holes in the ground, staring up in panic at one tiny unreachable spot of light. Go ahead and break! he thought, inflaming his luck, and as if acquiescing, the big oak gave him back a continuous *pop-crack-pop*, like canvas tearing, and the bough broke behind him. About six feet of the limb sank like a broken arm.

"Eeee!" he heard.

But he clung hard, and by some miracle, the branches out at the tip caught on a clump of weed on the hillside and the green wood held like a hinge where it had broken. He saw he had a tenuous bridge to a point on the cliff only four or five feet below where she stood. He slid down as fast as he could and kept his weight on the bough to keep it from pulling free from the hill. Slowly he levered himself up and flattened against the slope. His head was just at her feet.

Distraction plucked at his consciousness. In a movie, he thought, the bad guy would try to kick him in the head now.

Without a word she knelt and gripped the guardrail with one hand and reached out to him with the other. He took her hand in one of his and used the other to grab at the weeds, doing his best not to put too much of his weight on her. The stringy weeds held, and one foot found a niche. He wriggled and shinnied and at last got a leg up over the edge, and she pulled hard on two fistfuls of shirt until he rolled up onto the flat. At last he lay breathless on his stomach. Only then did he relax and let himself feel how close it had been.

"You must live right," he heard her say.

When he looked back he saw that the bough had sprung away from the slope and about a third of it hung straight down now, like the flag of a defeated nation.

"Thanks, kiddo. I guess it's not falling that's got my name written on it."

"Now you're mixing metaphors. What got your name?"

"Probably women."

When he stood up, he felt like a million. Luck mattered more than just about anything, he thought. But he knew that was the kind of brag you strutted out only after you'd had a big dollop of good luck.

They stood on a thirty-yard stretch of Mulholland that was untouched, but the asphalt fell away at both ends. Enough of the far shoulder remained, though, for them to make their way back to Skyridge. There, they found that a lot of the road had fallen the other way, too, carrying some of Skyridge down with it to the south of the ridge. They found a section of embankment that fell away gradually and they dug their heels to giant-step down the weedy slope, and soon they were on the unbroken part of Skyridge. They had crossed their Everest, Tenzing Norkay and Hillary. He wondered if she would recognize the names.

Just up the road an old woman sat on a lawn chair in the midst of the ruins of a house. She had an unlit cigarette in her hand and her arm went to her mouth and back down like a life-size mechanical coin bank.

"Mrs. Larkin," Lee called.

The woman didn't seem to hear.

"Mrs. Larkin!"

She nodded as they walked up but didn't look at them.

"Are you okay?"

"I found the photos," the woman said with a decisive little quaver. "The boat is gone, but I've got the photos."

"Can we help you?"

"Not just at the moment. We thank you very much."

Jack Liffey pulled Lee on. There would be a lot of hard-luck stories in L.A. that day, and at least the woman was alive.

The next three houses were pretty much intact and their spirits lifted. Then around a bend they could see the first bit of Lori Bright's still standing and Lee gave a squeal of joy and ran forward.

In a few seconds, though, Jack Liffey knew something was badly wrong. Lee had sunk to her knees on the road and let out an animal howl that ruffled the nape of his neck. When he hurried up to her, he saw that a fairly substantial steel-framed solarium was what had held up the masonry north wall of the house. The rest of the two-story house looked like a horse with a broken back. The middle had sunk a whole floor, and the south end where the entrance had once been had disintegrated completely. The rafters had tented up some of the house, but it didn't look like it was going to last.

She ran toward the house, calling "Momma!" and he caught up and grabbed her just before she dived into a gaping hole in the side wall.

"Let's check things out."

They paced around the perimeter of the house. While she

called, he studied where sections of floor and wall seemed propped up on something substantial and where they were only waiting for another tremor to settle. The trophy room onto the garden had survived, but it would never again be called high-ceilinged on some realtor's fact sheet. He could see no one was in the room. He checked the garage and found that all the cars were home, and he got a rusted-up pipe wrench out of the garden shed and shut off the gas.

If she had been in the front of the house, he thought, she was dead now, and if she had been right at the back, she would have stepped calmly out the solarium door and be sitting on the lawn. He decided if she was inside, trapped by rubble or a beam across her legs, she would be somewhere in the confused tangle at the middle, where the second floor had come down to mate with the first.

There was no answer to Lee's calls. He knelt and stared glumly into the lopsided opening that had once held the French doors onto the fountain alcove. Things were dark, but it seemed the best way into the tangle. He went back to the garden shed and got an old pry bar and a ball of twine he'd noticed.

"Jack, is she in there?"

"I hope not, but I've got to check."

"I'm smaller. I should go."

"I'm stronger. There's going to be some lifting and prying."

"We can do it together."

He shook his head. "If the house comes down on both of us, who goes for help?"

He tied the end of the rough twine to one of his belt loops and handed her the ball. "Don't hold me back but keep it a bit snug. I'll give you a double tug every minute or two so you know I'm okay."

"What's this for? I can't pull you out."

He met her eyes for a moment. "If it collapses, it'll help the firemen find my body."

Her face sagged and he could see a tear. She sat and hugged his leg. "Oh, Jeez. I'm so scared."

"I'm scared, too, kid. If there weren't a big eye watching me, I wouldn't do this."

"What do you mean—God?"

He shook his head. "It's inside. I probably saw *High Noon* too many times."

He gave her ankle a little squeeze and crawled over the broken threshold and immediately felt the cool. He let his eyes adjust to the dimness. There was a smell of plaster dust and something brassy at the back of his throat.

"Jack, tug so I know what it feels like."

He did.

"Break a leg. That's what the movie people say."

"My luck's still good."

He crept, moving his knees carefully through the lumpy mess, crossing what looked like a utility room. The washer and dryer were holding up the ceiling, leaving a tunnel. Then he wriggled into a tiled hallway where he felt a runner carpet under his knees, and where he could barely see. He wished he'd found a flashlight. A match would not be a good idea. Now and again, when he let his imagination work for a moment, he was almost petrified with fright. This was the fate with his name on it, his very own: buried alive in a space the size of a coffin.

He tugged twice, and heard Lee's faint voice. "Gotcha. Go for it!"

The world got confused now. Things were not at their accustomed angles and even the floor had given up the level and seemed to slant downward.

"Lori," he called softly. It was the first time he'd used her name, as if it carried a magic that he didn't want to waste. And he realized that he didn't want Lee to hear him using her mother's name, as if his voice would reveal too much.

"Lori. Speak to me." He stopped to listen. There was a throb from the walls that was probably his imagination. The silence was complete, not like a silence at all, but a profound absence. He rubbed two fingers together near his ear just to make sure he could hear.

"Lori."

He crept deeper into the dark and looked above him. Where the ceiling was gone, a little diffuse light was visible, and another foot on he could see the crack high above, giving himself a shiver. Not unlike the tiny high spark of light you'd see from down a well. Aftershock, he thought suddenly, his imagination exhibiting things starting to shift, the lighted crack widening abruptly, then snuffing out with a roar. If only they would schedule them at regular intervals.

"Lori!" He was using up the magic. He tugged twice on the twine, but it seemed slack and there didn't seem to be any response. He imagined Lee gone away, fallen asleep, attacked by a ravaging band of outlaw bikers who'd been unleashed by the quake. He could tell his mind was doing its best not to think too closely about the coffinlike walls.

"Lori."

The building creaked and he heard something settle hard. It was like a beast grazing unseen only a few feet away in an impenetrable jungle. He put his arms up involuntarily to protect his head, but nothing fell near him. As he went forward he felt a lassitude taking him over, something robbing the last of his energy.

"Lori, speak please. I can't stay here much longer."

He heard a small distinct sound, like a heavy sack dragged an inch across concrete. It did not sound like more settling.

"*Lori?* Are you in here?"

His hand found the jagged edge of the floor. It had fallen away or torn away, and he tried to see into what lay below.

"Lori?"

The dragging sound came again and he wondered if it was a rat. He tried to remember if there were any pets. Of course, it could be Anita or the gardener. Or an opossum that had harbored in the basement.

"Lori. It's Jack. Please."

And, strangely, it was not her name but his own that held the magic.

"Jack . . . Jack . . ."

It was almost without breath, and it came from a few feet below him in the dark. He wanted to laugh and cry.

"Lori! Are you hurt bad?"

"Oh, Jack. Don't look at me."

He laughed, he couldn't help it. "I can't see, Lori, it's dark. Tell me where you hurt."

There was a long wait. "How long has it been?" she asked finally.

"Since the quake? I don't know. Over an hour. We had trouble getting here."

"I can't hang on."

"Yes, you can." And then he remembered Lee. He tugged twice, then twice again, hoping she would take it for a sign. "Lee's here, too. She came back on her own hook. She wanted to find you. She was afraid for you."

"Honest Injun?"

It was such a strange thing to say he laughed again.

"She came to forgive you, of whatever it is she thinks she has to forgive you for."

He heard a sob, and in one strange moment, superstition run wild, he wondered if he shouldn't have said that, if the mistrust and suspense, the paralysis of emotion between the two women had been a kind of prop that prevented the final collapse. The floor began to tremble and he heard a ripping near his ear. The surface bucked and something crashed down below.

"Oh, Lord, no . . ."

Lee's scream penetrated to where he lay as the floor punched sideways, and then the whole house came in with a roar. When it was all over he was on his side, immobile. His head was wrenched sideways, and a surface pressed his cheek hard, but somewhere in front of him was one tiny, hard point of light. He could move his right foot slightly, but nothing else. Dust was choking him and rubble filled all the space around him. His fate had found him, he thought. The coffin with his name on it—and a terrible panic swelled inside him, swelled and then bloomed like a nuclear blast. It blew a plug and the terror rushed out with enough glare to light the world.

22

THE MORAL ORDER

HE REMEMBERED A WHOLE LOT OF FROTH ALL AROUND, A vanilla universe, white on white, billowing up with a medicinal smell and then a kind of white tunnel, and he wondered with a shiver if it was *the* White Tunnel, but he recalled reading somewhere that that was really just an artifact of the way consciousness decayed back from the edges of the visual cortex as the brain died, and then he figured if he was thinking stuff like *that*, he probably wasn't dead after all.

The dreams got very busy for a while, but they stayed pretty white and frothy and then they calmed down and he really worked himself down into them, and finally he opened his eyes to see, up close, the face of his daughter, Maeve. Her eyes went wide and she shrieked and ran away. It was supposed to be a welcoming male figure, he thought, his dad or his beloved uncle Seamus beckoning him into the Whatever, so again he reckoned he probably wasn't on the way to the Whatever. Dress warm, kiddo, he imagined Seamus warning him, and he chuckled. The idea of closing his eyes again was so delicious he did and he fell right back into the cotton fluff.

HE opened his eyes and saw a big brass belt buckle. ''Son of a bitch, he's conscious.''

Sergeant Flor had been leaning over him. Maybe he was going off to that place after all.

"It's important to be on time," another voice said, then he nodded off again.

THE next time he summoned the energy to open his eyes the room was full of women and they all seemed to start moving at once. Maeve and Kathy were there, and Marlena, looking wonderfully brown against all the Irish women, and they all ducked forward, looking close as if they'd just found a hair in the soup. Maeve gasped and beside her, amazingly enough, Lee Borowsky made an appearance, and they clasped one another and him all at once. If it was a hallucination, he wanted a *lot* more of it. He closed his eyes.

"Stay with us, Jack," he heard Kathy say. "We want you back."

Back? he thought.

He opened his eyes again. "Where back?" he said. A part of him realized he wasn't being very coherent, but it wasn't worrying him. His throat had hurt like a bastard, though, at the two words he spoke.

Kathy had an arm on each of the girls and was tugging them gently back. "It's like grunion," he thought he heard her say. "You mustn't frighten his consciousness away by being too eager."

He wriggled his toes and found his right leg wasn't responding quite right. He tried to peek under the covers.

"All bits here?" Again his throat objected.

Kathy seemed to have taken charge. She pressed a comforting hand on his shoulder. "You'll limp a bit, but you're all there. Praise the Lord."

"Whoever." He couldn't resist it. At least she hadn't brought along that doofus who taught social studies that she lived with now. What was his name?

Then all of a sudden he realized a woman was missing. He turned to Lee Borowsky. She stood arm in arm with Maeve, like sisters. They were almost exactly the same size, but Maeve was really big for her age. "Your mom?"

Lee shook her head, but she didn't seem weepy. He couldn't make sense of it.

"What?"

"She died, Jack," Kathy said softly.

He stared at Lee some more, feeling hollow and confused, and they couldn't seem to figure out what was bothering him. Why wasn't she more upset?

"It was two months ago. You've been in a coma."

"Show me a paper."

"Jackie, take our word," Marlena Cruz said. "You was gone far away. Mrs. Bright is buried and all, weeks ago. I got Loco, he's okay," she added quickly.

Lori Bright was dead. He couldn't adjust to it. He remembered something he'd overheard, something about a father who'd been an immortal, but only until the girl talking had turned sixteen. Lori was huge and durable and so vital that taking her out of the world should have made something collapse. Like a house. It just wasn't possible. He'd close his eyes and open them and then she would be there, smiling or beckoning or even raging at him for some reason.

He rolled his head and felt it was encased in something. "Skull fracture?" he guessed.

Kathy nodded. "Like going across the date line. Two months gone, just like *that*."

"If somebody hits you again," Lee said, "you get the time back."

Only Maeve laughed, a schoolgirl giggle.

"That's my girl." And then she burst into tears again.

Lee comforted her and Kathy told him that Lee was staying with them for the time being. She'd be going to live with her dad as soon as he got back from location at Lake Malawi, but for the moment she was in the back bedroom in Redondo. That was when the nurse came and chased them all out. The doctors wanted to shine lights in his eyes and make him move his toes and parse sentences and count backward and things like that.

He still worried about Lori Bright. When a light that brilliant went out of the world, how come he could still see?

"I sent my kid to Eagle Scout camp last summer."

"I didn't know they still did that stuff."

It was Lieutenant Malamud and Sergeant Flor again, standing off to the side, and he decided not to open his eyes.

"Yeah, the camp had a survival course, you know?" Malamud said. "Kick them out into the woods for a couple days. Tommy showed them all up. Ate bugs, made a shelter, the whole shebang."

Flor's voice started soft and then swelled as he came closer. "They didn't have survival camps when I was a kid. It was just called hanging out on the block, dodging bullets and shit. I bet this guy could use a good survival camp. *Esse*, I think he's awake. Liffey, talk to us."

Reluctantly he opened his eyes. "Hi."

"Your pals are here."

"Who?"

"Us, asshole. We're your pals because we haven't dragged you up to the jail wing at County. Not yet."

Malamud elbowed in and took over. "Feeling any better?"

"Better than what?"

"I guess being dead awhile fucks up your perspective. You had a busy time there, right before the big Hillside Quake."

"So that's what they're calling it."

"We're more interested in what *you* were doing. The Hillside Fault can take care of itself." Malamud's stare hardened.

"I can't remember a thing after my last birthday."

"That doesn't fly, pal," Flor put in.

"We know you got plenty of fond memories. I'll bet she was good in bed, with all that body on her. Did tricks, huh?"

He saw red, but realized in time they were trying to goad him. He remembered that they had called her the OMB, the Old Movie Bitch. "What am I supposed to have done that's irked you so much?"

"You've gone and upset what our captain calls 'the ethos.' He means the moral order of things. He's a real joker, he is," Malamud said. Even Flor looked puzzled. "Cops always got their own plans for the way things should work out, who should be winners and losers. You went and meddled with the moral order, and that's not nice. The captain is pissed, and when he's pissed, *we're* pissed."

He wondered if Monogram had been paying them off. "Really? I wish I could remember it, then."

"Stupidity is not a legal defense, guy," Flor put in.

"Did I kill somebody?"

They just glared.

"We're not just students of the passing carnival," Malamud said after a while. "If your fingerprints turn up in this thing somewhere, we *will* have your ass."

He relaxed. That meant they didn't know much of anything, they just resented his meddling. He would probably never know exactly what had gone down between Mitsuko and Monogram and G. Dan Hunt, and the part the cops had played in it all.

"I wonder what drives you, is it just revenge or some kind of honor?"

He remembered Lori asking him if he would choose courage or happiness. Forced choices like that were always false. "I wish I could remember. Sorry."

AFTER another rest he found a bunch of greeting cards and a book on the table beside him. He read the names on the cards—Art Castro, Chris Johnson, Mike Lewis. Old friends. The book was *Monty Python's Little Red Book*. It was big and blue. He wondered who would give him that. The flyleaf said, *Get well, dude*, and there was a small drawing of a beanie with a propellor on top. He smiled.

A friendly black nurse looked in and told him the neurosurgeon didn't want him overstimulated, so the visitors would be coming one at a time for a while. He thought about it for a while and figured it was a perfect opportunity for him to work out his relationship with all these women, one at a time, and he really meant to, but when the time came, of course, he didn't.

He felt a real warmth and even a little lust for Marlena, but he was still feeling guilty about getting starstruck and backing away from her. He let her tell him about Loco, who had got so hungry he'd torn open all the packaged food in what she called his "larder." He wondered where on earth she got that word. He figured he and Marlena would work something out down the line a bit and he didn't have to press things now.

Kathy pushed his buttons right away by starting in on a bunch of things he ought to do and things he ought not to do and maybe it was time to give up his ridiculous notion of being Sam Spade. He kept himself from getting angry, but the warming idea of making peace treaties with everyone had fled like a stepped-on cat.

Maeve was Maeve, and he wanted to joke with her forever, but she just kept bursting into tears. Anyway, he didn't think he had that much to clear up with her.

Lee was harder. She seemed to be storing away her grief over her mother's death, weighted down by her screwy brooding guilt over causing it with her anger. She was pushing it down deep in herself, the way he dealt with things, and he could hardly lecture her about it. He told her that the last thing her mother had heard was how her daughter had come back to forgive her. She screwed up her eyes skeptically and demanded a lot of cross-my-hearts, but at last she seemed to believe him. He didn't really know if it helped.

It was a totally unnecessary death, and that was what was always hard. Lori Bright could just as easily have been out on the terrace drinking lemonade when the Hillside Quake struck. He wanted to tell Lee what he'd found out himself, the hard way, that there was a moral order out there all right, but it certainly didn't come from Malamud and Flor. And it wasn't just or merciful, either, just necessary, and you had to let it be and go with it. But that was something you had to figure out for yourself. You could forgive the gods all you wanted for what they did to you, but you had no right to forgive them when they hurt somebody else.

The big thing that would go unsettled in him was with the woman who couldn't be there, he knew that. He ached for Lori Bright with every atom of his tingling, creaky body. Whatever it was she had, all that glamour and excitement, that sultry energy, that pain and confusion, that sexual heat that was only a marker for something else— he'd probably never sort out all the reasons he'd wanted her so badly. And still did, and always would. And he regretted the fact that he wouldn't be seen with her coming out of Spago or the Campanile. Some little kid pointing and saying to another little kid, But who's that guy with her?

He smiled. He'd probably missed his chance for good to be That Guy with Her.

It's never what it seems, he thought, brightening a bit. The movie star's got just as many heartaches as you do, and the whole thing is just a trick, and if you really let yourself know that, it's the only real victory.

Randy Wayne White

"Inventive"—*Playboy*
"Enticing"—*Entertainment Weekly*
"Dramatic"—*The Miami Herald*
"Compelling"—*San Francisco Chronicle*